THE DEVIL IN TARTAN

THE DEVIL IN TARTAN

1

CHAPTER

*It was on a fine June morning, with all the birds
singing and all the orchards afoam with blossom and the
lambs racing on the hillsides, when I rode for the first
time down through the fair valley of the Oquiddic River
and into the village of Brierbank. I was attended by
young Robin Kendrum, son of my father's wife, and a
likely enough lad, though inclined to be sullen, for he
liked not his chore.*

THAT WOULD MAKE a great beginning for a historical romance, except that I wasn't riding a milk-white palfrey in
the sixteenth century but driving a time-worn Dodge station
wagon in the twentieth. Robbie was not sullen but worried
about what lay ahead of him among his unknown relatives. I was
sorry for him, but rather looking forward to my job in Brierbank. At least I knew what I was going to do, but Robbie hadn't
the least idea what to expect, and since there's nothing worse
than some insensitive adult telling one how much fun it's all going to be, I kept quiet.

We had left Fremont at seven yesterday morning, and he had
ignored my few attempts at conversation until I gave up and
returned to my own thoughts for company. When he did speak, I
almost jumped.

"I suppose you know," he said with the tragic dignity possible
only for fourteen-year-olds, "that they've done this to get rid of
us."

"Done what, for heaven's sake?" I asked. For all I knew, this was the first time he'd spoken since he got up this morning. He'd accepted his mother's goodbye kiss in silence, and had been stiff of back and upper lip while shaking hands with my father.

"Shipping us out of the country," he said. "They want to get rid of us so they can be *alone*."

"I don't know about you," I said, "but I was hired to put all this research material together, and that's what I'm on my way to do."

"Ha!" he said scornfully. "Couldn't you have typed up all that stupid stuff back in Fremont? But they don't want you around this summer any more than they want me."

I was twenty-four, and resented being lumped in with him as a possible encumbrance to the happy marriage of my father and his mother. Besides, if I was to be stuck with him for the summer, I wanted to get the order of precedence made clear from the first.

"Listen," I said. "I'm a grown woman. Fremont's my home town, and I live my own life in it, no matter what my father does." I took a quick glance and saw him staring straight ahead. I had the uncomfortable feeling that he was close to tears. He was slight for his age, and his profile still looked childish and innocent, long black lashes and all. He must have hated those.

"I suppose you're right," I said, "about the advantage of being grown-up. I could have refused this job, but it appealed to me."

"Even with me included in it?" he asked bitterly.

"Yep!" That wasn't quite true, and it was even less true at this moment, with rebellion in the ranks from the start. "What would you rather be doing," I asked cheerfully, "if you had your druthers?"

He didn't answer at once.

The time was June, the morning fine, the road ran empty past green fields and woods, and off to the east there was a broad sweep of glittering sea. I'd have been enjoying myself without qualification if I hadn't been burdened with one resentful child who was probably going to sulk the whole time.

But of course he was the reason why his mother was paying me so much over what I'd have asked for the Kendrum Genealogy project.

Beside me there was one small, furtive sniffle, and then in a very steady voice he answered my question. "I always went to my grandmother's in Cohasset, and then my mother came for her vacation. The house is built out over the rocks, and if you're on the porch when it's rough it's like being on the deck of a ship. The waves crashed right under my windows sometimes, and the gulls woke me up. . . . And I knew all the kids."

The last six words were the most forlorn. I said, "Well, I can see how you'd miss it. But Fremont's a friendly town, and there's the harbor and all that life. Did you ever sail? You could learn how—"

"But I'm not *there!* I'm going somewhere else!" His voice cracked. "I don't know why they couldn't have let me go back to Cohasset, if they didn't want me around. My grandmother likes me."

"And your mother adores you. And Cohasset's still there, it's not going any place. Your mother wants you to know your father's family, that's all." But I could tell this wasn't cutting any ice with him, and I could sympathize, having known an abysmal shyness and stomach-wringing apprehension whenever I had to go into a new school or neighborhood, which had happened quite often in the years when my father's work as a civil engineer took us from one place to another. We came back to Fremont to stay before my mother died, and I was grateful to be able to go through high school as a member of the same class with which I'd begun the eighth grade.

"Our parents always think they know what's best for us," I said. "I still get it from my father once in a while, believe it or not. And sometimes they're right, though I hate to admit it."

"Well, they're not right this time!" he said fiercely.

"And you'll prove it if it kills you, huh? Hey, do you want something to eat? Your mother packed enough lunch to feed us for a week. I suppose she thinks we could stray off Route 1 and get lost in the wilds."

No smile. "I'm not hungry, thank you."

"I'll try to contain myself for another few miles, then. Look on the map and see how far we are from Prospect. That's where we cross the Penobscot."

He took the map and began sternly studying it.

"He'll be off on his bike, on his own most of the time," his mother had promised me. "And he's a very sensible boy, so you're not to worry if he's out of sight. But you're in command and he knows it."

It sounded simple in theory, but having been a kid myself and now being a fourth-grade teacher, I knew it could turn out to be anything but simple. "A nice youngster," my father had described him. But at that time he had never lived with Master Robert Bruce Kendrum; and I made his acquaintance at the wedding, only two weeks ago, a slim, smallish, dapper boy in a new three-piece suit; he had black hair and beautiful, solemn, gray eyes. He called my father "sir."

That was all I knew of him. Still, he hadn't been expelled from any schools, and Virginia seemed to be a down-to-earth, clear-eyed person who wouldn't blithely ignore any tendencies toward sadism, pyromania or kleptomania, compulsive lying, or even—God help us—juvenile alcoholism or a dalliance with drugs.

After crossing all this off I still wasn't exactly euphoric about his company, and I couldn't blame him for feeling the same way about me. He'd been sent away from his mother after having been the principal male in her life for three years, and forced into the company of an adult female who was also a schoolteacher. If *that* wasn't monstrously unfair, what was?

I couldn't endure the emanations. "Look, Robbie," I said

briskly, "let's have an armed truce and get along the best we can, huh? If you get to feeling absolutely awful, I promise you I'll get you back to Fremont. But let's give it a good try."

I didn't look at him, so I couldn't tell at once how he reacted, but it seemed to me that the vibrations calmed down a bit. At least I felt more cheerful, and the day got its June lustre back. Before we reached Calais we pulled off the road and ate some lunch, and each found a convenient patch of trees for our private purposes.

Still no conversation, but at least he wasn't beginning a hunger strike.

I think he expected more display at the border, and St. Stephen and Calais do seem all one in spite of the International Bridge, but I pointed out the difference in flags, and the signs printed in French as well as English. Morose silence from Robbie all the way across the New Brunswick countryside to St. John.

St. John, a big and busy port city, looked easy on the road map. But they must have rebuilt the city since the map was printed last year. Here even Robbie responded to the ever-growing atmosphere of urgency and panic. (Mine.) He sat up straight and began looking for signs, and got as excited as if we were on the lam after a bank robbery.

"That way! *That* way! Oh, gosh, you missed it! Go around again!"

True to form, when there were two ways to choose from, I always picked the wrong one; and the traffic was concentrated on our tail or bearing down on our nose, dreadfully self-assured and uncaring. Except that nobody blew his horn at us; I appreciated that.

There were no policemen to ask, and the detours were many. Robbie leaped out when we were stuck at a long red light and asked the people behind us for directions. When these petered out, down in a warehouse district, he loped across sidewalks and asked again. Everyone was kind, though amused; I suspected that watching tourists was a local sport. To me, hot and sweating now, the directions would have been unsortable tangles of second lefts and third rights, but Robbie blossomed out with a talent for clear thinking, as well as speed on those sprints during red lights. At last we were on our way out of the city, with the Sussex—Moncton signs clear, and we were jubilant.

We stopped for gas and rest rooms, and I treated him to the cold drink of his choice. After that I admired aloud the lovely pastoral scenes around us, and Robbie was impressed by the number of cows. I had decided, on my father's advice, to stop at Sussex rather than push on for Nova Scotia to find Brierbank after dark.

The motel he'd mentioned was the first one after we turned off the highway. It was small, it had a restaurant, and it was surrounded by emerald-green pastures with more cows. It also had only one room left.

The owner told me sympathetically I wouldn't be able to do any better in any of the other motels in town. He'd just tried to find rooms for a party of six. They'd gone on finally. While I was trying to think, another car drove in. I was too tired to go on for miles in the hope of finding two rooms; I hastily registered for us, took the key, and went to break the news to Robbie.

We might have been partners in adversity back in St. John, but now the bleak silence took over. He looked at me coldly and inarticulately, and I said, "We can ignore each other. You can have the television, and I'll read, unless I like what you've picked. Now I'm taking a walk into town to stretch my legs. Want to go?"

"No," he said with stark desolation.

"Want to get your bike out?" Too late I had a vision of him starting back on two wheels for Maine and Mother.

"No." He cleared his throat and said in a constricted voice, "I'll watch TV."

I left him, feeling like a rat, arguing with myself that he

needed to be alone. But in a strange motel room at four of a beautiful afternoon, curtains drawn, staring at some dismal re-run on television? I nearly went back and said, "Robbie, come on. And I mean it."

But I didn't.

2
CHAPTER

VIRGINIA had asked me about putting the genealogy data together back when she was still Mrs. Kendrum of Newton, Massachusetts, and newly engaged to my father. Collecting the material had been Robbie's father's work and entertainment in the year or so he'd lived after his second and crippling heart attack. It had all been done by correspondence with other Kendrums scattered over Canada and the States, historical societies, records clerks, and keepers of archives.

"Rob believed it was the one big, significant thing he could do for Robbie," she told me. "We were physically well provided for, and there's a trust fund for Robbie's education. But he was very angry with himself because we'd never taken Robbie to Brierbank. One always thinks there's plenty of time for these things, but that's true only if one makes the time. Rob kept up a correspondence with his relatives, but we hadn't been there to visit since Robbie was small, and we hadn't taken him. He suffered real guilt about this when he knew his time was so short."

I saw the sparkle of tears before she looked quickly away from me. But when she turned back she was clear-eyed and direct. "Robbie knows all about my family, but he *is* a Kendrum and his first American ancestor deserves to be more than a name on an ancient stone in the churchyard at Brierbank. Rob felt this with all his being. So I planned to take Robbie there sometime — as a matter of fact I'd been thinking about it for this summer, though I hadn't told Robbie. And then your father happened."

She smiled at me. My father was so happy these days, and I was so happy for him, that it never occurred to me to refuse the project. Besides, I had nothing lined up yet for summer work, and to live in my hometown like a vacationer abused my bred-in-the-bone devotion to the Puritan work ethic.

I could have organized all the material in the heavy file right there in Fremont; after all, it simply amounted to a mammoth tabulating and typing job. But then Virginia told me she'd been offered the use of a house in Brierbank for her vacation, and she was sure that the owner, Robert's youngest brother, would extend the privilege to me. If I wanted to go there, and take Robbie, she would make it worth my while.

"It's the house the first Angus built, after they grew out of the cabin. The cabin site is between it and the river. The family is friendly, the countryside is lovely. Halifax is about two hours away, and that's a fascinating old city."

She didn't have to sell me very hard. The money was good, if her young son didn't turn out to be a monster, and I had another very private objection to remaining in Fremont during school vacation. I wasn't keen on watching Micah Jenkins come and go on the *Mollie Pitcher* all summer.

Now in this little New Brunswick town I felt as far away from him as Europe was from Fremont Harbor, and weakly wondered if he'd eventually miss me and feel some slight lack in his life. But I knew he'd never notice even if some great natural disaster took away half of Fremont, unless it caused him some inconvenience like removing the Harbor Bar, the yacht club, and the tourists.

I walked back through town toward the motel, bemused by this strange but not painful sense of dislocation. If I'd been alone I could have given in to it, pondered it, savored it as a new experience. But Robbie was there. And he was the reason that *I* was there.

I knew he didn't want anything from me—no questions, no cheery adult patronizing. But I couldn't in all conscience ignore the kid. It would be better to annoy him than to isolate him in his self-pity. How well I remembered my phases when I wanted attention but was positively surly about it. My poor father!

When I got back to the motel, Robbie wasn't there. With a sinking feeling I checked on his bag. But that was still in the room, and his bike was in the back of the station wagon. I didn't really believe he was out on the highway hitchhiking toward Maine, but I was relieved when he showed up a few minutes later.

"Hi," I said. "Ready for dinner?"

"I guess so," he said dismally. He went into the bathroom and came out looking washed, his black hair damply combed.

We were almost the only customers in the restaurant. It was early, and the traveling men must have still been doing business or having their drinks downtown.

"I hear they have good roast beef here," I said.

Robbie scowled at the menu. "I've just been out talking to some cows. I was never that close to one before. They *like* you talking to them," he said sternly. "I'll probably never eat beef again."

"That's a dairy herd, Robbie. I mean, they aren't going to end up as hamburgers or roast beef in here. But I know what you mean." In deference to his sensibilities I decided on halibut and he did the same. He ate well and topped it off with coconut custard pie, which I had no room for. I decided he wasn't going too rapidly into a decline. Masterfully he told the waitress to put everything on one check, and I supplied the tip.

Back in the room, though he was still gloomy, he didn't forget his manners; he asked me what I'd like to see on television. "Have what you like," I said. "I've got some reading to do." I showered, got into pajamas and robe, and settled down on one of the beds with Robert Kendrum's file.

"Robert grew up in Brierbank," Virginia had told me. "But like most youngsters he wasn't interested then in what the old people might be carrying in their heads. The children knew a few certain facts about their ancestors, but God knows how much that had been handed down by word of mouth has been lost forever. Now, even though there's a great interest in family history among the modern Kendrums—well—" She shrugged sadly. "I feel it for Robbie."

The first thing I read that night was a note in Robert Kendrum's hand.

"I have an obligation," he had written, "to the one who is as much responsible for my son's existence as I am; the one who took such fearful chances on the unknown ocean, who lived through the killing heat in the south, endured ferocious winters in the north, and survived epidemics that could wipe out whole families in a week.

"Angus James Kendrum. In his time he'd been known as Angus Mor—Big Angus—to distinguish him from his oldest son, Captain Angus (of the local militia), and his first grandson, Angus J. So we called him that, familiarly. He was too far away in time to be considered any sort of grandfather. To us he was a young adventurer. My cousins and I played in the cellar hole of his cabin. We had an old skiff on the river and used to act out the story of his arrival by canoe, following the river up from Oquiddic Harbor eighteen miles away. All that we knew of him before that day was that he'd come from Scotland by way of Georgia. Otherwise he was a figure with no past until the moment he and his younger brother Calum and their friend Donald Muir canoed around the bend in the river, and he said, 'This is where it will be.'"

Angus Mor in Brierbank was well-documented by the recording of his crown grant in Halifax; his stone in the churchyard, his name in town and church records, the names and dates of his children's births in various old family Bibles. There was nothing *he* had written; he was illiterate.

Angus before Brierbank was a mystery. Brierbank was the English of a Gaelic place name in a Scottish valley that had been (and still was) Kendrum country. But a paid researcher there had found too many Angus Kendrums in the birth registers of too many little parishes, too many born around the time given on Angus Mor's stone. Angus was a very common name among the Kendrums, like James, Hector, Archibald, and so forth.

One obvious fact was that Angus Mor had come from the valley of Strathcoran. But how, why, and when? He'd have been fifteen at the time of the rising for Prince Charlie in 1745; quite possibly, if he were a big enough boy, he'd have been out for the Prince like the rest of the Kendrum men. Most of them had been massacred at Culloden as they tried to hold the line against Butcher Cumberland's dragoons. Their chief, the fifth Earl, had been killed, and those who'd escaped back to their valley expected to be hunted out and killed or sent into slavery. It was the same ghastly story all over the Highlands.

Another obvious fact was that the boy Angus and his younger brother had somehow gotten to America, to Georgia, after the battle on that miserable, bloody, April day in 1746. But what about the years between then and the arrival in Nova Scotia in 1760? They might have come as servants with some gentlemanly exile of the kind who set up their little Highland kingdoms in the Southern states, having been allowed their freedom for having sworn never to bear arms against the Crown.

Robert had gathered enough material on the life and times of the Scots in America to flesh out several historical novels. But in all his correspondence with strangers, or with distantly related Kendrums who sometimes had family yarns and legends to tell, he had never discovered anything about Angus James Kendrum in Scotland. And no passenger lists in the old shipping records showed these two as free emigrants, servants, or felons.

He'd clipped a scribbled note to this. "Just found out that after Culloden a number of Scots assumed other names for protection. *Smith* was extremely popular. It's possible the two boys lived and traveled under that name until they reached friendly territory."

I closed the file and put it back in my bag, arranged my pillows, and dreamily watched Robbie's movie without really taking it in. I remember thinking the background was appropriate for what I'd just been reading; it was a costume drama set in a haunted castle on windswept moors, with occasional invasions by enemy troops in eighteenth-century uniforms which sent the heroine racing up and down slippery stone steps with a guttering candle threatening to set either her fichu or her curls on fire. There was also the obligatory duel on the grand central staircase. Robbie was absorbed into absolute immobility. I watched, but my mind was elsewhere. Reading Robert Kendrum's notes I'd been as totally involved as Robbie was now. I felt now as if I'd been listening to the man talk, and that his words had touched into life another man born nearly 250 years ago.

Angus James Kendrum should have mattered to me only as the progenitor of thousands of descendants—the early Kendrums went in for huge families of sons—all of whom I would efficiently catalogue for the printer in a modern version of the begats in the Bible. But at this moment he and the man who remembered him were far more substantial flesh and blood than Micah Jenkins, for instance.

"Micah *who*?" I jeered. Silently, of course. "Brother, you're a long way off in all ways, and you don't give a damn, do you? Well, I don't either. I didn't add "So there," but I heard it.

Before the movie ended I got ready for the night so I could put my light off and snuggle down and allow Robbie privacy to walk out of the bathroom and past my bed in his pajamas. I did say good night to him, once I knew he was in bed, and he answered, but saved face by keeping it clipped and flat. He went right to sleep and I was glad of that, for both his sake and mine.

I lay awake for a while. Robbie was a quiet sleeper but I wasn't used to another person in my room. The setting was strange and my mind was active. If I wasn't driving the car I was muddling uselessly around in Robert Kendrum's file, and I began to get angry and apprehensive about lying awake the rest of the night. I'd brought a book along and it was on the stand by my bed; if I was still awake in a half-hour I'd put on my light and read. If it disturbed Robbie, too bad. I was the one who had to do the driving tomorrow.

After I made up my mind, I relaxed, and the next thing I knew I was dreaming. I did know it; that is the important thing to remember, that I always knew when I was awake and when I was dreaming. At least I'd know when the dream began, even though once I was plunged into its events they became for a while my only reality.

Lying in bed in this little motel in a farming town, I move from my first deep sleep into a stone courtyard; strange to me, no place I have ever visited before in my dreams. There's a sense of high walls rising, and sky overhead, but I don't look up at it. I just know it's there and probably sunny, but down here deep in a courtyard like the bottom of a well I move in cold shadow. I am trying to run but I am impeded in all my limbs, so I am like a television runner in slow motion or an underwater walker.

The curious angles of stone change like headlands passed in a boat, and suddenly an archway opens before me into a tunnel of darkness, but at the far end of the black passage there is the dazzle of bright sun on blue wind-whipped water.

I want to go into the tunnel and out to that dazzle, but I am afraid of the darkness between it and me. I'm also afraid to stay in this icy underwater shadow in the deep courtyard. I wasn't frightened at first, but now I am; I want to look in all directions at once, I'm aware of openings in the walls where something could be waiting for me to pass. There is a breakneck flight of stone stairs leading down from high up. I am cold and getting colder. I long for the warmth at the end of the tunnel, I am sickly shivering and struggling to move.

All at once a man stands in the opening, signaling me with a beckoning sweep of his arm. He is wearing a dark kilt and is bundled in a plaid. As if through cotton-stuffed ears I hear his voice.

"Come on! Hurry! Come on!"

My heart, my lungs, my head itself—all going to burst. I

want to go, but I can't move; and if I could take one step from where I stand, what would it bring down on me?

Help me! I try to cry with my leaden tongue, and I try to move my feet of stone.

I woke myself with my anguished strivings, and bounded up in bed panting and staring. I was completely disoriented. Waking in my own bed, I steer myself out of these things by celestial navigation, getting a fix on the stars outside my windows. Now I had to recognize the motel room dimly lit by the outside light showing through the translucent drapes. Robbie slept on deeply. I blew out a long puff of breath, shook my head, reached tremblingly for my robe. I had been sweating and now I was chilly. But the chill was nothing like the cold I'd felt back in the courtyard. I could still remember how it slowly engulfed me, the raw dead cold of a dungeon or a tomb. I shuddered in the robe.

Now I'd have liked a hot drink and some bright lights to exorcise it all, but that was impossible. I went into the bathroom and got a drink of water for my dry mouth. I parted the curtains and looked out at stars over the hill; blessed Orion, dearest of hunters.

The scent of the early-summer night came in to me, and I knew the cows were out there on the green slopes. Tomorrow we'd arrive at Brierbank, and Virginia had assured me of a good welcome there. At best it could be fun, at worst it would be a new experience, and either way it would still be absence from Micah Jenkins.

"From you I have been absent in the spring—" Not that he'd either have the time or the interest to notice once he began his summer's work as the glamorous blue-eyed skipper of a tall ship. But one couldn't help hoping. It came from being a closet romantic.

I went back to bed and got to work on my dream. It was not, after all, an unusual one for someone who's used to dreams vivid in both action and color. There've been times when I thought my dream life had a lot to commend it over my waking one. I have recurrent dreams about certain places I've never seen yet in real life, but would like to, and I've met some people I have never forgotten.

This dream and its ambience weren't going to leave me soon. The sensation of helpless terror, of not being able to run, is common enough in bad dreams, but this was different. I had all the physical reactions of having actually been through the experience.

I groped in all directions for reasons, and suddenly remembered Robbie's movie. Before watching that, I'd been reading Robert Kendrum's notes about the bloody massacre at and after Culloden. That accounted for the beckoning man's kilt. Put it all together with my creative imagination and I had the first chapter of a historical romance; I'd even included a staircase for the duel.

Great! I said. Now put yourself under by thinking up a story line. It shouldn't be hard, they all have the same plot. Let's see, there's this girl—

Normal healthy fatigue began to take over and I slipped gradually toward sleep, and then words moved in. At this stage, if you're overtired, some phrase silly or arcane can become an obsession. This time it was a name. *Angus Mor. Angus Mor. Angus Mor.* Like an incantation. Or a summons? On the brink between waking and sleeping I thought, I'm heading into his territory. So the beckoning man could symbolize him. But why that bleak and brutal setting, why the terror freezing my voice and my movements?

There was a possible explanation hovering like a timid ghost, just waiting for me to look straight at it, but I didn't want to. I've never taken very seriously my slight gift for ESP. I've never talked about it; as a kid I thought it would make me appear a freak to my peers. When I grew older and met up with the popular interest in such subjects I still didn't think my small talent was anything to brag about. Besides, you could lose it by exposing it, and such as it was, it was mine. It belonged to *me*, Noel Paige, and its modest accomplishments I kept to myself. They'd have probably disappointed most people; another good reason to keep them private in a world in which police called in professional psychics for help in murder cases and had once even asked a mare named Lady Wonder about a missing child. Nothing I ever dreamed or received was important, except when I located my own lost dog once when I was small. In the only accident I'd ever foreseen nobody was hurt, though it had been a very odd affair and I'd even seen the cars correctly—one had Arizona plates.

But I kept it all to myself. And I refused now to entertain the sky ghost of a possibility that I'd just had a genuine psychic experience.

I went to sleep instead, and this time if I dreamed I didn't know it.

3

CHAPTER

I WOKE UP knowing instantly where I was. Robbie was trying to get out without making any noise.

"Hi," I said, and he jumped.

"I'm going over to have breakfast, okay?" he said gruffly.

"Okay. I'll be over when I get myself together."

It was nearly seven when we pulled out onto the highway; a beautiful morning, glistening with dew, a few luminous patches of fog in the low places. We had no conversation, but Robbie had eaten a large breakfast, and I always feel that if any creature, dog, cat, bird, or boy, eats well, it's all right.

A few hours later the entrance into Nova Scotia provided us with the impressive display Robbie had expected at the border. We stopped at the first available spot for cartons of milk to go with our leftover sandwiches. An hour and a half later, driving along the Trans-Canada Highway with a little more traffic but not too much, we saw the Oquiddic Valley sign come up just where our instructions said we'd find it. We made a left turn off the highway into a dreamy, idyllic landscape of plowed fields in various shades of chocolate under the sun, leafy woodland, bowery orchards, pastures where sheep, cows, sometimes horses and ponies, grazed on turf which in this light had the lustre of grass-green taffeta. Hay meadows rippled in the breeze, and fragrance upon fragrance blew in at the car windows.

The road was narrow and winding, almost empty except for an occasional car or pickup, and once a group of youngsters on bicycles. They waved, and I waved back. Robbie didn't. He sat aloofly in his corner, staring hard at the hand-drawn map someone had sent Virginia.

We crossed again and again the narrow sky-reflecting band of the river as it flowed around the gentle loops of its course through the valley. We came finally to the Four Corners marked in red on the map. I wasn't prepared for the jolt the name *Brierbank* gave me when I saw that road sign. Angus Mor named this place! I thought excitedly. And that was the same river—that *is* the river!

I glanced at Robbie; his face was marble-cold and still. I wondered if he were trying to imagine his father at fourteen, riding these roads on his bicycle. But maybe he was so anxious about the plunge ahead that he could think only of himself.

Another sign. Brierbank Corner, four miles; Muir's Grant, six; Oquiddic Harbor, eighteen. We drove between woods full of birds until we came to a wide white-barred gate on the left, with a painted sign showing a glossy black horse, and over it the name "Maple Leaf Ranch."

"That's on the map," Robbie said tensely. "Ours is the next left after this."

"It's not the guillotine waiting for us, after all," I said. "Whenever I get nervous about something I have to do, I try to remember the people loaded in the tumbrils to go and have their heads cut off. Then I think how much luckier I am. At least I'll come out of it alive."

Robbie gave me a look of contemptuous despair, as if right now he'd rather be Sidney Carton than anybody.

The woods gave way to open fields again, we drove down a slight grade, and there were the white posts marking our turnoff. It was a hard dirt road running off to the east between pastures that climbed away from us on the left toward forested land, and fell away from us on our right down a long slope toward the river. From the upper pasture black and white cows watched us with solemn fascination. A little distance on we drove between two matching gates where the cattle could be driven across the road to the lower pasture. Beyond the gates a brook flowed through a culvert under the road and brawled foaming and beer-brown down the hill to the river.

Woodlot replaced the left-hand pasture, rising steeply to the northern sky, like our Maine woods in its mixture of hardwoods and evergreens. Ahead of us a newly shingled barn roof with lightning rods suddenly stood out above some tall old pines. We went around a mild curve. The house was on the right, at the top of the southern slope, and the line of venerable pines began at the road and went down past the western side of the house for a little distance. I turned off onto the newly graveled crescent of driveway and stopped the car at the back door. Straight ahead of us the barn faced us; not only its roof was new, but its doors and other trim looked to be freshly painted white.

The house was a familiar type to a State-of-Mainer, a roomy white clapboard farmhouse with a good-sized ell. That would be the owner's quarters whenever he came home for a weekend, as long as we were living in his house. We would share the kitchen.

We sat there, neither of us moving, and the silence came in on us, yet it was no more true silence than the solitude was emptiness. There were birds, a cow lowing back in the pasture, the rush of the brook we had passed, the light wind in those massive old pines.

"Well, we're here," I said tritely. I got out and stretched and looked all around me like one of those science-fiction people emerging from a space ship on a strange planet; I felt that far from home. Robbie got out, reluctant, holding himself stiffly. The back entry of the main house was unlocked, and I went through it and into a hall that ran through to the front door. The kitchen opened off it to the left. The house had been recently restored, Virginia had told me, and it smelled faintly of new plaster, paint, and lumber. The only sound was a clock ticking loudly in the kitchen.

I was alone. For all I knew Robbie was still standing like a pillar of salt by the car. Drawn by the clock as if by a welcoming voice, I went into the kitchen. The clock stood on a mantel shelf above a black iron wood range set against the ell wall. There was a full woodbox beside it, and two rockers were drawn up to it. Across the room there were a modern electric stove and refrigerator in a dull soft yellow that was a good match for the old-fashioned paint color on woodwork and floor. The kitchen went from back to front, old-fashioned in its spaciousness, with a roomy pantry in the northeast corner. I went in and admired its cupboards, open shelves, and counter space, and I looked out the window over the sink and saw Robbie standing up on the edge of the road apparently staring at the roof.

The cleanliness of the place positively sang, and most of the cooking utensils were shiningly new. A slight depression darkened my good mood. Keeping house for myself in my three-room attic apartment in Fremont was one thing. I was going to have to spend a little more time on it here than I was used to. Somebody else's house, and me not even an in-law connection of the family. I hoped Robbie's uncle wasn't one of those old-maidish bachelors who would be appalled to come home unexpectedly and find a day's dirty dishes stacked in the pantry, or that lovely satiny black iron stove in need of polish.

I went back out into the kitchen. Between the pantry and the wood stove there was a door to the ell with a thumb latch. At the southern end, where two windows looked down over the slope to the river, a long harvest table was set with two places, blue willow ware on bright mats. A pottery jug held daisies, buttercups, and red clover; there was a note propped against the jug.

Feeling a little like Alice in Wonderland reading her messages, I opened the note.

"Lunch in fridge and breadbox, tea and pot on stove," it said in a clear flowing script. "Welcome to Brierbank. We'll be expecting you to supper. Just follow the road past the barn and you'll end up in our dooryard." It was signed "Janet Kendrum. (Mrs. Archie.)"

Behind me Robbie said, "They don't have any TV. I wonder if they have any real bathroom in this place."

"Probably it's a two-holer out in the barn," I said callously. "Why don't you take a look through the house and see what you can find, then bring in our gear, and I'll start putting lunch on." I waved the note at the table. "Isn't it nice?"

He gave me a martyred look and disappeared through the nearest doorway into the front hall. I washed my hands in the pantry and put the shiny teakettle on to boil, found a crusty loaf in the breadbox and set it on a breadboard from the pantry, where I found also a knife in a handy rack of cutlery. In the refrigerator there were some essentials like milk, butter, bacon, and eggs. The prepared lunch was a bowl of hearty salad with a jar of homemade dressing beside it and a plate of thin-sliced ham.

The ominous warning of housework-to-come disappeared. I felt happy and adventurous. This arrival in a strange place with no one about but everything ready for us appealed to my romantic imagination. It would have been a lot better without this sulky kid, but if it weren't for him and his Kendrum ancestry I wouldn't be here at all.

He came running downstairs and said on his way out, "It's at the back, over that corner." He nodded at the pantry.

I went up the steep straight flight to the upper hall. Straight ahead of me there was a narrow, paneled door which I thought led into a closet under the eaves. There was a window beside it, and then the bathroom. This had obviously been made over from a small bedroom, so it was roomy. It wasn't fancy, but everything was new, everything worked, there was hot water and plenty of towels. Beside it there was a door into the ell, corresponding to the one downstairs. At right angles to the ell there was a wall of cupboards and drawers, painted a pale blue-green. It was broken by a door which led into a big front bedroom with one window facing east past the ell and two southerly ones above the kitchen windows downstairs.

The bare walls were off-white, the woodwork that same soft faded blue-green. Someone had done a masterly job of mixing paint and applying it to get that gently aged effect. The furniture was the painted Victorian sort, but under the plain white coverlet the mattress and pillows were modern, and the bed was made up. There were plain white ruffled curtains at the windows and braided rugs on the floor. This one has to be for *me*, I thought greedily, and then I remembered the teakettle, so I had to run downstairs before I looked at anything else.

The kettle was practically jumping up and down on the burner. Robbie had brought in the luggage and left it in the middle of the floor, and was now wheeling his bike across the yard. I rinsed the teapot with boiling water and made tea, then put my head out the door and yelled, "Lunch!"

He came with gratifying speed.

"Tea or milk?" I asked him, and he said in a deeper voice than usual, "Oh, I guess I'll have a cup of tea."

He had no intention of starving himself, and I kept him company all the way. He was the one who discovered the plate of devil's food cupcakes in the cake drawer of the breadbox, and ate three, with milk, for dessert. Ah, to be a skinny fourteen again. I reserved my cupcakes until later.

At the end of the meal I said, "I'll stack the dishes, and let's get our stuff upstairs to our rooms. Then we'll be free till we go out to supper tonight."

"Do we have to go?" It was a back-handed compliment for me; better the devil you know, and so forth.

"Robbie, they got this all ready for us. It's only manners to go and thank them. And they want to see you." He groaned. "You might as well take the plunge and get it over with."

He shrugged helplessly and picked up his bags.

My heart was already set on the room I'd seen, but the flowered furniture turned him off anyway, and he chose the room across the hall, also on the front of the house. His side windows looked west through the branches of the old pines toward the lower pasture, the cascading brook, and the main road well beyond. There was another bedroom behind his, empty except for some cartons and odd pieces of furniture that had just been pushed up against the walls. This room looked west also, and then out from the back of the house across the dirt road to the wooded hillside. Except for the bathroom, all the doors were ancient, and had thumb latches. The orginals, I guessed.

Robbie's furniture was plain, either very old or very good reproductions of old stuff. There was a woven Methodist Wheel coverlet on the narrow bed, hit-or-miss rag rugs, straight curtains of coarse natural-colored linen hung by tabs from the rods. There were good reading lamps beside the beds in both rooms.

I was too anxious to go outside to bother now with putting all my clothes away. When I left my room Robbie was standing by the hall window. I went and stood beside him and he didn't move away at once, but kept on looking out, inscrutably. The river glittered through a break in the shrubbery that marked the watercourse.

"We can swim down there, Robbie," I said. "At least your father said he used to. And they had an old skiff. I wonder if there's still one there."

He shrugged, and muttered, "I don't know." He turned away from me toward the stairs. I waited a few minutes to give him some sense of freedom. When I did go downstairs, his bike was gone from where he'd left it by the cellar bulkhead.

CHAPTER

I HAD EXPECTED that any kid would head first for the river. But Robbie Kendrum would have to come to terms with his new environment in his own way. Personally, I fitted into the *any kid* category.

On the way to the front door I looked into the living room. It was one long room like the kitchen—I suspected it had once been two small rooms—and empty of furniture. There was a newly paneled and bricked fireplace between the western windows. The floor shone like molasses candy, but its other woodwork was that same restful faded blue-green against off-white walls. Probably the owner had a choice collection of pictures, and spent his leisure time scouting for antiques. I hoped ungratefully that he wouldn't show up while Robbie and I were there.

I went out the front door, which was heavy and serviceable, with no fancy fanlight, and across a short stretch of recently mown lawn which abruptly became a field of daisies and buttercups. The wind had died out, the day was hot now, most birds quiet, the cows were probably lying down in the shade; I could hear the brook glissading downhill in its miniature rapids.

Micah Jenkins, Micah Jenkins, I intoned to test my other-world location. He came sharply into my mind as I'd last seen him, leaning against a post on the yacht club verandah, his arm around a small dark girl who was sparkling up at him like three strings of Christmas-tree lights of that insane-driving blinker variety. I hadn't meant to stare, I'd thought I was being casual—an indifferent glance flung in passing—but he intercepted it with those cerulean eyes, and his expression said as strongly as speech, "You had your chance."

The chance being his turning up at my attic door one night with his bedroll on his shoulder and walking in as if he lived there, or at least paid the rent. Mutual seduction under poetic circumstances is fine. Which was not this thing. I had the feeling I was supposed to welcome him with touching gratitude, and at once fall subserviently upon my bed.

"What are you doing here with that?" I asked ungraciously, and he replied with innocent astonishment, "Moving in."

"You are not," I said, and then added with the same brilliant wit that characterized my retorts at age ten or twelve, "Boy, you've got some nerve!"

We had a brief tussle. I am wiry, and he was weakened by the physical impact of his amazement at my reaction. He left with as much dignity as he could manage, having to go down two flights of stairs with that bedroll and meet my landlord on the sidewalk.

Goodbye, Micah Jenkins. If he could ever have forgiven me for my lack of appreciation when he'd been so generous, he could never forgive me Mr. Appleby's grin.

So I tested for him now, five hundred-odd miles away, and his eyes were just as blue, his head as blond, and his smile as devastating, his hips as lean and his motions as lithe, but since they weren't within touching distance I could tell myself that all these charms were merely nature's products, like the daisies I was walking through. The difference was that the daisies didn't take credit for anything. Micah behaved as if he'd designed and created himself.

I stopped on the path, or was stopped; I had come to a green dip in the field, the turf lumpy in places where it grew over the fieldstone ruins of chimney or foundations.

It had to be the site of Angus Mor's cabin.

I sat on the upper rim and looked down at the river coiling and shining on its way south to the sea eighteen miles away.

What time of year was it, what sort of day, when Angus Kendrum beached his canoe down there for the first time? Late spring? Early summer? The slopes would have been heavily wooded in those days, and he would walk up through the trees to this spot. From where he could still see the river, but it would be high enough to be safe from spring flooding.

I wondered if he spoke to his brother in English or Gaelic, and if Donald Muir had come all the way with them, or had stopped off farther south, in the place known now as Muir's Grant. But it was likely that all three men worked together to build each other's cabins. Maybe they all shared one at first, until the women came.

Supposing it was a day like this, the high tide of summer. What had Angus thought and felt? I remembered the paralyzing terror in my dream. If he had been one of those who ran for his life, there must have been a sense of journey's end, after all those years in the alien and sometimes killing heat of the Georgia summers. He could never have felt at home there, this exiled Highlander. No wonder when he came up the river he said, "This is where it will be."

I got up and went on down to the river. Below the thick-trunked alders the water flowed sibilantly by a small sandy beach, and there was a bank out a little distance around which the eddies swirled in a blaze of spangles. I took off my sneakers and tried the water; it was cold but no more so than the ocean and lakes at home. Across from me pasture land came down to a margin thick with buttercups. Far up the slope to my left, and eastward, someone was running a tractor across a plowed field.

I sat down on the coarse sand and shook warm handfuls of it over my toes. Swallows dived to catch unseen (to me) insects over the water. I lay back and watched them rise into the sky past the leaves. Drowsily I wondered what had become of Robbie, if he had got lost. Don't worry about him, Virginia said. Well, I wouldn't. He could ask directions, he had a tongue in his head.

Everything about me ran together musically in my ears: the river, the swallows' excited voices close and far, the distant tractor engine, the steady buzzing from the bees working in the flowers. I began to drift.

Weightless on the tide, I was still conscious of the river lapping at the sand bank and the swallows' aerial presence, but I was also standing on a height of rough turf with a cold wind blowing my hair back from my face, and I was watching the sea, not so much for a glimpse of distant islands as for a sail. It would be a dark coppery-brown sail.

So far, so good, I thought with drugged amusement; I'm out of the tunnel. To my right, dark water like a deep fjord, forested hills rising away from it toward snow-topped mountains as old as the world. A sea loch, that was it, a drowned valley into which the sea had poured. So wild, so harsh, and so desperately beautiful. No, *I* was desperate. But I was young, and I couldn't believe the parting would be forever.

There was the coppery sail, small among the boisterous crests, but the boat was steadily beating her way toward land. Behind me the others saw, and shouted. There was a general move down toward the shore somewhere. I felt it, knew about it, took it for granted, but actually saw nothing.

I put my hand inside my clothes at the breast and my fingers closed around the soft small leathery pouch hanging on a thong around my neck. That's all right then, I thought. Pulling my hand out I felt the coarse scratch of wool across my knuckles and, looking down, I saw the plaid wrapped around me and fastened on the left shoulder. The tartan had muted shades of blue and green, and a line of red like wild berries.

I thought—Noel thought—*Of course!* Then the despairing grief ebbed away and I woke fully there on the riverbank. I was groggy, hot, dry-mouthed, and disappointed because I'd waked up. I looked at my hand where I'd felt the rough wool, put it inside my blouse and closed my fingers as they'd tightened on the little bag. Now what was in *that*? I shut my eyes and tried to recall everything about it, went practically dizzy and numb with the effort, but it was no good. Everything had gone so fast, including the lightning illumination which had brought forth that *Of course*.

Bad-tempered and thirsty, I trudged up to the house. Robbie was in the kitchen having a mug-up of homemade bread and butter, and milk. I was restored by the airy coolness inside the house and a large drink of water pumped up cold and unchlorinated from the house's own well. I got one of my cupcakes and offered Robbie the other two. After a short struggle with his conscience (I like to think that was it) he took one of them.

"I've been down to the river," I said. "Did you see anything interesting?"

He lifted one shoulder and made that maddening sound that goes with it. "Gosh, that sounds smashing," I said. "I guess I'll go up and get my work laid out."

I went upstairs and looked over the stored furniture in the room behind Robbie's. I found a fairly modern and firm card table, which I set up by one of my front windows. I tried out chairs until I got the right one, and arranged my rugs under all the legs so I wouldn't scratch the new finish on the wide floorboards. Then I uncovered my typewriter, unpacked my paper and carbon sheets, the Kendrum file, my new pens in different colors to help me keep families categorized, my typing eraser, my box of paper clips. The card table wasn't big enough so I moved some of the stuff to a commode which in the old days would have held the washbowl and jug on top and the matching chamber mug underneath.

I felt as virtuous as if I'd done a day's work already on the project. Carried away, I put my clothes in the bureau and the closet, which opened into the storage section on the wall opposite the bathroom. There were dried-lavender sachets in the bureau drawers and plenty of hangers in the closet. Then I picked out a dress to wear to supper tonight with Mrs. Archie Kendrum, a thin cool outfit in a gold, yellow, and ivory print. I always felt good in it.

I knew who Mrs. Archie was, through Virginia's briefing. She was the widow of an uncle to five Kendrum brothers. Her children were well-grown and scattered, and she kept house for the eldest of Robert's brothers, Hector, who now owned the family farm. Then there came Alec, Robert, Stuart, and Angus. Robert had died from his bad heart three years ago; Alec had gone only this past spring, very early, when there was still snow in the woods where he was found. Heart again; it seemed to run in the family, Virginia said. Alec had left a daughter and twin sons.

Stuart, next to the youngest, lived in the village. He was a skilled carpenter and painter; in fact he had done all the work on this house, which had been rescued from a state of dereliction by the youngest brother, another Angus.

The house was known as the Angus J. House, for a grandson of Angus Mor, and it had gone to this man's daughters rather than to any of his sons. Some of the sons had gone to sea, to the States, or out west, and the eldest had fallen in love with a girl who'd inherited a big farm of her own. This was the property farmed by Hector Kendrum now.

So the house which Angus Mor had built eventually passed into the hands of heirs who might have carried Kendrum blood but not the name, and some had never even seen the place.

Whatever else the present Angus was, he was also a rescuer, and I appreciated that. Not only for the sake of the house itself, but because I could be standing in it now, gazing absently at myself in the Victorian mirror as if at my portrait in a frame, and hardly aware at all of Micah Jenkins. I'd been jolted out of time and space as I knew them.

I went out to the hall and called down the stairs. "Robbie, I'm going to take a shower. Do you want the bathroom first?"

No answer or sound. I shrugged and made the noise he'd given me earlier, got my robe, and went into the bathroom.

Later when I was dressing I saw Robbie down in the field standing on the rim of the cellar hole, hands in his pockets, motionless. I wondered hopefully if he were trying to imagine the cabin there among the great trees of the past. Not likely. He was probably being miserable, trying to fight off unmanly tears of homesickness and what he considered rejection.

"Oh, Robbie," I said softly. "It's not that, but you'll never believe it."

As if he'd heard me he set off toward the river at a run. I hoped he'd show up in time, but if he didn't I'd go along without him and he could ride down to the farm on his bike or not come at all.

Brushing my dark hair and coaxing it out around my ears, I was considering myself thoughtfully in the mirror again. Maybe this furniture had actually belonged to one of Angus J.'s daughters, and she'd looked thus in the mirror while getting into her Sunday crinoline, or curling her hair. Even if she hadn't, it was certain that some Victorian females somewhere had seen themselves in it, either with pleasure or dissatisfaction.

When I was in high school I decided my eyes were the color of sherry until I learned later on that there were many colors of sherry, and my eyes were really just plain light hazel. I've learned to make the most of them. They seem to change color with whatever I wear, and they're slightly almond-shaped; my eyebrows and lashes are naturally dark, I have a dimple in one cheek, never needed braces, and I have long legs and a long neck. I used to go through the catalog as a way of counting my blessings. Now I don't need to—not often, that is. Not after all the gifts my fourth-graders bring to my desk. There have been enough men interested besides Micah Jenkins to make up for the high school years when I could comfort myself only by saying my eyes were sherry-colored like Emily Dickinson's, but it takes a class of fourth-graders to make your ego really blossom like a rose.

Whistling, I put on my yellow dress and picked up a matching sweater, and ran downstairs. Robbie was just coming in the back door. He gave me a quick but complete scrutiny from head to foot. "I'd better put on something clean, I guess," he said. On his way upstairs he called back, "Hey, that swimming cove down there is neat."

"I thought so too," I called back, being careful not to sound overenthusiastic.

5

CHAPTER

AFTER IT PASSED the barn, the dirt road curved around a shoulder where a few twisted old apple trees were all in bloom, and ran on a slant across the hillside to the river. On the other side of the bridge we drove between hayfields and cultivated land. Everything wore a golden bloom in the late-afternoon light. As usual the barn showed first, a huge modern structure with a silo, surrounded by outbuildings for the machinery and the rest of the stock. Then came the white house, set among big pink-flowering apple trees, and one tall cherry with a couple of swings hanging from it. There were several cars and one pickup in the yard between the house and the outer buildings.

I turned in at the end of the line, and two big mixed-breed dogs came rushing at us, barking, but the sound seemed more sociable than menacing, as the tails kept wagging. Some cats of different sizes and colors perched on the back porch railing and steps were unperturbed. When we got out, with the dogs bouncing around us, five geese crowded up to a wire fence that ran past the back of the house and gave voice; beyond them a couple of cows watched us, and one of them mooed loudly. (All this welcoming clamor turned out to be typical of any Kendrum gathering.) There was a good deal of human noise in the house, and suddenly the back screen door flew open and the noise spilled out, bearing on its crest like a chip on a wave a slight, fast-moving redheaded woman, wearing an apron over slacks and a green shirt.

The cats scattered. The dogs flung themselves excitedly at her. People poured out behind her. I didn't have to look at Robbie to know his reaction. He'd liked the dogs but *this*—

"It's all right!" the woman called in a surprisingly hearty voice for the size of her. "None of us bite, dogs *or* folks! I'm Janet Kendrum." She gave Robbie's stiff shoulder a pat. "Robbie, I'd know you anywhere, you're the image of your father." She turned to me with her hand out. Her grip was hard. "Are you Nole or Nowell? We've been arguing about it."

"Nowell, like the first one the angels did say. . . . The lunch was so good, thank you very much for getting everything ready for us."

"I was happy to do it. Well, come and meet them all. Robbie, here are two of your cousins." She pulled them over to her, one on each side. One was Ross, the other Calum. They were a little older and quite a bit taller than Robbie, black-haired, long-legged in jeans and rugby shirts. They were identical twins, but one wore glasses and a moderately short haircut, the other had hair to the nape. The spontaneous grins were the same. They said, "Hi, Rob," and hands came out.

Robbie's response was grudging, but the twins didn't look offended; kids understand kids. Their older sister, Rowan Kendrum, had the same type of looks, a long face with good cheekbones and squarish jaw, a well-cut mouth on the wide side, gray eyes, and black hair. The strong features were scaled down in her. She was a good-looking girl.

Three younger children stared at us the same way the cows stared. They were Stuart's, two girls and a boy. Two had round rosy-tan moons for faces, and blond Dutch cuts. The other, one of the girls, had more of what I was already beginning to call the Kendrum look. Their mother was fair, pretty, and stout.

Mrs. Alec was a tall woman, plain but with a pleasant, gentle manner. Knowing that her husband had died only a few months ago, I thought I could sense the wellspring of sadness in her, not quite brimming over, always kept in control.

We stood around in the yard exchanging the kind of conversation that goes on at such times. The three children gazed alternately at me and at Robbie, who stared grimly at the curious geese and the articulate cow. Suddenly a soccer ball appeared, as if one of the twins had conjured it out of a dandelion.

"We were just kicking this around," he said. "Come on, Rob." They started toward the far side of the barn, with one of the dogs and the younger children. My hand itched to give Robbie a good hard shove between the shoulder blades. As if he felt my intent he took off. The remaining dog ran sociably with him, and I saw Robbie reach down to rub the dog's rough back.

"They'll make it now," Rowan said behind me.

"He's so shy."

"Why wouldn't he be?" asked Mrs. Archie. "Dropped down into this mess of relatives? . . . I'd better go check on my oven." The other woman went back in with her.

Rowan and I exchanged information; she was with an insurance company in Halifax, she usually stayed in during the week but had come home especially for this supper tonight. Her mother was a teacher and the principal of the Brierbank school "So you have something in common with her," she said. "But I never wanted to teach. I don't have the courage. Or else I'm just plain selfish," she added cheerfully. "I like being all on my own. Here come Uncle Hector and Stuart."

They'd been in the barn, and stopped outside while one lit his pipe. The family look was there, though he was a heavy, broad-shouldered man. "That's Hector," Rowan said. "Everybody's favorite uncle. Uncle Stuart's the one who's been working on the house. When I was little I thought he and Aunt Len were like Jack Spratt and his wife, and said so once at a family gathering. It went over big."

"I can imagine."

"Aunt Len thought it was funny, but Uncle Stuart didn't. Neither did my parents. Come on, once you've met them you'll have been through the lot, except for all the second and third and fourth cousins strewn around the countryside. And oh yes, Uncle Bob and Aunt Christy. They'd be here, but they're over visiting their daughter in Amherst for a few days."

Hector Kendrum was slow-moving, easy-talking, as if time had no meaning. "So you're going to write us up. Good thing it'll just be names and dates. Some of the family history would have the old folks turning over in their graves. Shake up some of the living, too," he added reflectively.

"Uncle Hector, you never told *me* any of those stories," Rowan said.

"And a good thing too."

"I'll get them from Angus," she threatened and he laughed. Stuart didn't smile and I had the feeling he wasn't any more eager to shake hands than Robbie had been.

"The house is beautiful, Mr. Kendrum," I told him, projecting as much charm as possible.

"I haven't finished the job yet," he said stiffly. "Angus shouldn't have let anybody in."

"I don't intend to hold up the work," I said. "Don't stay away on account of Robbie and me."

He was a perfectionist; that was easy to tell from the quality of the work, and to have someone in and out where he'd been working in peace would be as irritating as a hair down the back of his shirt. "We'll be out of the house most of the time when the weather's good, and when it isn't we can still find a way to clear out and leave you to yourself."

"Well, that's fair enough," said Hector, slapping his brother's shoulder. "How about a drink before we eat?"

"Well—" said Stuart. They turned toward the back porch.

"Noel's old enough even if I'm not supposed to be!" Rowan said loudly. Hector looked around, and Rowan thumbed her nose at him. "Authoritarian male chauvinist!"

He laughed, and Stuart looked austerely at all of us.

"How about it, Noel?" Hector asked.

"No, thanks."

The men went inside. "*Do* you want a drink and nobody will let you have one?" I asked curiously.

"I never touch the stuff, any more than a little wine now and then. But I'm twenty years old and making a good week's pay in Halifax, I have my own apartment there, and I come out home and get treated like a ten-year-old." She grinned. "Actually I don't mind that much. Makes me feel cherished. It also makes Halifax look good too when I go back."

We walked across the front lawn to the big cherry at the far side, and sat on the swings. Through open windows there came adult voices and occasional laughter. When that quieted for a moment we could hear the kids shouting and dogs barking over beyond the barn.

"I didn't know what to expect here," I said, "but it's even better than nice, it's great." I started to swing, not very high. "When I was little I thought a swing was absolute heaven. Whenever I got a chance, I'd keep at it till I was seasick. I had my own swing in one place where we lived, and my mother threatened to have it taken down because I'd get off it green in the face and staggering."

Rowan giggled. "I've done it too. And did you have to learn 'How do *you* like to go up in a *swing*, Up in the *sky* so *blue*—'"

She was interrupted by the kind of roar I thought I'd left behind in Fremont. A motorcycle was shattering the innocent hour. It charged past the house and made an assault on our ears, planed into a U-turn, and came to a stop, but not to silence, facing us. It kept on making enraged, threatening noises while the driver sat there camouflaged with helmet and goggles.

"Brierbank's answer to Hell's Angels," said Rowan. "My cousin Jamesy Kendrum, Stuart's oldest. He's not a bad kid, really. He just likes to look menacing." She yelled at him between cupped hands. "Shut her off!"

He did, but still sat astride, anonymous behind goggles. "Come on over, Jamesy, and meet the new girl," Rowan insisted. He took off his helmet and goggles and hung them from the handlebars, and slouched across the lawn to meet us, stopping to light a cigarette on the way. He was Kendrum all right, but not like the twins. He was older, perhaps eighteen or so, and was either discontented, disgruntled, or suffering from self-consciousness. He nodded jerkily when he was introduced. "Hi, Jamesy," I said, making it terse and offhand to get it over with for him. There was some faint scent about him apart from tobacco that I couldn't place. It wasn't important, and it didn't jibe with his get-up. Rowan was running on about something, and then she said, "And how's the new foal that's supposed to have such a great future?"

Then I placed the scent as that of a stable.

"Oh, he's getting prettier by the day," Jamesy said, brightening.

"Do you work around horses?" I asked with genuine interest.

"Yes," he answered without looking at me. "Well, I'd better get her off the road." He returned to his machine and walked it past the house toward the yard.

"Jamesy works at Basil Hammond's horse farm," Rowan explained. "That's the Maple Leaf Ranch. You must have seen it on the way. Basil's English and he thinks 'ranch' sounds horsier than 'farm.'"

Someone began ringing a handbell at the back door. "Supper," said Rowan. "Come on, I'm famished. Aren't you?"

I was.

The round-faced little girl was ringing the bell. "It's turkey," she told us, beaming; she looked ridiculously like her mother. The soccer players and audience came around the barn and I was pleased to see that Robbie was keeping up with the twins instead of stalking along behind them in stony solitude. Jamesy silently held the door open for Rowan and me and came in after us. The house smelled like Thanksgiving.

The women were hurrying back and forth between the kitchen and the dining room, and a table had also been set up in the kitchen. Hector and Stuart were standing out of the way across the room, with their glasses.

"Hello, Jamesy my boy," Hector called. At the sight of his son, Stuart's face actually hardened. I saw it change.

"Took the long way round, did you?"

"I came straight from work."

"Oh." It was a dry, harsh sound between a snort and a chuckle. "You took so long, I thought you maybe came by way of the Bain Place. What were you smoking when you came across the yard?"

Jamesy blushed, but it was a blush of rage. He pushed by Rowan and went around the table to his father; his slouch had changed into something more aggressive.

"Hello, Jamesy dear!" called Mrs. Archie, whisking in from the dining room. Jamesy didn't look at her. Rowan was taking wine from the refrigerator. The younger ones milled about us.

"Goddammit, it wasn't a joint," Jamesy said in a low voice. "Smell me. Go ahead, breathe deep." He thrust his head forward into his father's masklike face. "Tell me what else there is besides cigarette tobacco and the stink of horse."

"That's not a stink," said Hector. "That's one of the sweetest smells there is, isn't it, Jamesy?" He put his hand on his brother's shoulder. "Remember Sam and Johnny? How old did they get to be? The last time I cried was the day Grampa told me Sam was dead."

Jamesy turned away from the two men and sat on the couch under the window.

"If I was a rich man," Hector's easy voice rambled on, "I'd have me a team now and use them whenever I could. Just for the fun of it, y'know. Maybe it's not practical now, but it was all horses once, and farming went on, and life was a hell of a lot less complicated."

"Are you going to carve that first turkey," Mrs. Archie called to him, "or do you want me to start on it?"

"I dare you," said Hector, but he went on into the dining room. Stuart remained where he was, gazing down into his glass. In the light from the window he looked gaunt. Jamesy sat, hands hanging loose between his knees, staring at the linoleum. The two of them were so unhappy that I couldn't stand it, and I felt like a voyeur besides. I went to where Mrs. Alec was dishing up mashed potato and said, "What can I do?"

"Would you take this in, dear? And that dish of cranberry sauce?"

In the dining room the younger children watched Hector carve. The twins and Robbie were draped over the backs of chairs talking soccer. Mrs. Stuart was caressingly and impartially maternal to anything that came within reach, while this dreadful anger burned between her husband and son.

6

CHAPTER

JAMESY CHOSE to eat at the kitchen table with the youngsters, and I didn't blame him. Rowan asked Stuart to open the two bottles of wine. "Angus brought it over to me a few nights ago," she said. "It's supposed to be very good, something special."

"Where is he, anyway?"

"Oh, he had to fly somewhere on a job," said Rowan vaguely. "Pour yourself some first. I'll start the other bottle going this way. Have some, Noel?"

"A job, you say? More likely he knew where there was a better party," said Stuart. "With a lot more wine."

"What's the matter?" Hector teased him. "Can't you be jealous without showing it? You used to be able to tip it down, brother, before you got saved."

"Oh, Uncle Stuart, were you a swinger once?" Rowan asked mischievously. "Was he, Aunt Len?"

"I don't know. What *is* a swinger, anyway?" She smiled around the table. "He always wore his clothes well, he still does. And he could hold his liquor."

Stuart wasn't amused. He put down his fork, and drummed his fingers compulsively on the table. "I wasn't talking about liquor. Or my past. You all know what it is. The cities are loaded with it, and they can't wait to bring the filth out into the places that always used to be clean and safe."

"I don't think this is much of a conversation for the supper table," said Mrs. Archie. "We have a guest too."

"Coming from the States she must know well enough what I'm driving at. And she might as well know the disease has crept over the border. We've already had a drug raid in Brierbank— she'll hear that soon enough."

"And the Mounties didn't find a thing," Hector said soothingly. "They either got false information, or—"

"The people were warned and were able to hide the stuff."

Mrs. Alec said, "Stuart, we don't know that those young people at the Bain Place are using it for a drug distributing center. I can see the house from my kitchen windows, and there are never any strange cars there. . . . I'm often up in the night too, lately, and it's always quiet there."

"You never see evil, Priscilla," he said. "Even if outsiders never turn up there, who knows where they go in that van?"

"They take the weaving and the vegetables and the furniture orders to Halifax," Mrs. Archie said crisply. "The dear knows nobody has any chance of carrying on in secret in Brierbank. Not for long, anyway."

Stuart kept looking at Mrs. Alec. "You've got those twins out there." He nodded his head toward the noisy kitchen. "Would you be so calm if you saw them hanging out at the Bain Place? Could you tell when they came home if they'd been smoking marijuana, or trying the hard stuff?"

"I don't want them hanging idly around any place, Stuart," she said. "And I wouldn't want to smell beer or tobacco smoke on them when they come home—not at sixteen. . . . You know there were always chances for mischief in Brierbank if you knew where to look."

"And we never needed outsiders to tell us where," Aunt Len said. She chuckled and went on eating.

"Let's relax," said Hector. "I'm not about to evict my tenants without due cause. Listen to those young ones out there, and they haven't even got wine to get them started."

After that, the conversation was general. There was plenty of good food, the wine bottles were passed up and down the table, there was joking and laughter, and even Stuart relaxed and showed a more attractive facet of his personality. I could see his side; I hated seeing kids make the cheapest, most tawdry, and sometimes destructive, choices and think they were becoming sophisticated adults. The long hair, the jangling chains, and the rest of the get-up that went with the motorcycle must have appeared to him like symptoms of a fatal disease appearing in his son, and he was scared. He wanted to fight off anything foreign; he'd have built a wall around Brierbank if he could have. The tendency to panic is built into the system of a talented perfectionist. It was a tragedy if he couldn't take things easier, and save wear and tear on the "Kendrum heart."

Two brothers had already been killed by it in his generation. I wondered if Hector, sitting there so calmly and amusedly at the head of the table, often thought of it, and had consciously quieted himself. But maybe he was easygoing by nature, and he would live like some of his ancestors to be a patriarch of the clan.

The table was cleared—I helped, I had to move after all that food—and rhubarb pies appeared, more coffee, and tea. Most of the kitchen crowd was having ice cream with their pie.

"Are you getting enough to eat?" Mrs. Archie called to me.

"Enough so I'll need a marathon to work it off. Anybody for a jog to Oquiddic Harbor?"

"Oh, go out and run around the popple tree," she said. "That'll shake it down and make room for more. Run around the popple tree," she repeated with a nostalgic smile.

"Oh, they're full of those homespun sayings over Muir's Grant way, Noel," said Hector. "She's from there. They say Donald Muir was a redhead and peppered the place both in and out of marriage."

"And your father, my boy, and your grandfather were full of homespun sayings about redheads when your uncle first brought me home from the Grant. I didn't know if I'd be allowed to step foot in the door."

"Well, they got bravely over it," said Hector. "And think where I'd be today without that redhead from Muir's Grant to keep house for me."

"You'd be married," said Rowan. "You'd have been forced into it. I don't know what makes you and Angus so scared of the idea."

"I can tell you about Angus," Stuart said. "Why keep a cow when milk's cheap?" The wine had put a flush on his cheekbones and his gray eyes were very bright.

"Angus reminds me of the lilies of the field," said Mrs. Stuart. "Those clothes of his! Lovely!"

"What does he do? I asked.

"He's with a company that writes and produces documentary films for schools and television," Rowan explained. "You may have seen some of them. Anyway, he's putting a fortune into the Angus J. house. Most of his pay, anyway."

"And the Colsons wanted most of his blood for the old house in the first place," Hector said.

"Yes," Mrs. Alec agreed in her soft voice, "I wouldn't be surprised if he went into debt just to keep the house in the family. We're all grateful to him for that."

"He didn't go so far into debt that he had to sell his Jaguar," said Stuart pointedly. "And you wait, he'll be filling the house with wild weekend parties."

"Good!" Hector slapped his hands down on the table. "Just so long as he invites me."

"What the Gathering will do to the place," Stuart said gloomily, "I hate to think. They'll all want to tramp through it, and scratch up the floors and leave their dirty prints on the walls."

I felt self-conscious and wondered if I were washing my hands often enough. At least I was wearing rubber soles.

"Well, the groups can be supervised when they go through the house," Mrs. Archie suggested, "and nobody needs to go in for anything else, since he had you install those two toilets in the barn. And if it rains, the barn's big enough to shelter everybody. So stop worrying, Stuart. It'll only be for one day, after all."

Rowan and I took over the dishwashing. The youngsters all went out again, and the twins had coaxed Jamesy into the soccer game. The brothers disappeared somewhere outside; the three women walked across the road to see how the garden was coming along and then came back to the lawn chairs. We were left alone in the kitchen except for the hopeful dogs and cats. I made a collect call to Fremont and spoke for a few minutes with my father and Virginia.

I told them where I was. "I'd call Robbie in except he's playing soccer in a field somewhere. Some game—two men to a side."

Virginia was very pleased. "He's all right, then."

"I'd say so. He didn't think he would be until he met the twins, though. They've got magic." I winked at Rowan. "Kendrum magic."

Virginia laughed. "Oh, I know all about *that*! Give my love to everybody. Your father and I are talking about driving down in the fall."

"Oh, good!"

Back to the dishes. I washed, Rowan wiped. "What's the Gathering?" I asked her. "Something that happens every year?"

"No, this is the first time, but my father hoped it would be the start of a tradition. It's a big family picnic, with Kendrums coming from all over Canada and the States." She wiped fiercely at a plate, round and round as if to take the pattern off. I wished I hadn't asked her anything, but after a moment she went on. "Different people had talked about it, but my father was the one who got it started. All winter he wrote letters." She put the plate in the cupboard and took another, scowling at it. "So anyway," she said in a light, trembly voice, "what with the way things happened, the family wanted to call it off, but my mother and the twins and I agreed that he'd worked on it for so long it would be letting him down not to go through with it."

"I'm sorry about your father, Rowan," I said. "I lost my mother when I was nine."

"Oh, that's terrible for a little kid!" she exclaimed. *Terrible!* I'm so sorry, Noel."

"Thanks. Would you rather not talk any more about the Gathering?"

She shrugged. "No use avoiding the subject. Dominion Day's the first of July, and then they have the Highland Games at Antigonish, and anybody who's coming from a long distance this summer won't want to miss that. So the Gathering's scheduled for the tenth of July. Will you be here then, I hope?"

"Unless your uncle evicts us," I said.

"Oh, fabulous! Look, I've got some ideas of my own. I'll tell you!"

Virginia must have known about the Gathering and kept it from us, for fear of open rebellion from Robbie. If I didn't know about it, I wouldn't feel that I was deceiving him.

The evening broke up when the boys couldn't see the ball any longer. Jamesy roared out first, and Robbie and I followed. "See you guys tomorrow!" Robbie yelled at the twins as we backed around onto the road. He settled back onto the seat. "Uncle Hector says he'll give me a job if I show up early tomorrow."

"Are you going to show up?"

"Of course!" He sounded both startled and offended.

7

CHAPTER

I READ for a little while, but I could hardly keep my eyes open. So I put out my light. The bed was very comfortable, and I hadn't drawn my shades so I could see the stars in the southern sky, and wondered if they were reflected in the river. Some night soon I would walk down and see. I could hear the brook.

Faces, names, voices, sights, circled in slow motion through my mind, skaters to unheard music. Then, all at once, in my memory of that night, everything ended without any intermediate state, and the next thing I knew I was awakened from a sleep so deep that I thought I was back in my apartment and the landlord's daughter Linda and her boy friend were parked in the driveway with the car radio on.

But the windows were wrong, somehow. I struggled to orient myself, and all the time the music went on; the odd thing was that through the instinctive panic that goes with a sense of dislocation the music was registering on me. I identified fiddles and a banjo playing some kind of country dance. Scandinavian, Scotch, Irish? It wasn't Linda Appleby's kind of music. Recognizing that, I recognized the room, and decided that a car was parked in *this* driveway in Brierbank, Nova Scotia.

Maybe it had become a favorite stopping place because the house had been empty for so long and still was, most of the time. But my car was out there tonight, so they should know that the house was occupied. I didn't remember locking the car when we came home, we were both so sleepy, but I'd taken the keys, from habit. Still, I didn't want someone ransacking the car for what they could lift. Hoodlums here too? Well, it wasn't quite Paradise, according to Stuart Kendrum.

I got out of bed and went down the hall to the back of the house, pulling on my robe as I went. The white walls gave me enough light to go on. The music was very clear, though not loud, and by some trick of acoustics or my ears it seemed to come from downstairs, with the soft thumps and rhythmic sliding of dancing feet. I could have sworn I heard voices and sometimes whoops of laughter. All muted as if by distance.

There was no window open at the back, and neither was there any strange car in the yard when I looked down from the window outside the bathroom. It was then that the music stopped, and the returning silence broke on my ears like the wash from a fast boat that I never even saw passing by; only the wake was there to show that she had come and gone.

I looked down at the pallid crescent of the driveway, and the stretch of road between the end of the pines on one side and the barn on the other. On the other side the hill-climbing woods were a solid dark mass. Only the stars of the northern sky were familiar to me.

My feet were very cold. My scalp crept and tightened with cold; it went down my back like icy sweat. I hurried back to my room and put socks on my chilly feet, and got into bed with my robe on. I was tense and jumpy at first, but the snugness and warmth lulled me. It was all a dream, I thought. When I was overtired I often had forceful, convincing dreams.

But was I dreaming when I walked down the hall and heard the feet and the voices of the dancers?

Yes, yes, *yes*, I answered myself impatiently.

So why am I wearing socks and a bathrobe in bed? Was I sleepwalking?

You never sleepwalked in your life, and you're not going to start it now. Whatever happened, happened. It's over. Stop trying to dissect it and *go to sleep.*

Again I have no memory of starting to drowse, only of waking up again. A door opened and shut downstairs. Again voices, this time in conversation, but they never became clear, no words were isolated. I just *felt* it was a man and a woman talking. I sat up in bed, outraged. Had the house owner come home from Halifax in the middle of the night and brought a woman with him?

That wasn't the reason for the outrage, it was the lack of consideration; he knew we were here, and what time was it, for heaven's sake? Like an answer, the mantel clock struck once, which could make it either half-past twelve, one o'clock, or half-past one.

The voices were gone. I sat there hugging myself, trying hard to hear something—the creak of a floorboard, the movement of a chair—but there was nothing, and the silence from the other side of the ell wall told me no one was moving around in there.

I put my extra pillow behind me and lay back, not frightened but frustrated. On one plane I was still trying to find logical explanation, while on another plane something separate went on which I was trying to ignore. Don't be Nutty Noel, I sneered at myself. Talk about being spaced-out. Breathe deeply. Make up a mantra for yourself. Be your own guru. Guru guroo. Calloo Callay. What was the rest of that? Or the beginning—O Frabjous Day . . . I must look it up somewhere. Come to my arms, my beamish boy. Drifting now. Micah Jenkins, the Beamish Boy. And then the woman singing. Again no distinguishable words, and more audible in my head than outside it. I made myself lie still and listen. Gentle, quiet, minor, like a lullaby, and I could hear the cradle rocking.

I know I am awake. I shaped the words with my lips and at the same time folded down my little finger and squeezed till it hurt. The singing went on. The cradle rocked in rhythm with it, a small enough sound; one wouldn't violently rock a cradle.

There was a sudden explosion of juvenile laughter, just as

suddenly squelched. Feet running on stairs, not the front ones, but at the back of the house somewhere, and in the ell at the same time. I couldn't sort one from the other, the place seemed full of echoes, or else my head was. Thumps. Doors opening with the click of thumb latches. A solitary fiddle, plugging indomitably and slightly out of tune through the first bar of a reel, over and over, and then all at once—as if I could see it—the fiddle was taken out of the unsure hands; the phrase sang out clearly and sweetly under a dancing bow.

There were sounds which I realized much later came from the operation of a loom. Once there was a man's voice reading from the Bible, I was sure, because of the cadences, and I wondered, shivering, if he spoke over a coffin. I tried hard to catch a word, but I couldn't, any more than I could understand the group prayer that followed. But I knew it was a prayer, and it came to me—again from the cadences—that it was the Lord's Prayer.

I was praying too: Let it not be a funeral. Maybe the minister's come to dinner and he says a long Grace and invites everyone to pray with him while dinner gets cold.

I didn't know when I left off worrying about whether I was becoming Nutty Noel. I became completely absorbed in what I was hearing. The effect was of occupying a room in the center of a very busy house whose activities swirled round and round, over and under, heard, not seen, so real in every particular that I felt if I opened the bedroom door I would catch a glimpse of someone vanishing around a corner.

It was like Kipling's story "They," which I'd discovered by myself, and loved.

Sometime toward morning, but before daylight, everything ceased, and I knew nothing more was going to happen now. I was so lightheaded my brain seemed to be spinning behind my closed eyes, and my whole body was full of little pulses. But I could think clearly about it all.

I wasn't going to fight for logic. I wasn't going to argue for or against my own sanity. And I wasn't going to tell anyone who would wonder about my sanity. It happened to me, it was my own business. Tomorrow (today, rather) I'd write down everything I could remember, because even if I didn't intend ever to tell about this, I wanted my own record of it.

After that I threw aside my extra pillow, turned over, and went to sleep. I don't think I even dreamed. When I woke up the sun was strong in the room, birds were singing, barn swallows were chattering on the ell roof close to my east window.

Robbie had already taken off on his bike for the farm. He'd fixed eggs and bacon for himself, and plenty of toast and jam. I was glad to know he was so handy around the kitchen. I was also glad to be alone with my first cup of coffee. Solitude was exceptionally sweet this morning. I knew what was meant by feeling fragile. I really need more than four hours' sleep to be at the top of my form, and my lying awake last night hadn't been a matter of simple insomnia.

After some coffee I began to feel less fragile, less likely to have my head go whirling free into space if I turned it too quickly. I revived even more with a sandwich of home-cured bacon and Mrs. Archie's bread, enough so I fetched a notebook from my room and wrote down every detail I could remember from last night. In a separate section I described the dream at the motel, and the one by the riverbank. One can always find explanations for dreams; I was keeping these merely as curiosities, because of the color and detail and the part I'd played in them and the emotions I'd experienced as the unknown character.

But what happened last night was no dream. I wrote at the end of the account:

"It was as if I were caught in the heart of a house that has never stopped living and breathing since it was built."

8

CHAPTER

AFTER THAT, I put it all out of my mind. I composed a gro-
cery list, and went upstairs to make my bed; Robbie was
supposed to take care of his own room—his mother's orders.
While I smoothed out my sheets and blankets, I knew that I
would never again regard this bed as just a place for sleeping.
But I hoped I'd be able to take a nap on it when I came back from
shopping. Mrs. Archie was going to take me to visit the Bob
Kendrums in the afternoon, if they got home from Amherst this
morning. If I didn't get some sleep sometime today, I'd be feeling pretty insubstantial by two o'clock.

I passed their mailbox on the way to the Corner. This road
turned off to the left, and the Muir's Grant and Oquiddic Harbor road went on. The Corner itself was a meeting-place of
roads. There was a good-sized general store, a garage, the post
office, some fine old trees, a few modern ranch houses set among
older, more traditional houses with barns set behind them. A
shaggy pony was tethered on a front lawn, some small children
rode tricycles on a driveway; at the garage, a little knot of men
held a consultation over the exposed engine of a car. I stopped
outside the store, which had a black, white, and red sign over the
front door reading "Allan Swan and Son." I could hear women's
voices and laughter from inside. Leaning on the wheel I wondered dreamily if Allan Swan and Son carried that kind of cheese
you slice off a big wheel. . . . I could look across open fields
behind the houses on my right, across the road, and see a white

church halfway up a mild variety of hill, its square tower rising out of a billow of greens.

I started the car and drove on, being waved to by the tricycle riders and barked at without much conviction by a couple of middle-sized dogs. The pony watched me drive by. There was the hill road curving to the right, and I drove up about a hundred yards and pulled off onto a level parking place outside the church grounds. The building was clearly related to the country meetinghouses of home, except for the square tower topping the belfry instead of the steeple and weathervane. The front door was open to the warm air, and someone was practicing next Sunday's music on the organ.

I walked into the churchyard and began looking for Kendrum stones. I found many Swans, Rosses, Frasers, and Munros, and other names not in such numbers. Some of the stones were very old, the dates sometimes weathered away or obscured by lichens. Cemeteries aren't my favorite libraries, except when they're really ancient. The more modern stones cut too near the bone with me.

No Kendrums yet. I paused near the back of the church, looking at this part of the cemetery; a thick hedge of old-fashioned roses, still in bud, hid the pasture fence. Robins sang boisterously in the maples and in the church the unseen organ sang "Jesu Joy of Man's Desiring." A scalloping, singing flight of goldfinches suddenly swooped down on the seeded dandelions in an unmown corner.

"Looking for something?" a man's voice said, and I jumped. Stuart Kendrum was up on a ladder at the back of the church looking down at me. His face was shadowed by the long visor of his painting cap.

"Oh, hi!" I said. "I don't really need to see the stones, but—" I'd have felt foolish to bolt away now, as if I'd been caught trespassing.

He gestured with his paintbrush, and I followed in the general direction. "Over by the white lilac," he called after me.

I averted my eyes from the new, polished granite for Alec Kendrum, and headed straight for the white lilac. And there it was. The stone had been cleaned so that the lettering was clear, the message reduced to basic facts.

"Angus James Kendrum. 1730–1809."

I went down on my knees in the damp grass. I wished I had been alone to discover it, but then if Stuart hadn't called me I mightn't have persevered. The thing was—the paradox—that nothing gave Angus Mor flesh and blood like the sight of his name carved into the stone.

I was still staring at it when Stuart spoke from behind me. "Did you doubt he existed?" he asked dryly.

"No," I said.

"There are some who've said Kendrum wasn't his name at all."

"Do *you* believe that?" I twisted around to look up at him.

He shook his head, staring past me at the stone. I sat back on my heels. "Do you think of him a lot?" I asked. "Especially when you're working around here?"

His eyes, gray like the granite, flicked toward me. "As you get older, it happens that way. You get curious, y'know." He gave me a slight smile, either self-ridiculing or embarrassed. "There's Jean beside him."

"Jean, Beloved Wife of Angus. 1740–1816." Little flowering ground plants grew around the stones.

"Calum's not here, he went out west," Stuart said. "But Captain Angus is here, and Angus J. So are all of us who never left home, or who only left it for a war or to go to sea, and then came back."

I got up and went over to smell the white lilac. I was feeling strange, half-tranced from lack of sleep, and Stuart's voice was soft. "The ones who left," he said, "they're like a bunch of Johnny Appleseeds, they've sown Kendrums from coast to coast. But the funny thing is how the eldest son stayed in Brierbank each time."

"Yes," I said dreamily, shutting my eyes and breathing lilac. White lilac was different from purple. Who had set out the original one here? I wondered.

"But even with that, the old house would've gone out of the family if my brother hadn't bought it."

I opened my eyes, and had to blink to clear them. "Aren't you glad he did?"

"Well, it was either him or rich Americans. Or rich Canadians," he added with a wry mouth. "Not much difference, when money comes into a place like this and they try to turn it into a summer resort. At least this way the family gets to use the land and harvest the woodlot." He added offhandedly, "It's all Kendrum timber I've used on that house, as it was in the beginning."

"The place is a masterpiece," I said. "And don't let me keep you away from there, please."

He nodded. "I don't have much to do now, just some finishing up in the cellar. Storage place and so forth. It'll keep till I finish this job." He walked back toward his ladder.

"Thank you," I called after him. I don't know if he acknowledged that or not. I went out to the car and drove on up the hill and discovered the school, closed now, of course; turned around in the yard and went back down the road to the Corner and the store.

I wished I'd done my shopping first, so I wouldn't have to break the new spell I was in. If I didn't get some sleep soon I'd be having visions and hearing supernatural voices in the broad daylight.

Outside the store there was a decorated van which could only have belonged to the group whom Hector indulged and Stuart suspected. A young woman came across the road from the post office and put some packages in the van. She had a plain, bony face without make-up, and long straight dark hair parted severely in the middle, and wore jeans, a smock, and desert boots. She smiled and said, "Good morning," and so did I. Her manner was pleasant and she had nice eyes. In spite of her get-up she made me think of old pictures of those brilliant Victorian women. In the store a barefoot girl with really orangy-red hair in thick braids, wearing a full-skirted gypsyish outfit, was getting an ordinary list of supplies and paying with ordinary Canadian money.

She was kidding the grocer about some packaged goods. "Don't you know that's full of poisonous chemicals? And *that*? And *that*?" She kept jabbing with a forefinger.

He was elderly, and evidently used to her gibes; they were both good-natured.

"Say, I've been meaning to ask you," he said finally. "You're drinking all that raw milk over there—you ever had those goats tested?"

"We aren't fools," she said. "Those goats are the finest stock we could get, and we're taking no chances with them. Right now they're probably a lot healthier than you are, if you eat half the stuff you sell in here. Honestly!" she exclaimed to me. "There ought to be a government health warning on all that packaged junk!"

"You making a porridge of those three-penny nails, Eve?" he asked. They both laughed. He helped carry the load out to the van, and I walked around picking out items on my list. Eve was probably right, but Robbie and I would have to take our chances.

The grocer came back in again. "Are you Mr. Swan?" I asked.

"Senior. Son's out delivering. You're the historian, I take it."

"Thanks for the title! I'm really a glorified typist."

"That must mean a pretty one," he said gallantly. "Say, you ought to talk to Bob Kendrum."

"I'm going to see him this afternoon." If I don't go comatose first, I added silently. I had seen the wall telephone at the back of the store, and now a dull spark glinted through my fog. "Could I use your phone to call Mrs. Archie?"

"Go ahead." He told me what number to dial.

She acted happily surprised to hear from me, and that was very warming. "I'm at the store," I said. "Is Robbie coming home to lunch?"

"Oh dear, no, I'll feed the tribe here."

I kept from visibly sagging. "Is he really useful?"

"He certainly is. He's a good little worker. Of course he's going to stink of the barn when he comes home, I warn you."

"That's a good healthy smell," I said. "It makes you grow, they always told me."

She agreed, laughing, and said, "I'll be around to take you to Bob's." I thanked Mr. Swan for the use of his telephone, took my groceries back to the house and put things away, then went upstairs and fell onto my bed. I knew no telephone would wake me, and no traffic; the milk and feed trucks and other business vehicles usually came in off the Inverness road, to the east of the farm. It was the silent part of the day, except for the kitchen clock and the tiny, almost inaudible creakings and tickings of the house itself. Sunlight lay upon my floor and reflected on my ceiling. The brook sang in the distance and bore me with it into sleep.

9
CHAPTER

BOB KENDRUM was a great-uncle to the brothers, and he had been a very young uncle to their father. He had white hair and was just past eighty, but carried himself and spoke like a mere seventy or even younger. He wasn't tall but he was agile and wiry. His bifocals annoyed him and he let them slide down his nose and kept looking over them with bright blue eyes. He was one of those men whom it's very easy to imagine as a small boy, eel-quick, and mischievous.

He and his wife, Christy, a short nimble woman with curly gray-blond hair, had been working in the vegetable garden all morning, and they took us on the tour. From there we went on to the flowers. Everything was tightly fenced off from the bantams who followed us sociably around, some enormous, benign, elderly cats, a mixed collie-kind of dog, and a mongrel spaniel. A Jersey cow bawled incessantly for attention over the fence as we walked around.

"She's old," Bob said indulgently. "And spoiled rotten. We raised her by hand. She'll shut up when we get out of sight." But he made a detour to give her something he had in his pocket.

Christy called my attention to the heather in the rock garden. "Our daughter gave us the plants last year. And my, how it took hold! It knew a good home when it saw one."

"Like everything else around here," said Mrs. Archie. "It's a good thing you're not on the main road, Christy, you'd be running an orphan's home."

Bob was standing with his hands in his pockets, staring at the heather. "He brought heather with him," he said suddenly.

We all looked at him, mildly startled. "Who?" Christy asked.

"Angus Mor." He laughed like a boy. "It just came to me— swam up to my mind like a salmon coming upriver. Maybe my grandfather told me."

I thought without surprise, But there was no heather in bloom when he was watching for the sail. It was cold weather. There was something else in the deerskin bag around his neck. Something stolen out of the castle maybe; money, so they wouldn't go like paupers to America.

The queer thing was that I had instinctively attributed my dream experiences to Angus Mor, and was taking this reaction for granted.

"Of course it would all be dried up and dead before he reached Georgia," Christy said. "But I never heard of it before, him bringing the heather. You never told *me*."

"I never thought of it till right now. They say the older you get the more you remember. You want to visit me often, young woman." He looked over his glasses at me.

"Yes, the dear knows what you'll pick up," Mrs. Archie said, laughing. "If it's anything good, be sure to pass it on to the rest of us."

"Did you ever hear of his bringing anything else?" I asked Bob, trying to sound innocently casual. "Could they have brought any valuables—any money, maybe?"

"Depends on how they came. Besides, poor as they were and running for their lives, they wouldn't be likely to have much more than what they stood in. Maybe a sack of oatmeal, to live off on the journey, if they weren't too seasick to eat."

"Let's go in and have a cup of tea," said Christy, "and show Noel some of the old pictures, and the old Bible."

"Would it have Angus Mor's signature in it?" I asked eagerly.

"Why, he couldn't write, dear," she explained. "He always

made his mark. It's on all the records about his grant, Young Robert said, in Halifax, and even in London."

It took me a moment to place Young Robert as Robbie's father. "I remember about his not being able to read or write," I admitted, "but I thought maybe he learned as he grew older."

"Not if he was one of those bone-headed Kendrums," said Christy. "By the time he'd come up in the world from the cabin and built that house, he probably figured he'd done all right so far without an education, so why bother now?"

"Besides, he had enough booksful of learning in his head to fill a library." Bob steered me toward the front porch, a courtly hand under my elbow. "Men did in those days, y'know. They could lay out a house or a barn in their heads, and then hew everything out with an axe and an adz, and an auger bit to drill the holes for the pegs, and build as true and sweet as you could want. Watch the steps, m'dear. If you fall up them it means you won't get married this year."

"Gosh, I don't know how I'd survive that."

The dogs got in ahead of us, clearly used to attending tea parties. Bob went on seriously, "And he'd know most of the Bible by heart. Those men could recite it backward and forward."

"That must have been confusing for anybody listening," Mrs. Archie observed. She went into the kitchen with Christy, and Bob seated me at the square table in the comfortably cluttered dining room, and then brought a very old Bible, reverently wrapped in a faded old wool shawl. "My mother used to fold me up in this neat as a hen for the oven," he said. "Of course I was considerably smaller in those days." He disappeared somewhere else to get the pictures.

I unfolded the shawl and opened the Bible. In time-paled brown-ink copperplate as delicate as spider web, the first entry: To Angus and Jean Kendrum, a son, Angus James. May fifth, 1770. The other children came after that, and the deaths of some. I made my fingers as gentle on the frail old leaves as if I were reading Braille. I *was* trying to read something through my fingertips, but of course there'd be nothing now, after all these years and generations. My blind gesture was as instinctive as my earlier reaction to the heather.

"It was the minister always wrote those in," Bob Kendrum said. I hadn't even heard him come back. Out in the kitchen Mrs. Archie's hearty laugh resounded across chasms of airy distance. "The Reverend Iain Fraser. Y'see, by that time Brierbank was a village, and had its own church."

Angus Mor had watched these words being written down. He might even have been holding the child in his arms while he watched. In a time when most people married very young, he was a father for the first time at forty or so. It was likely that gray was already flecking his black hair—if it was black. I realized I was making him into the image of most of the modern Kendrums I'd met. When I began looking at the old photographs, I found enough family resemblance to back me up, unless the long-legged black-haired gray-eyed type had come into the family later than Angus himself.

Once the big teapot and the bone china cups came in, and the others talked over the photographs and discussed their subjects as we drank our tea, I lost Angus Mor and had to work hard not to resent it. There had been such a tantalizing, tormenting moment when I'd almost believed I could know what he was thinking as he watched the Reverend Iain Fraser writing.

"He might have been illiterate," Mrs. Archie said all at once, "but all his children had some learning. One of the girls even had a little school of her own. His eldest son Angus was a captain in the militia, and a surveyor. *His* son, Angus J., was postmaster for years.

"And he and Captain Angus were great fiddlers," Christy chimed in. "Oh, they played their fiddles for dances for miles around. Munro Kendrum over in Sidney has a violin he swears belonged to Captain Angus."

I had heard the fiddle, I'd heard the boy learning to play. Inwardly I was trembling again.

"That one would swear to anything," said Bob cynically. "If it *is* the Captain's fiddle, he probably stole it, or talked Eugenia out of it, which amounts to the same thing. She was always a little on the dim side."

"Now, Bob," said his wife. He gave her a defiant look and then handed each dog a whole cookie. She pretended not to notice. She said to me, "Eugenia's grandmother was Angus J.'s youngest daughter. He left the house to the girls, you know." She turned severely to her unrepentant husband. "At least Eugenia's family used the house as long as they *could*."

"As summer people," said Bob with contempt. "And then when Eugenia got past it, it was just left to wind and weather. They didn't have enough decency to hand it over to the family that should have had it."

Mrs. Archie said soothingly, "Well, at least Eugenia's grandchildren sold it to young Angus for a fair price, so now it's back in the family."

"Sold it!" he erupted. "They should have *given* it!"

"Never *mind*, Robert," said his wife. He pushed up his glasses angrily.

When I left Mrs. Archie off at the farm and drove home, I felt very tired. I'd been less exhausted after a day of teaching school. I couldn't understand it. But when I let myself remember how I felt in the churchyard or when I was reading the entries in the Bible, weariness rolled over me like fog coming in fast across Fremont Harbor.

But I would not surrender. Instead I put on my suit and went down to the river. The water was cold, but otherwise felt as silky as rainwater against my skin, and was more fun than a shower. I played around in it, knowing that if the current had any surprises for me I'd fetch up safely at the narrow footbridge for the cattle a short distance on, just past where the brook spilled into the river.

It woke me up and made me feel the way swimming always does, full of mindless good cheer and loving kindness toward the rest of the world. Even Micah Jenkins. This was my first thought of him since last night sometime, and it didn't last long now. Just an indulgent brush-off—Oh, *him*—and that was all.

There wasn't any clothesline for me to hang my suit on, and I couldn't find so much as an odd length of twine in any of the pantry drawers; a house has to be lived in for a while before it starts collecting useful cultch. I couldn't go down cellar and look because the bulkhead was padlocked. Finally I laid the suit out on the remains of the old stone wall where it emerged into the southwest sunlight from the shade of the pines. I added clothesline and soap powder to my new shopping list. Mrs. Archie was going to do sheets and towels and anything else I wanted to throw in, and I knew Robbie's clothes would have to go into her heavy-duty machine, but I preferred to do my own things by hand in the pantry sink.

I had put on eggs to boil before I started the clothesline search, and now they were hard-cooked. I built a substantial salad with torn lettuce, celery in thin slices, rings of onion, cubes of cheese, to be tossed together with the rest of Mrs. Archie's dressing. There was some ham left, plenty of bread and butter, and Mrs. Bob had given me some of the crisp thin gingersnaps we'd had with tea.

The twins dropped Robbie and his bike off; they had an old pickup, painted bright yellow, which could be heard long before it was seen. The engine was quiet enough, but everything else on it seemed to be loose.

Robbie reeked magnificently of barn and some related pungencies. "I've been helping to wash the cows before they get milked," he called on his way to the stairs, "and that's not all I've done today. Boy!" He came down smelling damp and clean. "I put my clothes in the hamper," he said to forestall me, and I hadn't even intended to ask, not being that much of a housewife and mother.

"Okay, let's eat," I said.

"Sure. Hey, you know what's in that big field across from the river from us? *Corn!* They feed it to the stock. Their own corn—you know, people-corn—is across the road from the house. I hope we're here when that's ready." He added gloomily, "But I doubt it."

"Maybe they've got an early variety," I suggested.

While he ate he gave me a complete account of his day and the plans for tomorrow. He showed me his blisters and a few scrapes and bruises. Afterward he asked me politely what I'd done, but my list sounded so excruciatingly dull compared to his that I made it short and vague, except for the swimming. I could tell that he pitied me, and I thought that was nice of him. I heard myself sounding like an unliberated role-typed female as I asked about his food preferences and made careful notes.

"And what kind of dry cereal?"

"None!" he said triumphantly. "I could eat eggs every day of my life."

Till you grow up and learn about cholesterol, I thought.

He carried his own dishes to the pantry and helped put away the other things, yawning. "Do you miss television?" I asked him.

"No way. My mother stuck some books in my stuff so I guess I'll go to bed and read a while." The last word was distorted by a yawn. "If I can get through a page, that is." Eyes watering, he grinned at me. "I hugged a calf today, and she nearly washed my ear off. And wait till you see the bull. They call him Billy Boy."

"He sounds adorable. Did you hug him too?"

He laughed, said good night, and slowly climbed the stairs, yawning loudly. I wasn't long in following.

10

CHAPTER

I T WASN'T quite dusk and I sat by my open windows for a while, listening to the brook which had already become a familiar voice in my life. I kept assuring myself that what had happened last night might never happen again. My first response to this was an anger and regret far stronger than ordinary disappointment. Last night I had experienced the sort of happenings about which I had often read, in accounts written by observers who were sworn to be sane, objective, and suitably skeptical.

I'd been interested in their stories, wondering frivolously how I'd react to cold spots or mysterious footsteps or crashes in the attic; I fondly called myself open-minded while knowing I was doubtful. And I'd never associated my small talent with the ability to tune in on such supernatural goings-on. I never even thought of it as a talent; it was just something that existed, nameless, as part of the way I was.

Now I was standing at a door which had mysteriously opened in a wall of air, and I was trembling on the threshold, half afraid to cross for fear I'd never get back, and terrified that the door would close again forever before I made up my mind.

I went to bed finally and read a little while. All this hard thinking made me tired, the way I'd been when I came back from Bob Kendrum's, and no wonder; it was like trying to think in a foreign language. I went to sleep without any trouble, and woke up to strange sounds.

This time I was prepared. First I checked to be sure I was

really awake; I was. Then I listened. Anticlimax. There was nothing supernatural about the small, cautious noises in the kitchen below. Maybe Robbie had waked up feeling sick from overwork and overeating, and was downstairs looking for something to take. I put on my robe and slippers and went out into the hall.

Robbie's door was shut. I leaned over the railing. A flashlight was moving around in the kitchen, the beam shooting occasionally out into the hall. While I watched, it became steady, and I pictured it standing upended somewhere. The cautious motions went on. Paper rattled secretively, there were faint clinkings.

I went down, also being cautious, because some stairs creak only in the dead of night. Slyly I approached the doorway nearest the foot of the stairs and looked around the jamb.

The flashlight stood on the wood range. An attenuated dark shape was at the refrigerator; the door opened and the light flared out like lightning, a hand reached in, something fell over with a clatter, and the shape whispered furiously, *Damn!*"

I started to laugh and clamped my hand over my mouth. But he'd heard my first gasp, and swung around.

"Oh, good God," he said in disgust. "Look, I'm sorry I woke you. I shouldn't have come in, but I had some stuff for the fridge."

"It's all right," I said, feeling lightheadedly silly. "I thought you were a ghost, that's all, till you opened the refrigerator. I don't think they can do that."

"I don't believe so. I don't think they carry flashlights, either. Look, I *am* sorry I got you up."

"I was afraid Robbie was sick, and he isn't, so I'm relieved. You must be Angus."

"I am, and you're Noel Paige. How do you do? I got back from Edmonton early this evening and drove right out. Do you mind if I put a light on?"

"Not at all."

He turned on a wall lamp by the stove, then looked at me

with a smile and said softly, "How do you do again? Welcome to Brierbank."

"Thank you," I said formally. "Can I make you some tea or coffee, or would you like to be left alone in your own kitchen?"

"I'd like some really good coffee, if you've got any."

"Your aunt thought of everything, even a good drip grind." Left to myself I'd have made instant, but I had a feeling one should never admit it to a walking clothes ad. I knew what Mrs. Stuart meant about the lilies of the field. I put the teakettle on to boil, and measured coffee into the top of the pot. "Would you like a sandwich?" I asked.

"No, thanks, I'm not hungry, just dry." His expression might have been called quizzical, or even downright amused, as if he knew what I was thinking about being caught in a bathrobe that had been brought along for warmth and comfort, not for midnight encounters.

I went into the pantry for cups and saucers, and put some gingersnaps on a plate. I could hear him moving about, and when I carried the tray out he was standing by the front windows with his hands in his pockets, looking into the dark. I put the tray on the table and returned to the stove to pour boiling water into the coffee pot. Then I waited for it to drip through, and studied him from the back as he gazed out at the night. He wore tartan slacks and a wine blazer over a white turtleneck. I had to admit he had the build and the carriage to wear them well, and he probably knew it. His black hair was a little longer than his brothers', but already I was recognizing the characteristic cant of the head and the way of holding the shoulders.

"Well?" he said suddenly, and turned around to face me. I realized he'd been watching my reflection in the glass.

"Well what?" I said. Micah Jenkins had given me a good indoctrination in male conceit. "The coffee's ready." I took the pot to the table, and poured. Angus pulled out the chairs.

"Perfumes of Araby," he murmured. "Or rather South America. I haven't had a decent cup of coffee for three—no, four days.

I was just wondering what you were thinking as you gazed dreamily into space."

"I don't know. I was listening to the coffee drip. Does it matter?"

"Yes, because you're not what I expected of a schoolteacher, genealogical writer, species of governess—"

"You really think in clichés, don't you?" I interrupted. "What should I have been? Cartoon-type schoolmarm? Comic valentine?"

"I apologize," he said seriously. "I meant only that you look too young to be all those things."

"I'm older than I look." I heard my own aggressiveness, and was slightly ashamed. "I love your house," I said in a ladylike manner. "Thank you for letting me use it."

"I'm glad to have you and young Robert in it. Have you been all through it?"

"Yes, except for the attic and the cellar."

"You'll have to see them too. We've saved everything possible, and there's a lot of beautiful eighteenth-century work besides what's out in the open like the stairs, the wainscoting, some of the floors, and so forth. And the barn! You'll have to see that. Good coffee," he said, raising the cup to me like a wine glass. "Angus Mor's son Captain Angus built the barn. They'd had several small ones at first, including a forge barn. That used to stand near the river, and it's where they made their own nails and tools. We don't know when they left off doing that, but the big barn out here was built in 1804. Captain Angus chiseled the date and his name on one of the beams, and that's still legible."

The back of my neck prickled. "Angus Mor was still alive then."

"Yes." The answer was left floating between us. I wondered if his nape prickled too. We were silent, sipping our coffee; absentmindedly he ate about five gingersnaps.

"You're lucky to have the barn still standing after all these years," I said. "Usually deserted barns fall down if they haven't been set afire by lightning or kids sneaking their first cigarettes."

"Yes, we've been lucky," he said. I liked him for his pleasure and pride in the property, and his respect for its past. When he talked about it in a soft, swift voice, leaning forward as if he had to communicate his passion somehow if only in these superficial ways, he was very attractive because he was being absolutely honest.

"More coffee?" he asked. I shook my head, and he refilled his cup.

"What about this Gathering? Is it going to be held here?"

"Yes. The Gathering was my brother Alec's idea at first, and then I thought, well, the house will be ready, why not have a sort of super housewarming for it? When Alec died none of us had the spirit to go on with it, until Priscilla and the kids insisted. Besides, the clan had been alerted, far and wide. If Alec could have managed it he'd have sent fiery crosses out instead of mere letters." His long mouth went up on one side. He looked away from me, down at the table, and I saw rather than heard him sigh. Then he said with sad humor, "If I'd done all that work I'd be damned if I'd want them to hold it without me. But—" He shrugged. "Anyway, it started out simply as a family reunion, with descendants of Angus Mor and Calum making a pilgrimage to the place where it all began. But by now it looks like a combination of the Edinburgh Tattoo and the raising of Prince Charlie's standard at Glenfinnan."

"It sounds marvelous," I said.

"Oh, I'm sure it will be," he said ironically. "There'll be a piper. I like *that* bit, I have to admit. He's a great old chap, not so old either. He's regular Army, retired; he and his pipes came through World War II with only a few scratches and rips. He lives over at Inverness. There'll also be a bevy of little girls to do their dances. And a lot of peacocking around; some of our kinfolk whisk into kilts at the drop of a Glengarry."

"Any of them in Brierbank?" I asked hopefully.

"Oh Lord, no. Even Alec never went that far. God, I wish he

were here!" he said. "I miss him like hell!" He pushed away from the table and walked restlessly around the kitchen, and I felt I shouldn't try to look at his face, or even be here at all. I was trying to think of a graceful way to disappear, when he came back to the table and said calmly, "Stuart disapproves of the whole affair. It brings too much of the outside world into Brierbank."

"I could see that. And I know how he feels. He's trying to hold onto something priceless that's slipping through his fingers."

"You've an old head on your shoulders."

"I don't know if that's a compliment or not."

"Oh, it is," he said, but I wasn't sure. My first response to him repeated itself, and I was about to say "Good night" in a severe tone of voice, just to let him know I hadn't come to Brierbank to get off on the right foot with the family swinger, when he laughed out loud and said, "I'm thinking of sending a special invitation to the Impostor."

"The *what*?"

"You don't know about him?" His peaked black eyebrows rose. "Isn't he in Robert's papers, or wouldn't my brother give the family legend even a paragraph?"

"No! Tell me!" I forgot dignity. I planked my elbows on the table, propped my chin on my hands, and stared at him. He sat down again, shut his eyes, and recited.

"Angus James Stuart Archibald Kendrum, Earl of Strathcoran by the indulgence of God. War cry: *Coire Brochain*, Corrie of the Broken Stones, a place name referring to an ancient battle. Clan motto: *While I breathe I fight*. Clan badge: rowan flower and berries. Clan crest: black bull's head, crowned with antique crown, *or*. Probably inspired when somebody stole somebody else's cattle, an ancient and honorable profession in the Highlands." He opened his eyes and grinned at me. "The owner must have caught up with the rustlers in the corrie of the broken stones, thus originating the war cry. . . . I suggested that

Hector's best bull be the star turn at the Gathering, wearing an antique crown, *or*, but only the kids agreed with me. Though Hector smiled."

"I think it's a lovely idea. Is he a Black Angus?"

"Smart girl. Alas, he's a Holstein."

"All right, we'll forget the bull. Tell me why the Earl is an impostor."

"The family myth is that when the Earl died at Culloden, Lord Kendrum and his little brother fled to America. Lord Kendrum, of course, had become the fifth Earl."

"Why couldn't that be Angus Mor and Calum?" I demanded.

"Because the boys' graves are in the family cemetery on the estate of Strathcoran. I saw them myself, about six years ago, and some other traveling Kendrums have seen them too. No, Angus Mor, who could neither read nor write, came from the valley of the rowans, all right, but he was probably a crofter's or gillie's son whose father fought and died at Culloden with the Earl, and the boys ran before they could be murdered for the name they bore."

"What about the real ones? Were *they* murdered?"

"No, it was some sickness that swept through the Highlands that year. The loyal troops never pillaged and burned at Strathcoran—the widowed Countess had some influential connections at the Hanoverian court. She was carrying a child when the Earl was killed; probably if he'd been alive at the time of the epidemic he'd have died too, and a cousin would have succeeded. But he became the next Earl at birth, and the other boys were in their graves by then."

"Poor kids," I said. "Poor Countess too, losing husband and sons in one year."

"Actually she was the boys' stepmother, but that's a minor point. It was a hideous time all around for everybody."

"You mentioned the valley of the rowans. What does that mean?"

"It's what the name Strathcoran means. The rowan, or

mountain ash, has always been a sacred tree in both Norse and Celtic mythology; in fact 'rowan' means 'rune.' The rune tree. It's still considered great good luck and a defense against witch-craft, a rowan by the house. I should set one out here," he said thoughtfully.

"That must be why they chose the flower and berries for their badge," I said.

"Yes, and there are still rowan trees in the glen. It's a beauti-ful place, a long valley with a stream running through it down from the mountains and opening into a sea loch. From out on the headland on a clear day you'd almost swear you can see out to Lewis and Harris."

My scalp was constricting so fast it was a wonder he couldn't see my hair rising. My head felt empty and full of echoes. I pressed my chin hard into my hands so they couldn't shake and give me away. The sun dazzled on wind-whipped crests, the cold burned my ears; I struggled to ignore it, to thrust it all away before it swept through this room.

"Why does anyone still hold onto the legend," I asked, "if all this history is known and documented?" The seas withdrew and the wind went down. "Because it's fun?"

"Would you want to give it up, if in your games and dreams as a kid you'd believed it, been a part of it? Yes, you could call it fun, but for some people it's like something bred in the bone. I've met very few Kendrums, outside of this earthy bunch still living on Angus Mor's own turf, who didn't claim the Strathcoran con-nection. Even those who don't believe Angus Mor was the fifth Earl say he was somehow attached to the castle, and not as a servant's son. That maybe he was an illegitimate son of the Earl by a local girl or a mistress. But in that case I'm sure he would have been acknowledged and educated. In those days a son was a son for a' that." He tilted back in his chair with his hands clasped behind his head and stared at the ceiling. "Sure, he was named for the Earl, but plenty of other male children have always been named for the chief."

"So did you name the present Earl the Impostor, or did the diehards do that?"

"Listen, there's a bunch of western cousins, and some of them are Americans, mind you, not Canadians, who not only believe the Lord Kendrum legend but that the Countess's influential friend at court was also her lover, that it was his baby she was carrying, so the new little Earl wasn't even a Kendrum."

"Which makes the present Earl a double impostor."

"You'd better believe it!"

We both laughed. "They're incredible," he said. "I've sat in with them over a couple of fifths of good Scotch. They're insurance men, politicians, industrialists, lawyers—and when they get a certain level of *uisquebaugh* in their blood they turn into wild Highlanders out for vengeance."

"If any of them are coming, you'd better not chance a meeting with the Earl."

"All dirks and claymores checked at the gate. Well, now you've had the family romance, scandal, tragedy, or fantasy, however you want to view it. You know, you're a great audience?"

"That's one of the nicest things that was ever said to me. Did you see the Impostor when you were there?"

"No, he's only home on his holidays. He's big in business over there, very rich by his own efforts, in spite of the Labor government. But I've seen photographs. He doesn't look like us. He's round-faced, fair, sandy, not terribly imposing in a kilt. But dear God, I'd like to get him to come. I can see old Stuart going into shock from pure rage. He can't even treat the business as harmless fun. Once Rowan said, fooling, 'Our cousin the Earl,' and Stuart laced into her as if she'd said, 'Our cousin the child molester.'"

"Then he must believe in the legend!"

"No, it's not that. Sometimes I think he's a closet Communist. Alec asked him where his sense of humor was, and he said it was no fit subject for humor and stalked out." He laughed. "I'd

love to get the Earl over here and see how he handles the true
believers on one side and Stuart on the other."

"Oh, the poor man," I protested.

The clock began to strike twelve. Would I get back to sleep
again with all this in my head? I doubted it. We cleared the table
together, and he told me again it was good coffee. "Do you mind
if I come in to cook my breakfast? I'll be quiet, if you sleep late."

"It's your kitchen. And we'll be quiet if *you* sleep late. . . .
Only I can't tell Robbie without waking him."

"Look, let's not worry about that, shall we?"

"All right, but I'd better rinse out this coffee pot."

When I came out of the pantry with the clean pot to set beside the stove, cool damp air moved through the kitchen, smelling of grass and the night. He had opened the front door and was
standing on the stone step. The brook sounded very loud. The
nearer daisies looked faintly luminous, but beyond them an im-
penetrable darkness filled the valley between us and the rise of
Bob Kendrum's woods on the far side.

Angus spoke in a low voice.

We ne'er shall tread the fancy-haunted valley
Where 'tween the dark hills creeps the small clear stream,
In arms around the patriarch banner rally,
Nor see the moon on royal tombstones gleam.

I hugged myself, not against the night chill coming in. "But
you've seen the valley, haven't you?" I said. As if he hadn't heard
me, he went on.

"I suppose this was the nearest to it that he could get. I would
be his, sealed, signed, and delivered. No laird could ever dispos-
sess his children, burn down his house, and turn the land over to
sheep." He came in and shut the door softly. "The Clearances
were even more brutal than the English, because it was their
own chiefs who did it to them."

"Did the Kendrum chiefs do it? I hope not."

"No, and that's a good mark for them, impostors or not." He
laughed. "I'll have to remind the romantic captains of industry of

that, the next time I get a chance. I can damn well see a few of *them* burning the crofters out if they saw money in it. Well, I should let you get to bed, and I'm groggy myself by now. Thanks again for the coffee and the willing ear. A good audience always goes to my head faster than good booze. Sleep well."

"You too," I said. He was already halfway across the kitchen to the ell door, picking up his flashlight on the way. The door had closed behind him by the time I put out the light.

CHAPTER

I FELL INTO BED as if I'd just run the Boston Marathon, too knocked out even to consider what had happened downstairs; not the arrival of Angus, but the discovery of a true tie between known fact and my dreams. I'll think about it in the morning, I promised myself, and I didn't remember anything more.

But in the morning I awoke depressingly early, and it was raining lightly. Why couldn't I have slept another hour, at least? It wasn't fair. This house would kill me yet. I had the wobbly, fretful mood that I get with lack of sleep. I felt also that I was extremely *plain*.

When I tottered to the bathroom I heard low voices downstairs, and felt even more victimized. I desired to come very slowly back to life with my first cup of coffee—alone. The last thing I needed this morning was an adult male assessing me by cold daylight as a naïve and dull girl from some quaint small town in the States. He'd been sincere about the house, but now I suspected he'd been having a fine old time quoting poetry to me at midnight, like Dickens' fat boy who said, "I wants to make your flesh creep."

"And the hell with you, Angus Kendrum!" I whispered loudly. It had a reviving effect. At least it started my blood circulating at a faster rate. I put on a golden-brown shirt that was supposed to do something for my eyes—maybe make them look less bleary—and matching slacks, tied my hair back with a paisley scarf, and went briskly downstairs prepared to cry, "Thank you for making the coffee!"

Be bright, poised, and unimpressed, that was the ploy. But he wasn't there. Robbie was just finishing his bacon and eggs. "Hi! Hey, you know who's here? My Uncle Angus. We ate together."

"I met him last night," I said without enthusiasm, now that there was no need to appear bright, poised, and unimpressed. But Robbie deserved better from me. "In fact," I said, "I woke up when we left Fremont. I went into the pantry for my cup and again, so I'm not playing with a full deck this morning. But I'll catch up. Looks like a good day for me to do some work and write some letters. What will you be doing?"

"Whatever Uncle Hector tells me. Of course there are always the barn chores," he said importantly, carrying his dishes to the pantry. "Hey, take a look at the Jag in the yard," he added, as he ran upstairs to brush his teeth.

He was happy, and that was a lot more than I'd expected when we left fremont. I went into the pantry for my cup and saucer, and looked out coldly at the silver-gray Jaguar. After that I was prepared to find fault with the coffee, turn it all out and start fresh, but it smelled good when I filled my cup, and it was hot.

While I was sipping, and life was slowly returning to limbs and brain, the twins' truck rattled and flapped into hearing, and waited on the road, panting hoarsely. Robbie came rushing downstairs. "So long!" he tossed out in passing.

"Have a good day!" I called after him.

The truck roared like a dragon trying to intimidate St. George, and finally got going. I buttered a slice of Mrs. Archie's bread, poured a fresh cup of coffee, and went upstairs and sat down at my worktable with my breakfast on the nearest windowsill. I wrote down Angus's description of the Strathcoran estate and clipped it to the account of my corresponding dream.

When I was doing this I had a sudden attack of gooseflesh, as if someone had dropped ice water on the back of my neck. *Nor see the moon on royal tombstones gleam.* They became the children's stones, old, tilted, half-buried in heather, showing gray and ineffably lonely in a cloudy moonlight.

I had to get up and find a sweater, then I walked around the upper floor trying to shake off the desolation the picture had brought me. I stood at the back window of the third bedroom looking out at the fine rain. I should go out and drive to a town somewhere, I thought, where people were in and out of stores. Maybe I'd buy bone china for everybody I knew, and get a head start on my Christmas shopping.

The dark-blue panel truck which I'd seen at the farm the other night came past the pines, and turned into the driveway, and stopped behind the Jaguar. Stuart got out. He went around to the back of it, and was taking out his tool carrier when Angus appeared from the direction of the ell. He managed to wear jeans and sweatshirt as if they were custom-made. Probably were, too, I thought, unpleasantly.

He and Stuart walked toward the house, Angus talking, using his hands in broad gestures as he had last night; Stuart listened, sometimes nodding. Once when Angus laughed outright, Stuart grinned as if he couldn't help himself, and Angus put a hand on his shoulder and they walked like this out of sight.

I felt too thick to work with words and dates, but I could wash the dishes and then decide what to do next (if I didn't decide to go back to bed). When I went downstairs, I could hear voices in the cellar, and from the pantry window I saw that the bulkhead doors were open. I didn't try to hear what the men were saying—I didn't care—but got busy with the dishes.

I had just finished scalding the coffee pot when the men came up the cellar steps. Stuart saw me through the pantry window and gave me a perfunctory nod. Angus smiled, and called, "Any more coffee?"

"There'll be some in a minute," I called back. Oh, what a smile on a rainy morning, I thought disdainfully. Does he have to be so damned sunny? I put water on to boil, measured coffee again, set out clean cups.

They came in the back door, and Angus said charmingly, "I didn't intend for you to wait on us."

"I have to," I said. "I drank up all the coffee."

"Only two cups here," he said. "Can't you manage another one with us?"

"You don't need me, do you, Stuart?" I said. "I know you're too polite to agree, but I'm catching up on my work this morning, so I'm going upstairs." I poured boiling water into the pot to the right mark. "That'll be ready in a few minutes. There's some of your aunt's good bread in the breadbox if you want."

It was a good exit line, but it was spoiled by the arrival of Hector and the three boys. The kitchen was suddenly teeming with male Kendrums. Even Robbie had begun to look taller, it seemed to me. Hector greeted me with such leisurely friendliness I couldn't rush off, so I offered him a cup of coffee.

"Haven't got time, thanks," he said. "I just stopped in to say hello to the boy with the itching heel. I'm going over to look at that truck Sandy MacLean's got for sale, and on the way back we're stopping at Basil's to see the new champion."

"He thinks he's bred him a race horse," Stuart said. "Already got him winning everything in sight in three countries."

"Oh, let him dream a while," Hector said. "Dreams don't cost much."

"You sure of that? That whole operation of his is like pouring sand down a rat hole."

"Well, it's his money," Angus said. "Who knows, maybe he'll surprise us all one day."

"Jamesy thinks this little feller's a winner," said one of the twins. Ross, with the glasses.

"What Jamesy doesn't know about horses would fill the library at Dalhousie," said Stuart.

"How are the Gemini doing?" Angus dropped an arm around each twin's shoulders.

"Great!" exclaimed the other twin, Calum with the hair. "If Uncle Hector likes the truck, we get a chance to buy his old one."

"It's time they put theirs out of her misery." Hector looked at his watch. "Come on. I told Basil we'd be there at eleven. Somebody's coming at twelve to buy a pony, he hopes."

"I suppose hope doesn't cost much either," Stuart said.

Angus looked at me and tipped his head toward Stuart. "Our brother the pessimist. Funny thing, he wasn't born gloomy, they tell me."

"Cute little tad, as I remember him," said Hector.

"One of us," said Stuart, "has to be a realist."

Angus hooted. Hector flapped his hand and went out, trailed by the boys. I went back upstairs, leaving Angus and Stuart in the kitchen. They were all normally soft-voiced, and I could barely hear their voices, even with my door open. The heater came on, just enough to take away the faint chill from the dampness. I sat with my chin in my hands gazing out at the fine rain falling steadily from the gray velvet sky. The distant greens were a pastel mist, and Hector's cornfield across the river was like brown corduroy. The swallows were not bothered by the delicate rain.

I wondered how the river looked in the rain. I thought of all the years the rain and snow had fallen on the cabin site, and it would have made me unutterably sad, except that I was getting so sleepy. I gave up finally. I shut the door into the hall and took off my shoes and crawled into bed.

Now that I'd given up, I felt wonderful. I cuddled down under the spare blanket, and let myself go. While I was still in that delicious halfway state I thought I heard a car drive out of the yard, but it wasn't loud. Jaguars purr, I thought mistily, and submerged.

I slept so hard that when I woke up it should have been the next morning at the same time. It was almost noon. I was rested, and came awake at once, with the feeling that something had aroused me, and that I'd been hearing it in a dream which now I couldn't remember, but the sound was still going on.

Someone was walking around upstairs, over my head. Maybe

Stuart had finished his cellar job for today and had gone up to look over the work in the attic. The narrow door at the head of the stairs, which I'd thought was a closet, must be the way up to the top floor. He could have come from the ell through the door by the bathroom, and gone quietly across to the narrow door.

But if he were just looking over things up there, why was he pacing? Worried about something? Anyone could tell his son was a problem to him. But why pace over a stranger's head? No; he was working out figures in his mind, and walking up and down while he calculated. He thought I was busy in my room, not sleeping, and I had told him not to consider me.

The light steps would go away completely, then return; go away, return. Go away, return. When I sat up and swung my legs out of bed, they stopped. But he couldn't have heard anything, it was just a coincidence. They didn't start up again. Maybe he'd completed his figuring.

The rain had become more of a mist now. I got my boots and slicker and sou'wester from the closet and went downstairs, and out the front door. The moist air was as warm and fragrant as that of a greenhouse. The birds were busy and noisy. I picked a spray of wild strawberries that showed scarlet where the path left the lawn, and went down through the wet field to the cabin site. I found a few more strawberries there, and felt suddenly happy.

I went on to the river. On my right the brook talked to itself, and the cows grazed on an emerald hillside. The alder leaves were fringed with silver. I walked around a smallish point to my left and then along the bank until I was opposite Hector's big cornfield.

A little distance below the foot of the cornfield there was an alder thicket, lively with birds whose calls were familiar to me from home. This gave way to a swampy strip at the river's edge, growing a thick fringe of buttercups and some sort of wild flags not yet in blossom.

Farther along to my left was the bridge over which we drove

to get to the farm. I was getting into some soggy territory on this side, so I turned around and went back. Whitethroat sparrows sang about Canada, and purple finches were exuberantly in possession of the old orchard behind the barn. I wandered along enjoying myself, gathering up good resolutions like flowers along the way: I'd write a good letter to my father and Virginia, I'd do a couple of hours' work this afternoon.

The momentum of this carried me all the way back to the front door. When I opened it, noise met me; the kitchen was crowded again. Robbie and I should have some lunch, I was ready for it, but what about all these extra men? Sandwiches obviously, if I had enough of the makings, only I didn't think so.

"Hey, Noel!" Robbie shot out into the hall. "Guess what!"

"I couldn't possibly."

"Hold it, Rob," either Hector or Angus called. I couldn't tell which, their voices were sometimes similar.

But Robbie rushed on. "Somebody shot at us! *Twice!*"

"You're kidding," I said, inadequately because I'd lost my wind.

"No, honest!" He was exhilarated. "Go on out and look at the places on the truck."

"I don't want to!" I snapped. I went past him into the kitchen, and he came behind me, babbling on.

"A foot higher and he'd have got Uncle Hector, and that meant *all* of us, because —"

"Robbie," Hector said quietly, "shut up."

Robbie slid past me and quickly perched on a windowsill. His face and ears were red. He was so mortified by the reproof that I felt sorry for him in spite of the disgusting sensation in my midriff.

The rest all watched me come into the room. Hector stood with one foot braced on the hearth of the wood stove, Angus half-sat on a corner of the table. The twins sprawled in chairs like long-legged puppets dressed as boys, except that their eyes were luminously alive in their immobile faces. Stuart stood in the middle of the room, his hands on his hips. He regarded me with exasperation. If the others considered a stranger the last thing they needed right now, at least they hid it.

"Get on with it," he snapped at Hector.

Hector spoke even more softly than usual. "It was when we were passing through the woods on the way out to the pavement. You know where Basil's road is built up above the ravine. I was going slow, because that dirt's like grease when it's wet."

"He'd pay five thousand for a horse, but he's too poor to put a guard rail along the steep side," Stuart said.

"I had the window down, so I heard the shot on the hill off to my left, and almost on top of that I thought a rock hit my door. But I had a feeling." He stopped.

"You had a feeling *what*?" Angus didn't raise his voice either.

"That it was no rock. A foot higher and we'd have been off the road and down in the ravine, four of us in the truck and landing upside down and maybe on fire. Then the bastard fired again." He glanced apologetically at me. "Sorry, Noel."

"*Jesus.*" The word was jolted out of Stuart. I could tell by the way the twins reacted that it wasn't his customary language. He was grayish-pale. "If you don't do something, I will!"

"If I knew who it was, for God's sake, I'd take him by the neck and shake 'im till his brains jingled! But whoever is fool enough to be shooting wild in the woods with a high-powered rifle isn't going to admit it. And I'll be damned if I can think who it is."

"I know who it is," Stuart said grimly. "Somebody looking for a deer out of season."

Angus said, "None of our well-known Brierbank poachers are that foolish with guns."

"I'm not thinking about any of them. Did you see that van anywhere, the one that belongs to that scruffy crew at the Bain Place?" They all looked blankly at him. "Well, no matter. They could park it in a wood road somewhere, and pull out after you'd gone by."

"They don't eat meat," the twin Calum objected, rising up. "They're vegetarians. They don't believe in killing."

"That's what they say," said Stuart with calm contempt. "But I'm willing to bet that's not how they *do*. So are you going over and put the fear of God into them, or better still, put them off the place?"

"You never give up on them, do you?" Hector asked mildly.

Angus said, "It could be anybody. I've been over to Inverness this morning, and I passed several cars coming this way that I didn't recognize. Some idiots from the city could be out driving around and thinking they could get a bird or a rabbit, or even a deer. There are plenty of places where a Jeep or a Land Rover could get off the road and into the woods out of sight."

"You could be right," said Hector.

"With any luck they'll shoot each other," the twin Ross said hopefully.

"What are you going to do, just let it *go*?" Stuart demanded.

"What can I do?" Hector asked good-naturedly. "It's too late to call the police. They probably came out of there right behind me and hightailed it for home. All we can do is write it off as a freak accident." He straightened up and took his foot off the stove hearth. "I'll call Basil. He should be told that somebody's been running around with a rifle on his property."

The twins got up, and Robbie, color normal now, left the windowsill. Angus began filling his pipe. Stuart creased his lower lip between thumb and forefinger, looking from one brother to the other. Suddenly he said, "Did you see Jamesy at the ranch?"

"Yep." Hector headed across the kitchen toward the back door.

"Was he around when you drove off?"

Hector stopped and looked back. Angus said, "Don't tell us you're suspecting Jamesy. What became of the hippies?"

Instant color stood out on Stuart's sharp cheekbones. "I just want to know how he's sticking to his job, that's all."

"He wasn't there when we left," Hector said. "He and the new chap, a nephew of Basil's from St. John, went off to whatever they were supposed to do next. Nobody told me what that was, and I didn't ask."

"Are you sure you don't want a drink to steady your nerves?" Angus asked.

"If they get any steadier I'll be paralyzed," said Hector with a grin. "Noel, I hope this hasn't scared you so you'll take the boy under your arm and run home with him."

"*No!*" Robbie protested. He glared at me. "I won't go!"

"I haven't said anything yet," I told him. I'd been sickened by Hector's sparse description of the car crashing down into the ravine and possibly exploding, but it was a matter of pride not to show it. "Sometimes a thing like this happens at home. Or we could meet a drunk on the highway, or a perfectly sensible person has a heart attack at the wheel. I'm not running."

But I had qualms. Should I consult with Virginia? Still, a normal life was full of near misses, and his mother didn't want to coddle him.

"I wouldn't go," Robbie said. "No way!"

"I'm going over there and look for empty shells," Stuart said.

"Good God, man, you don't think *Jamesy* fired that rifle, do you?" Hector was incredulous. "Took a rifle to work with him this morning in the rain on his motorbike, and then strolled off into the woods to pick off his uncle and his cousins as they drove by?"

Stuart flinched as if he'd been slapped, but went doggedly on. "He could have already hidden his rifle over there. If he was high on something, you don't know what he'd do. He was mighty resentful for a long time after you fired him."

"But he's a damn sight happier in the new job," Hector argued. "Basil says he's a dab hand with horses, and he hasn't had to be told not to smoke around the stables, either. So why should he still hold a grudge against me?"

"I just want to be sure. You don't know the boy." Stuart was unhappy. I was sorry for him, and wished I weren't there to make it worse for him. He must really hate me by now, I thought.

"Honestly, Uncle Stuart," Calum said, "Jamesy's not mad with Uncle Hector. He said so the other night. He says he likes horses better than cows."

Stuart's glance quelled him and returned to Hector. "Just the same, I'll be a lot happier if I can find a shell that came out of a strange rifle. Or maybe some other evidence that might be lying around. Tell me again just exactly where you were, and how you figure the distance and the angle."

Hector shrugged. "Got some paper, Noel?"

I supplied it and they settled down at the table with the boys hanging close by. Angus watched the group, arms folded, face unreadable. Hector was curt about the whole thing. "Talk about looking for a needle in a haystack," he muttered.

When he and the boys left, Stuart was studying the diagram. "Give the boy some credit, Stuart," Angus said.

I started discreetly for the stairs, but I couldn't miss Stuart's retort. "Do you think I don't *want* to? He's my oldest son! But if he's smoking that filth he's rotting his brain. He's got no sense of judgment left."

"If he *is* smoking a joint now and then, which you don't know for sure, it's not going to make him violent, Stuart. Take it from me."

"Yep, I imagine you're an expert by now. So you must know where they go from marijuana."

"It doesn't necessarily have to lead to anything else, any more than that cigarette of yours does. It's not good, but—"

"Speaking from experience, are you?"

"All I want to do," Angus said patiently, "is give you a little reassurance."

Stuart made a short, furious exclamation and went out. Before I reached my room I heard a truck door slam. I shut myself in and went to work.

12
CHAPTER

WHEN HUNGER drove me downstairs, the place was empty inside and out. Only the station wagon remained in the yard. I fixed myself an enormous lunch, and read while I ate. The affair this morning had lost much of its shock value, and would keep on losing it if Stuart couldn't link the shot to a drug-crazed boy. Angus was probably right about the effects of marijuana, and Hector was probably right to call it a freak accident caused by trespassers, who would never dare to come that way again.

I went back to work after lunch, and I didn't see anybody for that whole long Saturday until Robbie came home at supper time, left off by the twins. He brought a container of baked beans, still hot, some brown bread, and a dish of cabbage salad.

He and the twins had evidently worn out the morning's subject, and he was more eager to talk about everything he had done that day and the fact that Hector was going to buy the truck and the twins could now buy his old one. It could have been a Rolls-Royce, the way he talked. I went along with him on it, and we had quite an involved conversation.

"How about a game of gin?" he asked suddenly. "Or cribbage? Or checkers, maybe? My mother put them all in my stuff."

"Cribbage," I said. "I never won a game of checkers yet except when I was little and my father let me win. I'm not so hot at gin, either. But cribbage, now—" I rubbed my hands. He laughed, and ran upstairs to get the cards and the board.

We played for an hour, until we were both yawning and hardly able to see the cards through watering eyes. I skunked him twice and he was patronizingly generous about it, but I forgave him that. After all, it showed a certain gentlemanly attitude as well as a chauvinistic one. We had instant cocoa for a nightcap, and while we were drinking it he said diffidently, "Uh—the kids and I—and Uncle Hector too—well, all of us agreed not to say anything to Aunt Priscilla about what happened this morning."

"Oh sure, that's right," I agreed. "I won't say anything. Did your Uncle Stuart find an empty shell, do you know?"

"I don't know. He didn't come to the farm all day."

I went to bed as soon as he was out of the bathroom, read, fell asleep, and didn't wake up till morning. The Jaguar had returned sometime in the night, but there were no sounds of life in the ell. Robbie got himself up early as usual, fixed his breakfast, and was picked up by the twins, now driving the somewhat quieter truck, for the morning chores. They brought him back in an hour or so and waited while he cleaned up and changed his clothes. He was going to church with them, he said offhandedly, and I behaved as if this was the thing everybody did on Sunday in the country; I did it so well I wondered if the twins were secretly disapproving of me for not going. I salved my conscience by saying to myself, Oh well, next week I'll go. I really should. It's a necessary part of the whole experience here.

"Uncle Angus is having breakfast with Uncle Hector," Robbie said on his way out behind the twins.

"That's nice," I said. "Don't forget some money for the collection."

"I've got it." He looked handsome in his tattersall-check slacks and blue blazer. "Okay if I go home with the kids for dinner?"

"Fine, because I hadn't given a thought to Sunday dinner." We were invited to Mrs. Alec's for supper.

"We're coming over here to swim this afternoon, though."

"Fine," I said again. "You'd better step on it. I hear churchbells wafted on the breeze."

"They're too heavy for that," he protested, grinned, and went out. I was pleased with him. He was a nice kid, and acted as if he liked me, which made me pleased with myself. As for Angus Kendrum, I wasn't really disappointed because he was behaving just as I'd expected him to after our first meeting. We'd taken each other's correct measure, and therefore wouldn't see any more of each other than could be helped.

While I washed the dishes in the pantry, I could look out at the Jaguar shining and winking in the sun. "So he walked down to the farm, did he?" I said to it. "Probably ran. Or at least jogged. Cultivating his beauty. He and Micah Jenkins. One with his actresses and the other with his passengers. God, they'll be impossible by the time they're fifty, frantically trying to prove they're as great as they ever were."

All the while that I was raving I knew that I *was* disappointed. Our midnight conversation would remain isolated in time, like one of those satellites sent up to travel in space forever. So much junk polluting the once-purity of the universe. Beer cans tossed out along the road of the stars.

Better a mad tumble out of orbit and then incineration in a fast fiery end. The whole idea, especially the beer-can metaphor, was worth a poem. By the time I'd worked out a few lines, in blank verse of course, which was easier than searching for rhymes, I'd finished the dishes and was restfully indifferent to Angus Kendrum.

"Slobs in Space" would be a good title, I thought.

Until we went to the Alec Kendrum house for supper, the day was mine. I spent most of it down at the river, writing my poem, reading, swimming when the day grew hot, and falling asleep in the alder shade. I dreamed no dreams, had no visitations. I wondered if Angus's presence about the place had anything to do with it, either by inhibiting me or whatever influences were collecting about me.

This was the first time I had boldly acknowledged the possibility of those influences as something outside myself, and it was a little scary; it was like walking across a flowery lawn and catching myself at the edge of a cliff I hadn't known was there. But one needn't stumble into the fatal plunge. I had no intention of *that*. Still, I could have resented Angus's possible power except for what he'd told me about Strathcoran.

In midafternoon the boys came to swim. I left them to have the river to themselves. They were going to the farm for the evening chores before they showed up for supper, so I drove alone over to Brierbank Corner. I went up the hill past the church, and came to the school; the Alec Kendrum mailbox was across the road from it, on my right. A narrow dirt road led through the woods to the house. A neighboring farmer whose buildings lay out of sight over to the west rented the fields for hay and pasturage. There were only chickens here now, and an old pony the boys had long ago outgrown.

"She rules us with an iron hoof," said Rowan. "She has things all her own way around here. We'd never sell her because nobody else would put up with her." She gave me a carrot to feed Marjorie but I didn't trust that eye. Rowan gave her the carrot and then she was off across the field. "Besides," Rowan said tenderly, watching her go, "it would be like selling our own sister."

Bob and Christy Kendrum were already here, picked up along the way by some cousins who had driven out from Truro. They were catching up on family news (from all points of the compass, it seemed to me) in the house. Rowan and I sat on the long porch and took turns with the binoculars, looking down at the Bain Place.

Everything needed painting there, but the long rectangle of the garden showed lines of new green, and there was a good woodpile. The sheep and the goats were well-fenced off from the house and sheds.

"Maybe neither couple is married," said Rowan, "but they might just as well be. I mean, it doesn't feel like a den of iniquity when you go there. I'll take you next weekend and you'll see. Moira's the weaver and Jared's the cabinet maker. Eve makes wonderful bread, and knows all about herbs. Her husband—or man—or companion, or whatever—is the gardener. It's strictly organic, of course."

"Where's his marijuana crop?" I asked, scanning with the glasses.

Rowan giggled. "Don't ever let Uncle Stuart hear you say that, or he'll think you want to be a customer. They *don't* raise it. If any of them smoke it—well—" She shrugged. "I know other people who do, too. That's their business."

"Unless they supply it to the kids around here," I suggested, "and I've just spotted a motorbike parked behind one of those big oaks near that red shed."

She grabbed the glasses from me. "Looks like Jamesy's, all right. But it never occurs to Uncle Stuart that Jamesy might hang around there because he likes them. They're *interesting*, Noel." Her gray eyes were as earnest as Robbie's could be. "And Jamesy isn't just a nutty kid who wants to spend his life racing around on a motorbike, even if that's what his father thinks." She lowered her voice even more. "Don't mention seeing it over there."

Stuart and his carload were just arriving. The three children burst out of the car and set off at a run for Marjorie's pasture.

"Don't you kids go inside that fence!" Rowan yelled after them. When they didn't slow down Stuart whistled, and it was like bringing a troika to a sudden violent stop.

"If one of you gets a hoof in the face you can go around toothless till you can pay for your own teeth!" he told them. "With a broken nose, too! So mind your railings."

"That's telling them," said Rowan with a grin. Stuart shook his head and went on into the house. Aunt Len gave us her bemused and tender smile.

"Aunt Len's not made of solid flesh, she's a mixture of cloud and marshmallow," Rowan observed. "Very frustrating for Uncle Stuart sometimes, I should think."

The boys came in, and Hector and Mrs. Archie arrived a little afterward. Jamesy showed up, not smelling of pot as far as we could tell. Angus was the last to come, as if he'd timed his entrance; a symphony in rust and gold today.

Rowan went in to help her mother; I said I'd do dishes. I stayed outside on the porch swing, holding a half-grown kitten, while all the family talk went on. The Truro cousins hadn't seen Angus in some time, and evidently considered his work very glamorous and exciting, but he was jubilant about a fresh conquest.

"I've been working on Emmie Durang," he said. "Drinks yesterday, drinks today, and I've finally talked her out of that shell-carved blockfront desk. I'll have to take about six coats of paint off it, but it'll be worth it. Solid cherry underneath. And the original brass pulls too." He was jubilant.

"How much did that set you back?" Stuart asked.

"That," said Angus solemnly, "is a sacred secret between Emmie and me. Let's just say that when I can afford it she's got a butterfly tavern table I want."

"She's used it for a plantstand for years," said Mrs. Archie disapprovingly. "It's a mess."

"Some bargain," said Stuart, "if you have to drink your way to it."

"Oh, I dunno," said Hector. "Sounds like fun."

At the table I was between Bob Kendrum and the male cousin from Truro, Gilbert Kendrum. Bob acted delighted to have me beside him. He was both jolly and courtly, pouring my wine and asking if I had enough of everything, urging me to try some special pickle or preserve, have another roll.

Then Gilbert Kendrum asked him his opinion about some political issue and the two men began talking past me, which gave me a chance to eat, listening contentedly in on one conversation and then another; there were several going on at once around the table, and a good deal of laughter. I didn't have to know whom they were talking about to enjoy myself. Maybe I'd get a look at some of these eccentrics before the summer was over.

"Well, young lady!" Bob said to me, and I prepared to refuse anything else because my plate was still loaded. "Have you seen any ghosts yet?"

I know what they mean about the jaw dropping. Mine did; the question was utterly unexpected. He was mischievously pleased by my surprise. I widened my eyes and asked innocently, "Should I have?"

"*Robert*," said Christy severely from across the table.

Flushed and beaming, he ignored her. "If you're tuned in right, you should."

Christy sighed. "Gilbert, will you put that wine bottle out of his reach?"

"I don't want to stop him now," said Gilbert. "*Are* there ghosts in that house?"

"Ghosts in any old house, my boy."

"But how can I tell if they're there? What should I listen for?" I asked. The other conversations had stopped as if the one word *ghosts* had killed them all with one blow. Everybody looked entertained except Christy, who was trying to catch Bob's innocent blue eye and not succeeding. "What do they *do* in the Angus J. house?" I persisted.

"What ghosts usually do," Angus said. "Rattle chains. Moan. Weep endlessly."

"And drip water like the ghost of the governess in *The Turn of the Screw*," said the woman cousin from Truro, who was a librarian.

"Make tables walk across the room?" suggested Mrs. Archie.

"Knock once for yes, two for no," said Rowan, "or is it the other way around? Throw dishes and move furniture. Pictures fall off the wall."

"That's a poltergeist, if there's any such thing," I said. "And the table tipping and knocks are spiritualist tricks. All separate from real"—I hesitated—"real honest-to-goodness ghosts."

"I thought for a minute you were going to say real flesh-and-blood ghosts," said Angus.

"She's just getting into the spirit of the thing," said Hector. There were some obliging groans; I uttered one of them. If Bob was going to drop any fact at all in the midst of all this, I wanted to catch it, but I didn't want anyone to suspect that it meant anything to me.

"Did you ever personally know of ghosts in the Angus J. house?" I asked him. "If you've got a good ghost story you can't back out now. Can he?" I appealed to Rowan.

"No, he can't. We're listening, Uncle Bob. So give."

"*Bob,*" said Christy softly. "None of your fairy tales now. We don't want Noel scared out of her senses if she hears a board creak in the middle of the night."

Thanks to the wine, or some other exhilaration, I almost said, *But you don't know what I've heard already.* The basic instinct of self-preservation saved me. I smiled at Christy and said, "I don't think there'd be any nasty characters haunting that place. It has such a good feeling."

Gilbert Kendrum said, "What about the theory that ghosts are entities that hang around the places where they died violently?"

"There weren't any murders or suicides in that house that I ever heard of," Hector said. "Did you, Bob? You, Gib?" Both men shook their heads. Bob was subdued now, fussing with his glasses, as if Christy had gotten to him at last.

"Couldn't there be souls who stay around places they loved?" Rowan asked. "Or to watch over someone? Where did this belief in guardian angels come from?"

"Wishful thinking," said Angus. "I suppose that in the old days if anybody survived plagues, pogroms, and great natural disasters, he'd be inclined to think it was more than just luck. He'd think he had supernatural protection even if the rest of his family or village or army didn't."

"Never mind the old days, a lot of people believe in it now," said the librarian. The conversation shifted away from ghosts. I kept quiet and ate. I'd get around to see Bob the first chance I had, and wouldn't it be wonderful if I could talk to him alone? I longed for a confederate who would take charge of Christy; clearly, there were matters she didn't think Bob should talk about. I knew this could be as much wishful thinking as Angus's guardian-angel theory, so I pigeonholed it for now.

Or I tried to, but it wouldn't be thrust quite out of sight.

"What are you thinking now, Noel?" Angus's question seemed to have been asked twice. Startled, I looked up to see him in Rowan's place across the table from me; she had got up to take off plates.

For this moment everybody, even Bob, was occupied with somebody else, and it gave us an odd solitude, even isolation.

"I'm thinking about food," I said rapidly. "Making room for that cake I saw in the kitchen."

"No, you weren't. I can tell. That expression didn't mean cake, even coconut layer cake." He got up, just about ready to laugh at me, but keeping it to himself; at least that was how I read him.

It could be said in Micah's favor that he was mostly inarticulate.

13

CHAPTER

WHILE ROWAN and I did the dishes, she invited me to come into Halifax and spend Tuesday with her. She was owed a day off and could take that one; I could ride in with an aunt who commuted during the summer months. When I agreed, she called her aunt and made the arrangements then and there.

"Know what we're doing tomorrow?" Robbie asked on the way home at dusk. "We're going to rip shingles off a roof." He sounded as if he could hardly wait.

"Don't tell me your uncle's going to have you kids up on top of the barn."

"Nope, but I'd like that. I've got a good head for heights," he bragged. "Gosh, I wonder how far you could see from the top of the silo."

"Well, don't try it unless you ask your mother first," I said. "What is this building? A small chicken house, I hope."

He laughed, all triumphant male. "A little barn. It's over on the Bain Place."

"How come? I thought the tenants did all the repairing."

"This is something different. It's way off by itself, near the river. A woodlot hides it from the house, and it's in a kind of valley besides. It's what's left of a small farm that got annexed to the Bain Place a long time ago."

"Is it safe for you boys to be climbing around on an old place like that? Excuse me for making responsible noises, but it goes with my job."

"Uncle Hector and Uncle Stuart went all over it a while

back," he said. "Uncle Hector says it's too sound and solid not to be saved. He may fix it up as a camp and rent it to somebody who wants peace and quiet by the river. Those people from Truro, Mr. and Mrs. Kendrum, hope he will do it. They'd like to use it."

"Shall I fix a lunch for you?"

"Nope, Aunt Janet'll tend to that." He yawned loudly, and it was contagious. We were both yawning and laughing foolishly about it by the time we got home. The ell was lit up.

Robbie went straight to bed. I could hear faint sounds next door, so I stayed in the kitchen, consciously giving Angus a chance to come in and tease me about ghosts—that private moment at the table had fairly promised it, unless significant and promising glances were simply part of his normal equipment, like Micah's intent blue stare. Setting the table for breakfast didn't use up much time, so I made some tea which I didn't really want. I went up and got my notebook, and sat down at the kitchen table to read over my last notes. If I had luck (or a guardian angel) I'd soon have more to add to it.

Be objective, or you'll never sleep tonight, I warned myself. But suspense had me by the throat. It was like Christmas Eve when I was small, an anticipation of astonishments so unbelievable that the wait was almost agony.

There was a tap on the ell door and Angus put his head in. "Cheerio! I'm off."

"Drive carefully," I said sweetly.

He cocked an eyebrow. "Yes, Auntie." The door closed behind him. I sat there staring at it. I had wanted to say something to him, I didn't know what. If he'd challenged me about phantoms, how objective would my response have been, with that notebook lying under my hand? How strongly would I have been tempted to knock that consciously whimsical grin off his face?

Listening to the Jaguar driving out, I realized my narrow escape. I could have given away the works and hated myself in the morning.

But I went to bed in a bad mood anyway. I treated myself to a long warm bath, and after that I wrapped up in my robe and sat by my windows, listening to the night. I heard a plaintive bird-call strange to me, a fox barking, and the sound picked up by one of Bob Kendrum's dogs over beyond the river and the woods. Then quiet, except for the brook. There was the scent of new-mown grass. Fireflies like drifting sparks in the dark. I grew heavier and heavier, and went to bed.

Sometimes I fall asleep directly; occasionally, if I'm over-tired, I float in this half-waking, half-dreaming limbo. The technical word, which I came across in a weird kind of novel once, is hypnogogy. In the hypnogogic state you're likely to see and hear strange things in odd, isolated fragments that you can't relate to yourself as you can relate most dreams. Or your body receives a sudden strong jolt of mysterious energy which makes you jump, and thoroughly wakes you up.

Tonight I didn't jump, but I heard someone walking down-stairs. I wasn't alarmed, I didn't care. I was floating free.

A woman's face appeared.

It didn't evolve eerily out of swirling mists as they do in the movies. It was all at once there against the black area between the dim shapes of the starlit windows. Red hair flowed dishev-eled over some sort of dark wrap that bundled her to the ears. Greenish eyes with pale lashes stared from a white face, so con-torted by some passion that you couldn't say whether she was beautiful or ugly, young or old; you could be sure only of the eyes and the strong, thick, hot-colored hair. I remember being not afraid but enthralled.

There was a name, *Francis*. I didn't know if she said it or not, but it was there, like her. She said, "Your father is dead."

I bounded out of bed, my hands shaking, my teeth chatter-ing. She was gone, but not the words. *Your father is dead.* I was frantic. "Oh God," I whispered, "why isn't there a telephone in this place?" I could hardly stand, my legs were so unsteady, yet my heart was working so hard that seemingly it wouldn't let me keep still without its exploding in my breast.

Somebody would call the farm, but not in the middle of the night. They'd say, Let her sleep, she doesn't have to know until morning that her father is dead.

But I wanted to drive to the farm *now*. Never mind rousing Hector and Janet, I had to call someone in Fremont and find out. Maybe he and Virginia both—a flash fire, a car accident—

I couldn't wake Robbie, he was only a child, and if something had happened to his mother he shouldn't know until the truth couldn't be avoided. "Damn you, Angus," I said through my trembling jaws. "Why couldn't you have stayed?"

I'd have given anything to know someone adult was on the other side of the wall.

Downstairs the clock began to strike midnight. At first it sounded faintly through the drumming in my ears, and then, like a large and soothing hand stroking my head, came the assurance that my father was all right. It was someone else's father, or nobody's at all; the woman with her flowing red hair and hard jade stare was simply a figment of that hypnogogic state. Like the name *Francis*. I didn't know any Francis.

With a groan of relief I fell back into bed and pulled up my extra blanket and curled up. The silence of the house was now as restful as sleep itself. When had the pacing stopped? I examined the question with what I hoped was scientific detachment; was it just before or just after the woman appeared? Had I really heard it, or had it been part of the limbo condition, or my own heartbeat?

Too much of a problem to fuss with. I drifted again, luxuriously, and then the weeping began. The sobs wrenched excruciatingly up from the gut, scraping all the way so you'd expect them to be made visible with blood. My own belly muscles contracted in spasms, my own lungs were laboring. There was a knowledge of shattering grief, shot through with fragments of unintelligible words. But one thing was clear—the voice that tried to speak them was that of a boy.

Robbie. Surrounded by men who reminded him of his father,

he had been attacked in his sleep by an old sorrow set loose. I was out of bed again and past the hall before I realized there wasn't a sound behind his door. I laid my ear against the paneling and finally heard a faint rustling as he turned over, and then the quiet, sighing breath one sometimes gives in deep sleep. There was no suggestion of the short hard breathing that follows heavy weeping.

But talk about gut reaction—I was aching with it, and my face was wet too. I huddled in my blankets, hugging my knees. That sense of terrible grief was still with me, but I knew it didn't directly touch Robbie or me.

I kept thinking, It's all right, it's not *your* sorrow, it will go away. But it didn't.

Then something else arose with such power that it toppled and drowned the desolation, and I came struggling and gasping to the surface buoyed up by this new passion.

Hatred. An exhilaration of it; a lustful itch in my hands to take someone by the throat and joyously, effortlessly, *kill*.

I knew I was wide awake this time, and if I wasn't careful, if I let myself be swept along like a chip, I'd lose something priceless and never get it back. These were genuine experiences, unless I was crazy as a coot and didn't know it.

I couldn't settle down to sleep now and I didn't care if I never did. I went downstairs and made myself a large cup of cocoa, then sat in a rocking chair with my feet on another chair, drinking in the dark. I tried to analyze the happenings. I knew I had never seen that woman in my life, and I knew I had no boarded-up rooms in my brain preserving all kinds of terror. Earlier I had called her a figment of the hypnogogic state, but what if she belonged in somebody else's memory?

I gripped the hot mug hard to keep from slopping the cocoa, I was so shaky. If she existed in someone else's memory, so did the rest of it.

Angus Mor had been fifteen when he left Scotland, and it had been a boy whose weeping I had heard and shared until my chest ached. After the hurricane of anguish, he'd have hated whoever had destroyed his father, hated Fat "Butcher" Cumberland, and most of all hated the Scots who supported the German Georges instead of the Stuarts.

Who was the woman, then? His mother? No mother had ever been mentioned; she couldn't have come with the boys. Perhaps she died long before, and this woman was someone else, an aunt or a neighbor. No, the stepmother! Angus had mentioned her.

I had no doubt now that I had received someone's memories, or at least glittering and painful fragments of them. Was Angus Mor the pacer in the dark? I wondered, trembling; and in his lifetime had he paced many nights because he had memories that wouldn't let him sleep?

I stared wildly around the starlit kitchen as if something else were there. But whatever had been with me tonight, it was gone, exorcised perhaps in that one crashing climactic moment of hatred. I was left high and dry and felt like bursting into tears.

I longed to talk about the whole thing with someone, but nine people out of ten would think I was off my rocker, and the tenth would come zeroing in on me with a Ouija board or a covey of mediums. Some scholarly, hard-headed, incorruptible researcher was called for, and there might be some such person connected with Dalhousie, but this was somebody else's house so I couldn't do a thing about it.

Besides, I didn't really want to. For now, it was all mine. It was between me and Angus Mor. If he wasn't aware of me, I was aware of him now, and in no doubt whatsoever.

I went back to bed to sleep like the victor of a great battle.

14
CHAPTER

WHEN I WOKE UP to the cheerful noise of the swallows, my first thought was that if I'd actually picked up some of Angus Mor's memories, and the red-haired woman wasn't my own creation, she should have had an accent of some sort, or have even spoken in Gaelic; in which case I wouldn't have understood her.

But then I realized that for Angus she'd have had no foreign accent or unknown language, so I'd received the *sense* of the words in my brain.

Robbie had already gone. I fixed a large breakfast because I was terribly hungry, as if I'd done a lot of traveling the night before. Well, I had. Way back to 1746, if I was sane. They say you can't tell if you're going round the bend, but I always thought I'd know. Having had my valid ESP experiences as a kid, slight as they were, and done some reading on the subject, I was able to be open-minded about some pretty far-out theories. If a dog can hear a whistle that people can't, why can't certain human beings be born with superfine receiving systems? Of course you'd have to accept the belief that nothing which has ever happened in this world is lost, that somewhere the wake of its passage still foams out its invisible ripples, and that an old house can be like one of those mysterious ridges far inland that were once beaches upon which salt combers broke and left their proofs behind.

I could imagine someone like young Angus, for instance, listening to my reasoning with an indulgent and patronizing smile, slowly shaking his head; I could even imagine my father doing it. No, he'd be saying in alarm, "For heaven's sake, Noel! Have you been *smoking* something?"

But I wasn't going to tell either of them. So I could reason in circles or like a wildly jumping checker player if I wanted to, I thought smugly. I enjoyed my breakfast and brought my notebook up to date.

As I wrote I saw that I could have created the walker; there could be natural reasons for the sound effects. I wanted to get down cellar and see. Angus had made this big talk about my seeing the cellar, the attic, and the barn, and then he'd stayed away from me the whole time. He'd simply decided I wasn't worth any more attention. Well, at least he was honest about it— I could give him good marks for that.

I wondered how I could get into the cellar. It seemed odd that Stuart should have the only key; the padlock was new, and two keys always went along with a new padlock.

I tried the door into the ell, and was immediately ashamed of myself, because Angus had left it unlocked. So he trusted Robbie and me. I bargained that if I could see any duplicate keys from the door I'd borrow one; if not, I wouldn't step over the threshold to go search.

The door opened into a comfortable, masculine sort of room; shelves of books and magazines, a big cluttered desk with a typewriter and a good lamp, some pleasantly saggy chairs pulled up to a Franklin-type stove which used the same chimney as the wood stove in the kitchen. Stairs went up across the far end of the ell. There was a window beneath them that looked out at the old orchard.

Directly to my left a small lavatory backed up to the pantry wall, and the door to the yard was around the corner from it. And on the wall between that door and the first window there hung a narrow strip of waxed pine with hooks screwed into it, and on these hung five keys with wooden tags lettered in black.

Somebody once said that "cellar door" was one of the most beautiful sounds in the English language. I knew it was. Now if only Stuart didn't take it into his head to show up. I could say I heard a funny noise down there, but how would I explain going into the ell for the keys? Stuart would suspect me of looking the whole apartment over, upstairs and down, and he'd tell Angus so.

Don't come, Stuart, I ordered him sternly. I went out my own back door and unlocked the padlock. Six stone steps led down to a new, heavy, inside door which stood open. The cellar was light and roomy, but didn't extend under the ell. Its fieldstone walls had been painted up with fresh mortar, and the cement floor was new, with a gutter where the hill water could run through in the spring when everything was thawing. Under the pantry and kitchen end, there were a modern oilburner and a big fuel tank, the electric pump and pressure tank, and a new hot water heater.

All around the cellar there were shelves, mostly new. A spacious cold cupboard had been built in the northwestern corner. A long bench ran under the southern windows, piled with stuff that was evidently being sorted. I saw at first glance some old canning jars of greenish glass, and plenty of other ancient bottles that would have driven a collector mad. The bench itself was old, the wood dark and scarred with wear. There were many drawers under it, some in bright new wood. I poked curiously into some grimy wooden boxes beside the bench. One was full of old iron; hinges, big hooks, latches, and so forth. The others held the miscellaneous cultch any cellar collects over the years. I love to paw over such stuff, but I was nervous about being caught, in case Stuart was no good at mental telepathy; besides, if he *should* receive a powerful message telling him to stay away, he'd probably rush right over.

The surprise was a flight of steps going up to the floor above, because I hadn't seen any way down from inside the house. I went up the steps, which were old but sturdy. On the fourth one up, I could put my palms flat against what lay overhead. I shoved gently, and felt a trapdoor move. Up another step and I could sight through a bright slit along the hall floor toward the closet under the front stairs, across the kitchen threshold to my left, and on my right to the sill of the rear door to the living room. I kept pushing, and something slithered softly away. I remembered a hit-or-miss rag rug out there by the back door.

I lowered the trapdoor, backed hastily down the narrow steps, ran across the cement floor, and scampered up the stone steps out into the dazzle of the morning. I just managed not to slam the bulkhead leaf down. I snapped the padlock, returned Angus's key to its hook, and rushed back to the hall and the trapdoor.

The hinges had been set flush with the floor and painted the same color. On the side that opened there was a neat little indentation at the edge of the center plank, holding a small brass ring just big enough to hook a finger in. I did so, and swung back the trapdoor the whole way. Of course there had to be an indoor entrance; who in the middle of a Nova Scotia or Maine winter had ever wanted to run outdoors and open a bulkhead to get down cellar and fetch up potatoes or salt fish or a jar of last summer's garden stuff?

I shut the trapdoor and put the rug over it. It passed through my mind that if anyone had wanted to make me nervous he could have come in from the outside and up through the trapdoor to make ghostly footsteps. I couldn't really believe Stuart would be up to anything like that. Maybe Jamesy, if he felt mad enough at the world. He hadn't yet looked me straight in the eye. If he could get the key, I'd be a handy object for him to take out his spite on, if he felt like kicking his father but didn't dare.

Well, it'll take more than pacing to scare the hell out of me, my boy, I thought, and if you start rattling chains I'll wrap'em right around your Adam's apple and make cider out of it.

I felt good when I started out for Bob Kendrum's. I wasn't going to tell them anything, I was just going to ask to look at the old Bible and pictures again, and maybe—if Fate or luck had anything to do with it—Bob would get wound up before Christy could stop him.

I didn't want to drive by the farm without speaking to Mrs. Archie, so I went back out to the black road—they called it "the pavement" here—and turned south. Less than a mile away I saw Bob's mailbox and made a left turn across the pavement and onto Bob's road.

Bob himself was ahead of me, as if he'd just been up to put mail in the box. I slowed down, admiring his straight, cocky way of carrying himself. He'd been in a Canadian Highlander regiment during World War I, and I could imagine him in his kilt. The dogs were dashing ecstatically in and out of the woods. One of them, circling back to Bob, saw the car and began to bark. Bob turned around, and I put my head out and waved. He grinned and moved to the side of the road, calling the dogs to him, and waited for me to catch up.

"Hello, there, young woman! Janet's taken my wife off somewhere, and I don't expect you were coming to see *me*."

"But I am," I said. "Because you can tell me what I want to know. You and your friends want a ride home?"

"I never turn down a ride with a good-looking girl. You sure you want these two?"

"Just put them in the back seat. They can't hurt anything." They jumped in, breathing hard with happy excitement. Bob shut the door on them and came around to get in front with me. The air was fanned into motion by two ardently waving tails, and my ear was kissed.

"They like to ride," Bob said fondly. "They don't get much chance these days since I've given up driving my own car. Well! What was it you wanted to know? Watch out for the potholes."

"They make me think of home," I said, navigating with skill. "I want to know about the ghost, or ghosts, whatever it is in the Angus J. house." I had decided in an instant to use the blunt approach, so he wouldn't have any time to back off.

He was so surprised he actually stuttered. "Wha—what—"

"You said something last night, and I didn't have a chance to follow it up. Look, Mr. Kendrum, I'm not nervous, I'm just curious."

His blue eyes looked no older than Robbie's or the twins'. "I'd tell you if you promise not to let on. Christy would be real annoyed with me. Of course she's not a Kendrum—she's a Tolmie—so whatever there is over there, it wouldn't mean the same to her as it does to me."

"You mean you've heard something?" I didn't jump at it. With great control I brought the car to an easy stop in the dooryard.

"No, I've never spent a night in that house. But my father had some tall tales. We took 'em as gospel when we were kids, but later I couldn't make up my mind whether he was drawing the longbow or not." The dogs began fussing, and he had to get out to open the door for them. We went up onto the porch and sat down behind the pots of flowering plants on the railing. The pet cow was not in sight this morning so we escaped being bawled at.

Bob got out his cigarettes and offered them to me. When I refused he said, "Smart girl. But I'm too old to worry about them now."

"Tell me some of your grandfather's stories."

"Well, y'know—maybe you do, young as you are—there are things you've believed all your life, but you don't know how they came to be in the first place. Who started them, or what, y'know. Like the yarn about the Earl. And Calum and Angus and Donald Muir *walking* all the way from Georgia. In Calum's line, all those folks growing up in the west, thousands of miles from Brierbank, they'll swear on it, chapter and verse. We believe in the ship, we *know* about the ship, as if Angus Mor himself told us only the other day. Somebody in Calum's line didn't get his facts straight, but we know the truth because we're right at the heart of things."

"I know what you mean," I said. I wondered how long

Christy would be gone. This double life of mine was keeping me in uncomfortable suspense.

"How about a cup of tea?" Box said suddenly.

I don't like tea in the morning, but I said I'd love it. You can get really confidential over a cup of tea at the kitchen table, and we did.

"My grandfather was Murray, Angus J's youngest son," he told me, "and he went to sea. He never lighted in one place long enough to marry until he was pushing forty. My father was his last young one, born in 1862. I came along in 1895. Grampa was hale and hearty till he was about ninety, so I heard some things straight from him. Later Father passed on to me what Grampa'd told him about when he was a boy in that house. One thing was the pacing. Somebody walking the floor at night when he knew everybody was asleep. He never could figure out who it was, Angus Mor himself or Captain Angus, or somebody else."

I didn't think I showed anything, but Bob set down his cup hard and said abruptly, "*You* heard him?"

"I don't know," I said. Somebody could be making use of the legend. "Does the family know about it?"

"Well, I've mentioned it sometimes over the years, and it's likely Father did. But you'd know if you heard the walker." I thought he was relieved by my doubt. "It didn't sound like anything but what it was. . . . If you hear anything else at night there it's only the voice of an old house."

"The voice of an old house," I repeated. "Maybe the walls *can* talk, if you know what to listen for. Was there anything else besides the pacing?"

He polished his glasses, giving me a sidewise look as if sizing me up for something. Then he poured more tea into my cup without asking. A high-pitched crowing had been going on outside for some time, and he tilted his head toward the sound and listened with a smile of pleasure. "Hear that banty rooster. He hollers all day, telling everybody he's cock of the walk. I love that sound."

He was either trying to think up a good story or he didn't

want to tell me anything more. I took another doughnut just to use up my nervous energy in chewing.

Bob said suddenly, "Once Grampa woke up and heard a man and woman arguing in low voices, and it wasn't his father and mother. Funny thing, it was as if they were talking inside his head."

I swallowed. Too big a piece of doughnut for a throat that wanted to close tight. "What were they saying?"

"He couldn't make much sense of it, he was so shaken up by hearing 'em at all, y'know. He just caught words here and there. He always said afterward he wished he'd listened hard." I do too, I thought, but not mournfully. Even if Christy should walk in now, I'd have gotten what I came for. Bob was going on. "And oh yes, once there was a woman singing to a baby, so low and soft. *His* mother couldn't carry a tun in a basket. He said this wasn't frightening, it made him feel sleepy, and sad too, y'Know. . . . Something about the tune. Then the first time he heard people talking Gaelic, over in Pictou, it was, he knew that was the language of the song."

I have heard her! I almost told him. I braced my elbows on the table and gripped the cup between my hands hoping the contents wouldn't slop out over the edge. In a minute now I'd be blurting out everything I'd heard in a stammering rush, and I didn't want to.

But, incredibly, Bob was too busy with something else to notice anything strange about me. "I'll get his picture. You saw it the other day, but it'll look different to you now." He pushed back his chair and jumped up. On the way out he said, "He was born with a caul, y'know. Maybe that's why he—" I couldn't get the rest of it as he disappeared. I put my cup down with great caution and took several long breaths. I must not tell, no matter what else Bob told me, and I knew it wasn't just an instinctive caution but a deep possessiveness.

Bob came back with the picture. "It was taken in New York. He was master of the *Clementine Moir* then. She was a big old four-sticker."

He'd been a young master but many of them were young in those days, I knew from my Maine background. There he sat in a genuine "captain's chair," wearing his sailing master's clothes before a painted backdrop of harbor and vessels, looking out at me with the fixed, penetrating gaze they all have in those old photographs. The eyes were oddly light-colored under the black brows. His thick black hair was parted on the side, longish over the ears. The nose was aquiline, and high cheekbones planed down to a long and cleft chin. The mouth was austerely straight but one had the impression he might suddenly smile.

The whole thing, pose and expression, gave him the tone of one of Raeburn's aristocrats, an arrogant but probably good-humored young man absolutely at ease with himself.

We looked at each other across a century and more. Did you hear the fiddle and the dancing? I asked him. Did you see the red-haired woman? Who was Francis? Did you ever wake yourself up with that boy's sobbing? Did you—

Bob chuckled. "Hard-bitten young cuss, isn't he? He doesn't appear like a man who'd be hearing such things as he heard."

"I think he looks full of secrets," I said, "and he's watching that photographer ducking in under the black cloth and thinking, 'You may know how to operate that infernal machine of yours, but I have listened at the door into another world.'"

Bob sat back as if I'd slapped him. "God, girl, the way you say that gives me the cold grue."

"Hey, I'm sorry." I managed a good laugh. "I was just being theatrical. Does he look anything like Angus Mor, I wonder?"

"They always said he did. He had two crowns in his hair, too, and they claimed Angus Mor did. I missed out on the Kendrum looks, taking after my mother's family. They run small and fair. Maybe that's why I'm so partial to my banty rooster. He's little but he's loud. That was always me." He laughed at something he was remembering privately. "Reason you see the same looks cropping up now is because some of the Kendrums married the same type. You take my brother Malcolm, he was six foot four, and he married this tall girl from the Annapolis Valley. There wasn't a one of their young ones under six foot, girls and all, and most of 'em had the black hair and the Kendrum nose."

I still held onto Murray Kendrum's photograph, studying the face. Bob didn't seem to think this was strange. He rambled on, smoking, feeding doughnuts to the dogs. "Well, you've got all the facts on the family branches. You must have seen that some second and third cousins married now and then. Young Angus says the early Kendrums were like the Rothschilds, they always married Kendrums. Well, it wasn't quite like that. He says a lot of other foolishness too, which I won't repeat."

"I can imagine," I said dryly.

"Oh, he's a good boy, and I'm glad he's got the house. Too bad *he* wasn't born with a caul; no knowing what he'd pick up if he'd light long enough." He turned sober, almost reverent. "Y'know, when Grampa was a boy growing up in that house, his grampa Captain Angus died, and Angus Mor had died before Grampa was born. For Grampa, the house was full of the two of them. They still read from Angus Mor's Bible, and used some of his tools, including the ones he brought from Georgia with him. His last pair of boots stood in a closet. And Captain Angus's fiddle!" He laughed like a boy and slapped his hands on his thighs. "He heard *that* in the middle of the night, and got up and went to see if it was still in its case or playing all by itself! His father was in bed and snoring, so it couldn't have been *him* fiddling, though Captain Angus had taught him, y'know."

I know, I answered in my mind. *I heard one of the lessons.* I was past gooseflesh and shuddering now. I had accepted the truth of what I knew. "And was the violin in its case?" I asked with a smile. "I hope not."

"That's what he hoped too, but the minute he put his feet on the floor, the music stopped. But he always swore he wasn't dreaming."

I hated to hand the picture back. I could have talked to you, Murray, I told him. I could have told it all. But it was time to break up the session while I could still hold onto everything. Mrs. Archie might bring Christy back any time. Reluctantly I laid the picture down, with a grim sensation of shutting a door in Murray Kendrum's face—or in my own. I began fooling with the dogs, just so I would be able to keep glancing at the photograph; I wished Bob would take it away.

"Did your father go to sea too?" I asked, not really caring; I just wanted to get out of there.

"He tried it, but he never got over being seasick. So he came back to Brierbank and bought this farm from somebody who was selling out and going to the States. And now I've no one to take over from *me*," he said. "We were never lucky enough to have boys, and my brother's boys are scattered to hell and gone— when they show up at the Gathering it'll be the first time they've stepped foot in Brierbank since they were brought here as babies to see the grandparents." He wasn't despondent; he'd had a number of years to face facts. "We'll leave it to young Hector, but who's *he* got to hand it on to? Y'know, I'd make my place over in a minute to any Kendrum lad who showed a love for the land and some intelligence with it, but where is he?"

"The twins—"

"Oh, they'll be going to university and coming out professional men."

"Robbie may have the feeling, but he's too young to know. What about Stuart's boys? Jamesy?"

Bob gave me a disgusted look. I was beginning to feel sorry for Jamesy; unlovable he certainly was, but it must be awful to know it. "He's good with horses," I offered, weakly.

"I won't argue with you there. That's a gift, like playing the harp, and just about as useful. A horse farm these days is a luxury business, and it's a far cry from a working farm." He walked discontentedly around the kitchen, hands in his pockets. "Five brothers in the last batch, and only five sons amongst them! It's disgraceful! Young Angus should be marrying and breeding, but all he thinks about is having a good time. Even his work's a game." He stopped pacing and fixed me with a bright bantam eye over his glasses, his white hair standing up like a cockscomb. "He's taken a fancy to you."

"Oh Lord!" I laughed, and got up from the table. "I don't think so!"

"I was watching him over at Alec's the other night," he insisted.

"That," I said, "is just his act. I've met men like him before."

I looked down at the haughty, ruggedly handsome face in the photograph. For me, henceforth, it would be the face of Angus Mor. What was it like when he smiled?

Irritatingly, I got young Angus's smile, and I didn't want *that*.

15

CHAPTER

WE PARTED like old friends, and I promised again I
wouldn't tell Christy, or anybody else, what he'd told
me. I was too strung out to go back to the house, so I turned left
by his mailbox and drove to the Corner. Robbie and I each had a
letter from a parent, and I had a postcard with a schooner on it;
Mollie Pitcher under full sail and, if you squinted one eye and
concentrated, Micah was discernible at the wheel, capless so his
blond head would show in Glorious Postcard Yellow.

For one blinding instant I thought that Micah had suddenly
missed me and had made the unheard-of effort of finding out
where I was. But the message was from my landlord's daughter,
saying she had achieved her heart's desire (for this year): a summer job cleaning windjammer cabins on Saturday afternoons.

I wrote her a note of congratulations. My card had a mare
and a foal, so she could think I was in a Canadian blue-grass
paradise. In Fremont your own horse was as much of a status
symbol as your own sailboat, be it dinghy or racing yacht.

At the store I passed the time of day with Swans senior and
cygnet, while I bought crackers and cheese and a bottle of to-
mato juice. Then I drove out toward Muir's Grant looking for a
good stopping place. I found a spot where a dwelling had once
been, but the buildings were long gone. All that remained were
the dooryard maples. I drove in and ate my lunch here, and
wrote down everything I could remember that Bob had told me.

After that I was ready to drive back to the Angus J. house.

There I settled down to work all afternoon on what I was being paid to do. It wasn't exactly a mind-stretching exercise. What the whole thing would amount to in the end was a superior tabulating and typing job. I had to make a couple of carbon copies, which guaranteed stretching the job out, as I wasn't an infallible typist and would have mistakes to correct in triplicate.

There were at least two persons right in Fremont who could have taken Robert Kendrum's material, organized it, and gotten it ready for the printer in a very short time indeed. If Virginia intended to pay well for the typing job, it was generous of her to offer it to me and then add more for the supervision of Robbie, who would probably have done very well simply left at the farm with Hector and Mrs. Archie.

I couldn't have been more grateful for the offer, because I'd gone through the Looking Glass just as surely as Alice ever did. So this was turning out in some ways to be a labor of love.

Angus Mor's descendants numbered in the thousands, even though Bob Kendrum thought his kin were falling down on their task of filling the earth with Kendrums. All those great families of sons in the earlier generations had certainly gone forth and multiplied. After I'd been writing in and crossing out for a couple of hours I found that I'd misplaced a whole family — Archibald, b. 1819, m. Susanna MacLeod, b. Pictou, 1822, and they'd had eleven children all of whom had lived to grow up and marry and beget.

At that point I gave up the whole thing and went down to the river for a swim.

Robbie was left off by the time I was making macaroni and cheese for supper. He'd had a glorious day ripping off shingles. Never had so much fun in his life, he told me. Hector had shown up at noon with a large lunch for them, and had ripped out some poor boards and replaced them with new. They had gotten the whole thing covered with roofing paper and one course of shingles laid. He and the twins had taken a swim in the river, and the people from the house had come to swim too.

"Ross says they skinny-dip when nobody's around, but they wore suits today. Hamish—that's one of the guys—is trying to teach the little kids to swim, and this big dog of theirs kept trying to save them. Uncle Hector sat on a log smoking his pipe and laughing like anything. He kept telling the dog to go get 'em. Then the dog would come back out and shake all over him."

Robbie, laughing, was not recognizable as the small boy fighting misery. He seemed even to have grown a couple of inches, and when he described the work they'd done, he was brusque, masculine, comfortably important. Virginia might possibly feel a pang of loss. But like me she'd probably have allowed herself to be instructed on just how one ripped off shingles with a shovel, and with great strength of character she wouldn't caution him about stepping on rusty nails, falling off the ridgepole, or crashing through a rotten board.

My supper was a big success. Robbie helped to clear the table, still talking. When I could get a word in edgewise, I asked him if he'd like to go to Halifax with me tomorrow. He was astonished.

"We've got that roof to shingle!"

"I just thought I'd mention it," I said humbly. "So you'd know my heart was in the right place."

"Anyway, the twins are going in with Rowan for Dominion Day, and they asked me. It's like our July Fourth," he explained kindly, "and they'll have a big parade, and all kinds of stuff." To show that his heart was also in the right place, he added, "You could probably go too if you wanted."

"Thanks, but I guess I'll see what they do in Brierbank."

He was too polite to look relieved.

Nothing happened that night, and when I woke up early the next morning I appreciated the hours of solid sleep, but I was worried for fear nothing more would happen, that I'd ruined everything by talking to Bob, that for me Angus Mor had returned to being simply a name on an ancient stone under which his very bones could have long since disintegrated.

The possibility was as bleak as bereavement; the fact would *be* bereavement. I felt frightened, and peculiarly weak. But I had no time to give in to it now. I was to meet Rowan's aunt, Miss Ross, out at the end of the dirt road at seven o'clock.

Robbie had already gone to the farm. I made a decent breakfast for myself and enjoyed it in spite of my anxiety. The sleep had done me good, and I was resolved to have a good time today no matter what. I just wouldn't think about tonight until tonight came; and if I were not intended to hear anything more than I'd already heard, well, I was fantastically lucky to have heard anything at all.

Rowan's aunt was a long-boned, good-looking woman in her forties. There was a family resemblance to Rowan, though her beautifully casual short hair was light brown and had probably been blond when she was small. She was the executive secretary to the president of a big oil concern whose home office was in Halifax; she had started out in the company at nineteen as a filing clerk.

"They used to kid the life out of me about being a country girl," she told me. "I boarded in Halifax with relatives and went home weekends, and on Mondays somebody was always sure to ask me how many cows I'd milked that morning." She laughed. "Many's the time I've gone straight to the office after flying in from London or the West Coast, and said, 'Who's going to ask me about my cows this morning?'"

She kept a flat in Halifax but she had a small house in Brierbank and preferred to commute in good weather. She was interested in my background, and she'd visited Fremont by yacht once and had never forgotten its beauty. She knew why I was in Brierbank; I guess the whole town knew.

"I remember Robert," she said. "He was always quiet, but had such a nice smile. We all went to school together here, you know. Alec was a dear man, and we'll never get over losing him. And Hector is dear too, in his own way. Stuart was always dour. Now *Angus*—"

I saw the corner of her mouth tuck up, and she smiled at the road ahead. "Angus is in a class by himself. I don't know what unkind fate kept me from meeting someone like him when I was twenty-five. Though when I was twenty-five someone like Angus wouldn't have given me a second look."

Me neither at twenty-four, I thought. "Angus Mor is the Angus I'd like to have known," I said. "I've got a lot of questions to ask him."

"Don't try a seance," she advised me. "They all come out sounding just alike and bubbling about Summerland." We both laughed. I was feeling better by the moment.

"I wish he'd left journals," I said, "but they say he couldn't read or write."

"And in all his ignorance he once owned half of Brierbank," she said dryly. "You've probably discovered by now that Angus's daughter Elspeth married an Ian Ross, so I'm descended from the Founding Father too."

"Is there anybody around here who isn't, besides me?" I asked.

"Goodness, I hope you're not feeling deprived. Maybe we can have you made an honorary one." We were laughing again but I thought, Yet I may have heard him walking and talking, and none of the family have, except Murray Kendrum over a hundred years ago.

Rowan's apartment was in an old house in a quiet part of the city. It's impossible to "do" Halifax and Dartmouth in a day; they need a week or more if you want only to begin to know them. We decided to save Dartmouth for another day, and we had a leisurely morning in Halifax, taking our time wherever it suited us. We stopped for midmorning coffee and pastry, and walked that off in time for lunch.

I wanted to take Rowan to eat in the nicest place she could suggest, and she picked out a very splendid hotel. "It practically costs the earth just to get into the dining room," she said, "but it's not your treat, it's Angus's. I only have to sign something afterward. Already I feel as cosmopolitan as all get-out." She laughed at herself, but I knew she was telling the truth. If I thought dear Uncle Angus was smugly scattering blessings from afar on two naïve girls, I certainly wasn't going to say so.

"How did he get in on this?" I asked, trying to sound merely curious.

"Oh, I had it all fixed up for us to have lunch with him today, but he called last night and said he had to go to New York. Something unexpected, and he was awfully disappointed." She gave me a luminous look intended to convey the personal measure of his disappointment.

I'll bet, I thought cynically. He probably thought it up out of desperation.

"You shouldn't have told me he'd even considered it," I said. "What the mind doesn't know the heart doesn't grieve for, or however it goes. Just think, right now in far-off New York some lucky girl is being dazzled out of her skull."

Rowan giggled. "How I'd love to be his personal assistant and chase him around from one place to another. Once in a while I mention it, just to see him blanch. He has two stock answers." She held up a finger. "One, he's afraid I'd be swept off my feet by some unscrupulous actor, and he'd never forgive himself." Another finger. "Two—and finally—always said very sternly, he doesn't believe in nepotism. Come on, let's pick out something costlier than rubies, and make him sorry he wasn't here to restrain us."

It wasn't quite that expensive but it was good, and I got as much kick out of the surroundings and the service as Rowan did. We acted as if we lunched like this all the time, and we even drank a toast to Angus. Neither of us could think of anything witty or memorable to say, but Rowan said she'd tell him about it, and he would be touched.

I wondered if he already had a personal assistant rushing from place to place with him, and if she was the live-in kind—so handy if you want to give dictation in the middle of the night, I thought with juvenile spite. I tried to figure out how to ask without sounding interested. That was impossible so I gave up.

After lunch Rowan took me to a book and record shop run by people she knew; I bought my father a Harry Lauder album, and for Virginia a very nice little watercolor, all matted and framed, of boats, wharves, and water at Terence Bay. After some pleasant puttering around in this shop, Rowan wanted to take me to another favorite of hers.

"Just for looking, though," she warned me. "It's a very expensive hobby shop."

The very expensive hobby was Highland dress, and the window display was magnificent. "You mean some people will show up at the Gathering dressed like *this*?" I asked. "I can hardly wait."

"Well, probably not into the velvet and lace and silver button and fancy sporran bit. But the kilt, yes, and a plain leather sporran, the proper hose and brogues. With a *sgian dubh* tucked into one sock, of course."

"Of course," I agreed in the same tone. "What's that?"

She giggled. "A knife, in case the guy needs to defend himself or sharpen a pencil or something. Hey, come on inside, and I'll show you the Kendrum tartan. They've got a wonderful old pattern book, with all the authentic tartans woven in silk. They're nice about letting us poor folk come in and look."

We went through a revolving door to a broad lobby, into which the kilt maker's shop opened. Across the lobby there was a row of three elevators. One had just arrived and a small group of people were leaving it, scattering out and heading for the main doors. Some were solitary, preoccupied, and in a hurry. A couple of women stopped to start or finish a discussion. A child said plaintively, "I didn't cry, so now can I have my ice cream?"

Stuart Kendrum was among them. I wouldn't have recognized him dressed for the city and among strangers, but Rowan called his name.

"Hello, Uncle Stuart! What are *you* doing here?"

Then I picked him out at once, noticing that he wore clothes as well as Angus, though he was more conservative. I was sure that he'd seen us first, and could have done without us.

He didn't smile, just gave us an austere nod. The lighting in this place didn't do much for him, I thought, wondering what it did to my coloring. "I had business," he said forbiddingly.

"You can't fool *me*," Rowan teased him. "You're having a kilt made to wear to the Gathering."

He repeated, "I had business." He turned his head as if to look back toward the elevator doors, and then abruptly stopped the motion. He nodded at us again and walked on toward the revolving door without another word. The instant he was outside Rowan rushed me across to read the directory beside the elevators. There were three law firms, two doctors, and some company names that gave away nothing about their business.

Rowan inclined first toward the legal names. "Maybe it's some problem he doesn't want to take to Mr. Chisholm in Inverness," she murmured. Her forefinger slid reluctantly toward the first doctor. "I hope it's not—oh gosh, Noel, did you see how bad he looked? Like a man who's just had a terrible fright?" Her hand dropped to her side as if her arm had lost its strength. She had gone pale, and this time I didn't think it was the lighting. "What if there's something really wrong, really *bad?*" she said in a low voice. "And he's been worrying all this time, and now he's found out there's something to worry about?"

"Oh, come on!" I said. "A lawyer's more like it. Maybe he's trying to do something about Hector's tenants and he never dreamed anybody from home would catch him at it. That would give him a nasty shock all right."

"*No*. It was more than that. I knew it right away, even before I saw those names. I knew it when I was making that damfool talk about a kilt. Noel," she said solemnly, "Uncle Robert's gone, and my father. Uncle Stuart could go the same way, and it could happen to Angus too, and Uncle Hector." Her eyes filled with tears; she was really upset. "I don't know what we'd all do without Uncle Hector!"

I cursed the coincidence that had brought about this meeting and ruined the day. There was a horrid logic about Rowan's deduction. His lips had seemed to have no blood at all. And where was he now? He'd disappeared among the sidewalk strollers like someone plunging into the sea. Maybe he'd gone in somewhere for a drink to steady his nerves. I had a hideous picture of him driving back to Brierbank with his new knowledge burning in his brain.

"Well!" I said heartily. "Are we going into that shop or not?" I hate people being hearty to me, but now I know why they do it.

"All right. Yes." Most of her gloss had gone. She wasn't at all interested now, and I knew she had gone back two short months to the finding of her father's body in the woods. I took her elbow in a relentless grip and almost shoved her toward the shop door.

Inside, the splendor vibrated like music. I'd never seen so many different tartans in my life, and all that went with them once they were made into kilts. "My God, the colors make my mouth water," I murmured. Rowan wasn't making a sound or a motion. I gave her elbow a pinch. "You mean your Uncle Angus is actually able to resist all this?"

I heard a small, tremulous chuckle and felt as relieved as a mother hearing her baby's first cry. "The kids and I told him he's probably had a complete outfit made, in secret, and he's going to appear in it at the Gathering, and knock everybody's eye out."

"In a flash of lightning and a roll of thunder, if he can manage it," I said, "and he probably can."

We brooded hungrily over the women's gowns and skirts in both street and evening lengths. We looked at badges and brooches and buckles; bagpipes; *sgian dhus*, plain and fancy; bonnets, Balmoral and Glengarry; hose, diced and plain; sporrans, simple or elaborately fitted. At lace and velvet and silver buttons and braid. "No, you can't tell *me*," I said, "that Angus Kendrum really wants to pass up a chance to be a peacock. There must be something wrong with his legs."

Rowan made a sound between a snort and a sneeze and clapped her hand over her mouth. Recovery was almost complete. She asked if we could see the pattern book and we were left alone with it in a quiet corner of the shop. She showed me the Kendrum tartans. One was a dark hunting tartan, green, blue, and black; the next had thin lines of red and yellow crossing an infinite variety of shades of green and blue. I remembered how the red had showed up in my dream, but no yellow.

"The sett is one of the most complicated," Rowan said. "There are so many gradations of color in it. Trust the Kendrums not to keep a thing simple, if they can make it difficult. It was plain enough at the beginning, but people kept adding to it." She turned this swatch over and I saw the tartan of my dream. "Kendrum Ancient," she said.

"Well, they're gorgeous," I said. It was odd how at a distance from the house in Brierbank I could accept my experiences as a normal part of my life. I couldn't believe they were over, but I wouldn't dwell on it.

We restored ourselves afterward in a place that did a real English tea, and walked that off at the Citadel and on the Common behind it with its spectacular fountain, and then went to the Public Gardens. We were young, we were healthy, so the effect of the meeting with Stuart was long gone. That didn't mean Rowan wouldn't worry about him from time to time, and I would wonder about him too, but the cloud had moved on. We agreed not to mention the encounter to anyone else, and then we didn't speak of it again to each other.

16

CHAPTER

I LOVED HALIFAX, and Rowan was so pleased she offered to spend a few days of her August vacation in town if I would come in and stay, and see everything else there was to see in the twin cities, including some nightlife.

She delivered me to her aunt's elegant office at five. I could think my own thoughts on most of the ride home, as Daisy had another passenger, a Brierbank woman who'd been visiting in the city over the weekend.

Wednesday was raw and cloudy, and I kept a wood fire going, and worked all day at the kitchen table. Thursday it was still gray, and I worked until midmorning, when I drove Mrs. Archie and Christy to Inverness. They took me sightseeing in two fine old mansions with gorgeous gardens, and I took them to lunch. Later I spent a lot of money on bone china cups and saucers and mugs decorated with my friends' birth-month flowers.

Friday the sun came out again, strong and hot. I put in a long morning's work with the descendants of one Alexander Kendrum's fourth daughter. They'd been almost indecently prolific, and certainly the present generation wasn't doing much toward lowering the birthrate in Australia, South Africa, and California, just to mention a few places where they'd come to roost.

In the afternoon I went down to the river for a swim. Afterward I wandered along the bank without much conscious thought, simply existing in the warm, moist, earthy, flowery atmosphere. It was a peculiar state for me, because my mind had been so frantically busy ever since that night in the Sussex motel. It was suspended animation; a *waiting*.

There had been no hauntings or visitations or even memorable dreams since I'd talked with Bob on Monday. Waking each morning from a sound sleep, I would be disappointed, but I wouldn't let myself be afraid and maybe create some sort of psychic smog that could foul up the works. Once I woke in the middle of the night, but all I heard was the clock striking very slowly; it needed to be wound. I couldn't make that into a message, and I caught myself almost praying, *Angus, if you're here, give me a sign.*

The answer was a nothing so solid that it was a fact in itself. No one was as absent as Angus Mor when he was absent.

As I wouldn't allow the fear and anxiety, I wouldn't allow frustration. It wasn't easy, but having to concentrate on names and dates was a great help. On this Friday afternoon I strolled along the riverbank feeling comfortably vacant until a familiar sound penetrated my torpid consciousness.

A motorcycle was nearby, and in a wrong place for a motorcycle.

Hector's cornfield. It couldn't be. It must be on the road beyond, going through the woods toward Bob Kendrum's. It *had* to be, and the woods were both magnifying and echoing the noise.

I shaded my eyes with both hands against the afternoon sun and looked across the river, above the buttercups and the alder swamp toward the even furrows of the cornfield, no longer lovely and rhythmical but darkly scarred in angry arcs and slashes and marks of Zorro, as Jamesy's motorbike charged back and forth across it, sending up a bow wave of fine brown soil.

He wore neither helmet nor goggles, and I imagined that I could see his face like a grimacing mask with fiercely bared teeth.

I stood there with my mouth open. Then I saw the boys appear at the top of the field, Robbie first; I hadn't known he was such a sprinter. They were yelling, not that I could hear them over the snarls of the motorbike, but I could see their hands at their mouths. Hector came behind them. On one of his mad roundabouts Jamesy must have seen them, because suddenly he skidded into a sharp turn, front wheel in the air, and then plunged off straight down through the field toward the alder swamp. The boys ran along outside the plowed ground and Hector wasn't too far behind them; he was surprisingly fast and nimble for a big man, and I thought, He must have a pretty healthy heart. I'll have to tell Rowan, only what if he drops while I'm looking at him?

The bike disappeared into the alder swamp and raged its way through. The pursuers also disappeared into the alders. Then the bike came bucking into view, protesting in earsplitting crescendoes as it was forced through sodden spongy soil, over roots, and across half-fallen alders. The way Jamesy was bouncing in the saddle his spine must have been jarred beyond all sensation from tail to skull. He reached the buttercups and with one final burst of noise drove straight into the water.

The silence came on like sudden deafness, until I heard the boys yelling back in the alders. Fascinated, I wondered how far Jamesy could drive underwater, and if he was high on something he'd probably attempt it. But he appeared on the surface treading water and apparently trying to see where the bike was. The boys came bounding out of the alders, and when they saw Jamesy you couldn't miss their relief.

"He's all right!" they shouted at each other, and back to Hector. "He's okay! Hey, Jamesy, you nut, are you out of your *skull?*" They said other things too, slogging along the water's edge. Jamesy started for the shore, clumsily—probably handicapped by heavy boots and soaked jeans—and they were all making grabs for him when Hector arrived. He reached over the tangle of boys' arms, took Jamesy by the shoulders, hauled him up onto the bank, and shook him.

It was a hard, vigorous shaking, and Jamesy offered no resistance. He looked to be absolutely limp. Hector dropped him suddenly and strode off into the alders. Jamesy stayed where he was. The boys took off their sneakers and jeans, and in their undershorts plunged enthusiastically into the water and began getting the bike out. Jamesy did not seem at all concerned. He crawled back into the alder shade and I could see him sitting there with his head in his hands. The boys struggled mightily and uproariously, and finally got the motorbike out and wheeled through the buttercups onto firmer ground. They tried to interest Jamesy in it, but he still sat with his head in his hands. Finally they walked the bike through the alders the way Hector had gone. After they disappeared, though they were still audible, Jamesy got clumsily to his feet and trailed after them.

It was such an incredible performance from start to finish that I stood there spellbound for quite a few minutes, watching where Jamesy vanished as if I expected everyone to take curtain calls. Gradually the boys' voices faded away, and a faint suction around my feet made me feel as if I'd be literally rooted to the spot if I didn't move. I stirred myself and climbed up to the top of the bank, and walked home through dry meadow grasses.

When Robbie came home for supper he told me Jamesy had been fired from the Maple Leaf Ranch, and blamed Hector for it. "He thinks Uncle Hector told Mr. Hammond that he shot at the truck that day. Well, he didn't," Robbie said indignantly. "Uncle Hector wouldn't do anything like that if he didn't know for sure. He just told Mr. Hammond that somebody was firing wild out in the woods. That Jamesy's a real nut. He thinks everybody's after him."

"Do you think he was high on something, maybe?"

"I don't know that much about it. Could be, I guess, but the twins don't think so. They say he's always been like that, only now he's worse." He groaned. "That corn was all up, and just as pretty and green. Wow, what a *sick* thing to do."

"How was your Uncle Hector afterward?" I asked.

"He was pretty mad, but he got over it."

"I meant—did he feel all right?"

Robbie looked surprised. "Sure. Why not?"

That was a relief. "What happened to Jamesy finally?"

"He took off toward the Inverness road. I didn't know if the bike would run or not, but I guess it didn't dare to do any different, the way he tromped on it. I don't know what he'll do now. Uncle Stuart's going to be plenty mad at everybody, and at Jamesy most of all." He went upstairs for his shower. When he came down again, and we were eating supper, he said thoughtfully, "Sometimes I'm kind of sorry for Jamesy."

"Me too," I said. We didn't go on to discuss reasons, but I remembered Stuart's face as I'd last seen it, and I didn't know whom to pity more, father or son.

The walker woke me up. With Jamesy still in my mind, I thought hazily that he'd gotten into the house to bother Robbie and me, just because he wanted to strike out at someone. Or else he wanted to do some damage to his Uncle Angus's property, having turned against all his family. But as I came fully awake and listened, I knew it was the authentic pacing.

I lay listening to steps going back and forth, the hesitation when he turned at one end of the kitchen or looked out the front windows into the dark before going on again. I heard him on the stairs, and then overhead, till the house was full of footsteps.

I'd heard them overhead on that foggy, sleepy morning when the shots had been fired, and I'd thought it was Stuart walking back and forth as he worked out figures in his head.

I was sure it was Angus Mor. I *wanted* it to be Angus Mor, so it had to be. But I knew with a little guilt that I wasn't being purely objective. If there was a walker, I shouldn't name him until I knew for a fact who he was. The one thing I could righteously claim was that at least one other person admitted to hearing him. I got into an argument with some imaginary doubters and heard myself becoming mad and flustered, and while I was reminding myself that I should remain poised and self-confident in the face of ridicule and skepticism, the pacing stopped, and I went to sleep.

17

CHAPTER

SATURDAY AFTERNOON the boys had a soccer game at Muir's Grant, and Robbie came home at noon to clean up.

"Has anything more happened with Jamesy since yesterday?" I asked him.

"Nope. Ross asked Uncle Hector if he told Uncle Stuart yet, and he said no, and he wasn't going to. He says it's between him and Jamesy, if he can get hold of Jamesy and make him listen to some common sense." He shook his head. "Poor old Jamesy. What a crazy guy."

Driving him over to meet the twins, I told him Rowan and I were going to the Bain Place that afternoon.

"They're okay, I guess," he said. "Not real hippies. Hey, while you're there, go on down and take a look at our roof."

"Hey, I will."

"Uncle Hector's going to get Uncle Stuart over there sometime this weekend to decide on making it into a camp."

"I wouldn't mind renting it."

"You'd have to get on the waiting list. What's the matter with the Angus J. house?"

"That belongs to your Uncle Angus, and he's only letting me, no kin of his'n, use it because of the work I'm doing. If I wanted to come back here on my own, I'd have to rent a place. You can always stay at the farm."

"Hey, I'll bet you could too," he said in what was for him a burst of enthusiasm. "They like you."

"Well, thanks, Robbie," I said temperately, and decided to quit while I was ahead. It's always nice to be liked, and in some circumstances it's much nicer than in others.

Mrs. Alec was away for the day. Rowan and I saw the boys off in the truck, threatening to attend the game and scream hysterically on the sidelines. "And hug and kiss you when you come off the field." Rowan promised, "and I'll say to everybody, 'Aren't the Twinnies *adorable*? They're my little brothers!'"

"You know what'll happen to *you*," Calum said menacingly. "The adorable Twinnies may just drop you head first down the nearest well."

We walked down to the Bain Place by a charming roundabout path that led through the woods for most of the way. We didn't have to go near any cows, for which I was glad, and when we cut across a shady corner of the pasture where about twenty-five sheep grazed or lay down under the trees, Rowan assured me there was no ram to worry about. "They don't raise lambs, just wool for Moira's weaving and knitting. They aren't all of the same breed, because she likes different kinds of wool for different things." Knowledgeably she named them off; the only ones familiar to me were the big, black-faced, stocky-legged Hampshires, because my aunts had a pet one who lived into a tyrannous old age. He used to snatch anything edible out of my hands and send me howling into the house.

The Bain Place was shabby, but only from lack of paint and grooming. I saw new lumber in corner posts and doorsteps, some new windows, and bright patches of fresh shingles on the roofs. Old perennials and flowering shrubs grew and spread as they pleased. Some small naked children played in and around a big washtub of water in an untidy but abundantly blossoming orchard. A variety of free-ranging poultry, some with young, coexisted peaceably with the cats and an immense black Newfoundland who turned the whole dooryard scene into a Landseer.

The two couples had an easy cordiality. Hamish, who looked scholarly behind his beard and glasses, or because of them, was the farmer, and his big garden was his pride. He had a good market for his organically grown vegetables. We were introduced to the goats, who were very self-possessed and looked searchingly into our eyes; one expected them to offer hooves to shake.

Jared reminded me of a professional athlete, maybe a tennis player, and the shorts he wore this hot afternoon enhanced the illusion. His workshop was in one end of the barn, exquisitely orderly and fragrant with cedar; he was making a chest on order. Two captain's chairs were almost completed.

The dye shed was separate from the other buildings. As much as possible Moira used natural sources for coloring the wool, so we learned a little about that. Moira was the one who reminded me of a Victorian intellectual. In the house the big sitting room had been turned over to her looms, her spinning wheels, her hanks of finished wool.

Eve, who had kidded the grocer about his goods, ran the kitchen. She also baked breads on order, sold herbs from her own garden and special blends of teas, and put up jellies and preserves in season. She made wines for their own use.

One small room was an office where the bookkeeping was done at an old rolltop desk. It was an extremely orderly office; it even had a filing cabinet and shelves of books. That alone should have impressed Stuart Kendrum. The whole place would have favorably impressed him, if anyone could have got him there.

But maybe not; I've met people whose prejudices are written so deeply on the granite of their brains that nothing in the world can erase the grooves. He'd have thought the naked three-year-olds were indecent or that Jared was smoking hashish in his pipe. At the least he would suspect them of getting smashed every night on homemade wine and swapping mates in one continuous orgy. Hamish and Eve were a couple, and so were Jared and

Moira, and if I didn't see any wedding rings it didn't mean they didn't exist, even if only in figurative form, which sometimes is stronger than the literal form.

We had tea on a trestle table down in the orchard near the children's tub. It was one of Eve's mixtures, mysteriously spicy and delicious, made properly with boiling water in a preheated china pot, poured into thin cups, and stirred with worn old silver spoons.

"All this is part of the ancestral loot," said Moira. "We haven't gone back to the Stone Age, regardless of public opinion." There was thin-sliced bread and butter, and the children had molasses cookies.

"Every time I come over here," Rowan said, "I feel so darned futile. As if I was frittering my life away fighting off a cloud of black flies. Selling insurance, for heaven's sake!"

"Listen, love," Jared said with a smile, "*we* have insurance. Wouldn't be without it."

"That still doesn't make me feel any better," she said. "But when I go back to Halifax I'll recover, until the next time. Because I really love it there."

"Then you're fine," said Eve, "because loving where you are and what you're doing is the big thing, isn't it?"

"What do you do, Noel?" Jared asked me.

"I teach fourth-graders. I like it, I know I'm good at it, and my kids like *me*."

"Well, then," said Hamish, smiling benignly in his beard. "We like this life. We love it. But being able to make a decent living from it is what makes it a good life. I'd be a liar to pretend otherwise."

Would that impress Stuart? I wondered. No, he'd probably be contemptuous of their customers, or think they didn't exist. Poor Stuart, I thought dreamily under the apple trees, watching the Renoir-play of light and shade on the children's flesh, listening to the bees in the blossoms and the quiet voices around the table. The Newfoundland lay near the children.

Poor Stuart, I hoped he wasn't sick. But it was a kind of sickness, to be perpetually and obsessively worried. . . . After Jamesy's behavior yesterday maybe his obsession had a right to exist. . . . Forget it, it's none of your business. Just enjoy.

Another sound broke through the gentle ones about me. It was dulled by the house and barn between us and it, and then it suddenly stopped. I realized when I saw Jamesy coming down from the house that I'd been hearing his motorbike coming along the dirt road that led in from the pavement.

He had almost reached us before he knew that Rowan and I were there, and in the small interim I saw a different Jamesy, half-smiling, eager, and so unconscious of our alien presences that he had the vulnerability of the sleeper who doesn't know he is watched.

"You're just in time, Jamesy!" Hamish called to him.

Then Jamesy saw us. He looked as if he had crashed face-on into an invisible barrier. Shock and then fury—or furious disappointment—contorted his face. He turned and ran back toward the house.

Rowan jumped up and yelled his name through her cupped hands. Hamish called too, the Newfoundland rose up barking. Jamesy kept on going and disappeared around the house.

"Oh *damn!*" Rowan whispered. Her eyes were full of tears. We heard the motorbike start up and take off past the barn and along the rough road that went on onto the woods.

"Don't worry, Rowan, he'll be back," Moira said.

"But right now, this minute, is the time that counts," Rowan said. "Everything's going wrong for him and he's coming all apart."

We all listened, looking off blindly to where the sound was dying away in the woods. "Too bad," Jared said as if to himself. I didn't think he was talking about what had just happened.

"Sit down again, Rowan, and have some hot tea," Eve urged. "This happens. Somebody else is here and Jamesy rushes off, but he always comes back."

"Maybe he'll meet up with Hector at the old barn," I said helpfully. "Hector wants to talk to him." Too late I remembered that Stuart would probably be with Hector, so the "common sense" conversation wouldn't get off the ground. Rowan was staring sadly down at her cup. "You can't do anything, Rowan," I said before I thought, "because you're not the reason he's miserable."

"I never *was* able to do anything, even when I felt kindly toward him," she admitted. "But when you grow up you look back and think maybe you were stupid and blind and impatient, and—"

"Young," said Moira with a faint smile. "And you're not ninety years old now, Rowan. You can always start being his friend."

"I *have* started," said Rowan honestly, "but if he doesn't know it, what good will it do him?"

"That's a moot question," said Hamish, joining fingertips together. "Shall we moot it?" Which for some reason made us all laugh. We did discuss it though, in generalities. If enough people had positive, friendly, concerned feelings for an unhappy and disordered person, would the combined emanations have some influence on him? We weren't in total agreement, but it was a good lively argument that led away from Jamesy into anecdotes and examples and quotations; thence by devious ways we came up against other kinds of influence and whether they existed or not outside of the brain that was being influenced.

"Like Joan of Arc's voices?" Eve asked. "What about these people who hear someone telling them what to do? How do we know they're not right?"

"Now you get into the bi-cameral theory," Jared said.

"What's that?" I asked, anxious to get away from supernatural voices. He was happy to explain, and I listened with deceitful avidity and even asked him to give me the name of the book he was quoting so I could get it from the library.

Later we all walked back to the house carrying the tea things, and he gave me the name and author. I promised myself I would read the book just to prove to myself I was honest, and I would write to Jared when I had finished it.

Except for the upset about Jamesy it had been a lovely afternoon. We decided to extend it by taking the road through the woods and inspecting the boys' new roof, as Robbie had wanted us to do.

The road lay in shade now, and the still air had a warm resinous scent. The birds were becoming active, getting ready for night, and their calls echoed in the woods, and squirrels signaled our passing. We didn't talk much, except to agree that the two couples were worth knowing. Otherwise we walked alone in our own thoughts.

We had been on a gentle descent all this time; quite suddenly we came out through thinning trees and saw the leafy borders of the river before us. There was an old cellar hole on a knoll to our right, and the barn beyond that, its silvery green roof incongruously new above its age-darkened sides and the narrow old door at this end. Our road passed between it and the riverbank, and went off into the woods again, toward the pavement.

Below the barn the river widened into a pool. It was all in green shade now; the water was the color of dark peridot, dusted with a sparkle of light when something disturbed the surface.

The angle of the barn hid its yard from us until we were halfway along the side, and then we saw Hector's new truck parked at the northern end of the building.

"Well, look at that!" Rowan exclaimed happily. "He *is* here! Hi, Uncle Hector!" she called, heading around the corner. "You in there? Oh!" She laughed. "Excuse the yell, I didn't know you were so close."

I caught up with her. Hector looked at us without speaking. He was sitting on a sawhorse outside the big open doors. There was something odd about him; he looked different, like a Kendrum but yet not like himself, and his color was strange. It reminded me of Stuart, that day in Halifax.

It was like being kicked in the stomach.

"Are you all right?" Rowan was almost too frightened to speak.

He nodded, and his mouth twitched in a faint grin. He waved a hand at us and said wheezily, "Just lost my wind, that's all."

She ran to him and took his hand. "But *why*?"

"Not—my heart." He took another wheezing breath. "Just knocked the wind—out of me. Fell."

Rowan sagged onto the sawhorse beside him and leaned her forehead against his shoulder. He put his arm around her. Now, with fear diminishing in me and his color coming back, I could see why else he looked different. He didn't have his glasses on.

"Did you lose your glasses when you fell?" I asked.

He nodded back toward the open door. "In there somewhere. Hayloft ladder gave way under me. Rotten. Thing broke. Damfool trick to trust my weight to it." He took a deeper breath, experimentally. "Didn't break a rib, I guess." He gave Rowan a hug. "Sorry I scared you, love. You came along too soon."

"Never mind. I'm so relieved I feel drunk. I could fly! Whee!" She giggled. "Hey, are you sure you don't have a concussion or anything? Hurt your back?"

"I'm not seeing double, I'm not dizzy. And if I'd broken anything, how could I hug a pretty girl this close?"

I went into the barn to find his glasses. Of course they were nowhere near the foot of the ladder, and I had to step around and over the new lumber and ladders the boys had stored in here. I found the glasses on the floor between the rungs of an aluminum extension ladder, and one lens was severely cracked.

"Oh damn," I said, but a cracked lens was a small thing beside the possibility of a cracked skull or spine.

Outside the door Rowan said, "Were you here when Jamesy went by? He rushed away from the house when he saw us there."

"Yep, I heard him go tearing by. I was back in the tie-ups,

getting some idea of a layout before Stuart showed up. He never did get here, by the way. Maybe he was turning in off the pavement when Jamesy charged out, and they had one of those eyeball-to-eyeball confrontations."

"Well, I wish they *would* get things talked out," Rowan said. "They just can't communicate at all."

I lingered in the barn, trying to imagine it illumined with big windows and light walls. The hayloft could be turned into a balcony, or a sleeping loft with a skylight so you could watch the stars. I was in love with the idea already. You wouldn't need stairs up from the main floor; there might be some over in back, reached from that narrow door we'd seen at the other end as we approached. I remembered a barn laid out like that at home. Out here, a sturdy ladder would do to save space, and kids would love that.

Dreamily I wandered out with the glasses. "I'm on your waiting list of hopeful tenants, Hector," I told him.

"Put her down first, Uncle Hector," said Rowan.

"No, I know Gilbert Kendrum's first," I said firmly. "But can I be next?"

"You are." He accepted his glasses philosophically. "Could be worse. I've got spares at home. Can you find a place to roost, Noel?"

"Sure." I took the other sawhorse.

"The twins told Mum and me about Jamesy going crazy in the cornfield," Rowan said.

"I want to talk to him about that. Yesterday I was a mite out of patience with him, you might say. I did call up Basil last night and asked him what the story was. He said he'd heard his nephew and Jamesy were either smoking or sniffing something, and he called them in to talk about it. The nephew's been in trouble at home in St. John, but it wasn't with drugs, as far as Basil knows."

He ran out of breath and took a minute to get started again. "Anyway, he wasn't going to accuse the boys, he just wanted to talk it over with them. He says the nephew is a cheeky type, but he's never had any fault to find with Jamesy, and he'd have accepted his story. Trouble is, Jamesy exploded before Basil got six words out and took off like a rocket. Basil wanted to get hold of him somehow. I suppose he's been trying today."

"Well, he certainly hadn't reached Jamesy by the time he showed up at the Bain Place," Rowan said. "Because Jamesy was miserable, you could tell. Who was it gave Mr. Hammond all this choice information?"

"He didn't say. I had a feeling it was somebody he'd had to fire a while back, trying to make trouble for him and the boys."

"And succeeding," I said. "It just goes to show that no matter how many people are sympathetic to a kid like Jamesy, and want to help him, some despicable character can wreck him."

"Let's hope it's not a total wreck," said Hector. "I'm not giving up and I don't think Basil will. He feels guilty as hell about it."

18
CHAPTER

WE RODE OUT to the pavement with Hector and refused his offer to drive us all the way to Rowan's house. "You'd better get home quick and start soaking out the sore places," Rowan said maternally.

"I'm stopping around at Stuart's first. See what's happened to everybody."

"If those two killed each other, you'd never find out from Aunt Len. She floats around on a higher plane than the rest of us."

"Oh, is that it?" Hector grinned.

A neighbor picked us up in a few minutes and delivered us to the Alec Kendrum mailbox, and we walked in to the house. Mrs. Alec was home from a visit with a cousin at Oquiddic Harbor. Some boy had just called to ask Rowan to a dance that night, and she called back and asked him to bring a date for me.

The twins dropped Robbie off after chores, and he brought baked beans with him again. "Aunt Janet says next Saturday night we have to come down and eat with them. She stopped in this afternoon to ask you but you weren't here. Then Uncle Hector came home all lamed up, so he's going to bed early."

"I know about *that*," I said, rather triumphant at being practically an eyewitness.

"Gosh, that ladder held us all right."

"Well, you kids are a lot lighter than your uncle. And probably that rung had just reached the fracture point."

"Gosh." He shook his head. "More narrow escapes around here."

"Yep. So *you* be careful. Who won the game?"

"Brierbank, of course."

"Of course," I agreed. "I should have known. Do you mind being left alone tonight?"

He looked insulted. "Are you kidding?"

"You probably wouldn't mind having TV tonight."

"Who needs it?" he asked with disdain, spoiled somewhat by a big yawn.

I put on a full-skirted dress printed with red strawberries, sandals, and tied back my hair with a red ribbon. Rowan and two men came for me around eight in her date's car. Terence Tolmie was a stocky, sunburned, blond young farmer, a partner with his father in the egg and poultry business. His friend was a real Scot whose family had emigrated last year and was raising sheep over near Inverness. His name was Murdo MacKenzie, and he had very red hair and freckles. I could hardly understand a word he said, but his grin was as broad as his accent and his shoulders. He was a feather-light dancer with a strong arm for swinging.

The orchestra was good: a flute, two fiddlers, an accordion, drums, and a piano. The musicians could spell each other and have time to dance too. The square dances were new to me, but not for long. Of course the boy's breaths, and that of some of the girls, began getting alcoholic as the evening went on; it was almost always more noticeable after they'd been outside to cool off. But nothing affected their feet. This kind of dancing exorcised practically anything, the way the tarantella was supposed to make you work off the poison of a tarantula bite.

A fight broke out in the dooryard between two boys, one of whom had shown up with the other's girl, and it spread like an epidemic until the brawniest and loudest among the noncombatants convinced the warriors that the Mounties had been called.

That stopped the war, but the Mounties never did show up, having never been called. I was disappointed.

"Oh, Noel, they don't wear those red coats now except to show off," Rowan said. "It wouldn't have been any different from your Yankee police stopping a brawl."

On the way home Terence meekly let Rowan drive. My partner in the back seat became drowsily amorous in a mixture of Gaelic and English. He was not aggressive about it, and the last time I disengaged myself he muttered something which could have been either poetry or a mild curse, and began to snore against my shoulder. I managed to wind down a window part way to let out the fumes.

Terence was docile too, and very sleepy, so the drive was a quiet one on nearly deserted roads once we'd left the parking area outside the dancehall. There was enough of a moon to frost-whiten roofs and new-mown fields. Rowan and I agreed in soft voices that it had been a super dance, and then we were lulled into silence by the shush of tires on pavement, the entranced stillness of the moonscape through which we traveled, and our own normal tiredness.

Just as I began worrying about Rowan's falling asleep and going off the road, we came down the hill past the church. Above the motionless dark masses of the maples, its square tower in fresh white paint fairly glittered in the moonlight.

Rowan slowed the car almost to a stop. "I always used to think the bell was alive up there," she murmured. "Listening, just waiting for the right touch to make it speak."

"It knows we're here now," I said.

"Who?" Terence muttered, sitting up straighter. "Are we home?"

"No, love," Rowan said maternally. "Go back to sleep again." Terence obediently sagged. My partner sighed, and wrapped his arms tighter around me. We drove through the sleeping Corner, and when we had left it Rowan began to sing in a hushed but clear and true voice.

> *From the lone shieling of the misty island*
> *Mountains divide us, and the waste of seas—*
> *Yet still the blood is strong, the heart is Highland,*
> *And we in dreams behold the Hebrides.*

My throat squeezed shut. Everything the dance had exorcised was back with me; and I knew it for what it was, a longing so painful that it was ultimately terrifying, like the mere prospect of torture. After what I had been allowed to see and hear—and if this was all, if the door in Time was locked for good against me—how could I ever cope with the return to the limited, mediocre *me?*

Then the incongruity smacked me like a cold jellyfish. What was Noel Paige doing here, wrapped in the arms of a drunken Highlander and mourning for the ghost of a dead one?

Rowan was still singing.

> *We ne'er shall tread the fancy-haunted valley,*
> *Where 'tween the dark hills creeps the small clear stream,*
> *In arms around the patriarch banner rally,*
> *Nor see the moon on royal tombstones gleam.*

I had to speak, just to see if I could break the grip on my throat. "Angus came out with that week. What is it with you Kendrums at midnight? The patriarchal genes remembering the patriarchal banners?"

"Angus would say it's the ham in us. Or the Gael. . . . Ever since I was a little kid and we learned the poem in school, the stones in the churchyard have reminded me of that verse, especially by moonlight."

"I like the tune."

"You won't believe this, but Angus made it up years ago. He used to play the guitar and sing."

"Somehow I can't imagine it," I said.

"He's been trying to live it down for years." She laughed. "He's full of surprises. He's going to get one too. I'm collecting a group of the older schoolkids to sing the whole 'Canadian Boat

Song' at the Gathering. Wait till you hear them belt out 'O then for clansmen true, and stern claymore!'"

Murdo surged up with a shout, dropping me and glaring wildly about him.

"I think that was the MacKenzie warcry and he's looking for his stern claymore," I said. "Hey, Murdo!" I patted his substantial arm. "The war's over. Relax."

He asked me a question in Gaelic, muttered his own answer, laughed to himself, and slumped back against my shoulder, this time without the hug.

"My God," Rowan said softly, "I'd better keep still. No knowing who's inhabiting that wild Highlander's skin when he's asleep."

Terence had slept through it all.

We turned off the pavement and onto the road to the Angus J. house. The resting cattle looked like boulders in the moonlight. The black woods were turned by the night into a holy or haunted hill. There should be a ruined chapel at the top, I thought; I could imagine the dull pale light falling through broken arches.

"If Angus hasn't come home, I'll go into the house with you," Rowan said. "I always hate to come into an empty house where there's no telephone and no dog."

"You mean you worry about crime in Brierbank?" I teased her.

"Gosh, no, not way out here, and with no rich recluses who keep millions of dollars in their houses, or big collections of diamonds. It's just a feeling I have."

But I thought of Jamesy, abhorring my presence at the Bain Place that afternoon; I was sure it wasn't Rowan's fault that he rushed away.

"But it is the Angus J. house, after all," Rowan was saying.

"What's so special about that?" I sat forward, dislodging my sleeping beauty, who nearly tipped into my lap. I gave him a shove and he fell back into a corner.

"Oh, nothing," said Rowan vaguely, "except it's so far from everybody, and you could meet a moose crossing the yard, or even a bear."

"Gee, thanks!" I breathed. "I can hardly wait! So if a bear is waiting for us right now, a heck of a lot of good you'll do me if we're both afraid to get out of the car."

"We'll shove the boys out first and while the bear's sniffing them and being stunned by the fumes, you can rush into the house." We giggled like a couple of fourteen-year-olds.

Angus's car wasn't in the yard. Neither was a bear, nor a moose grazing on the lilacs. Rowan and I went in by the unlocked back door, turning on lights as we went. I was sure at once that nobody was in the attic or cellar. I went up to listen at Robbie's door and after a moment I heard him turn over.

"No bear upstairs, either," I said when I came down.

"Disappointed?"

"Crushed. Want a mug-up?"

"I'd love it but I have to get those two home."

I walked back to the car with her. Instinctively we hushed our voices rather than mar the night; the brook seemed louder than normal, as if it were an enchanted stream full of mystic voices, entirely suitable for the windless moonlight and the black hill rising across the road. I could almost see that ruined chapel at the top.

Terence woke up when Rowan got into the car and said in a perfectly sober voice, "I must be getting old when I can't hay all day and dance all night without being knocked out by a couple of drinks. Want me to drive?"

"No, thanks. If you drive we're sure to meet the law, with you and Wee MacGregor back there smelling like Auld Sporran or The Fiery Cross or whatever brand you were drinking."

"I never saw the name on the label, but it felt like a fiery cross going down," said Terence. "Corners, flames, and all," He shuddered.

"Talk about self-torture!" said Rowan. "See you tomorrow, Noel."

"Shall I drive around and pick you up? Because I don't know the way to your aunt's."

"Yes, come on over. Fourish, so I can get home to supper."

I watched them out of the yard, and then went into the house. I was hungry, and cut and buttered a thick heel from Mrs. Alec's graham loaf, made a big mug of cocoa, and took them up to bed with me to have while I read. I became very sleepy all at once, with that good physical tiredness that makes any bed feel like a cloud in Paradise. I put out my light and stretched out with a sybaritic sigh. But I had just begun drifting on my cloud when I was jolted back to the old barn, looking around on the floor for Hector's glasses.

The transition was so vivid I could smell that pungence only to be found in old barns where the ghosts of hay and animals remain. The wide doorway behind me framed a square of summer bloom and light, but it didn't take away much from the shadows inside. I remembered that from the afternoon, and how I moved around the lumber and the ladders, kneeling at different spots so I could closely cover the area.

This was no hypnogogic state—I was wide awake and recollecting in detail. Now I know what had been wrong that afternoon—I'd been too shaken up then to take it in. Now, in detachment, I looked up at the ladder when I came to it, and there were no rungs broken on it. It looked to be very sturdy indeed. The wood was dark with age, and the rungs showed the polish of wear, but not one of them was broken.

Badly jolted both physically and emotionally by the fall, Hector had lied without thinking how easily it could be checked. Of course he hadn't expected us to show up and for me to be so helpful about his glasses. No, later when he'd gotten his wind back he'd have gone back in and found his glasses himself, and he'd have had time to concoct a believable story to explain his soreness.

But I remembered now how quickly he'd dismissed Jamesy, and how realistically he'd cussed the ladder and his own foolishness for trusting his weight to it. So I was positive he'd been pushed off the edge of the hayloft by someone who'd come up the stairs in the corner, and it was a wonder he hadn't broken his neck.

He knew he'd been pushed and by whom. Jamesy had roared by, parked his bike out of sight, and had come back through the woods.

I was so wide awake then I thought I'd never get to sleep again. It's a family affair, I lectured myself. Forget it. Hector understands Jamesy and pities him. If the fall had killed him he wouldn't be here to be understanding and pitying, and Jamesy'd have lost a friend. . . . Maybe Hector could convince him that he hadn't gotten him fired and that he should go back and talk with Basil Hammond. Of course if Hector had broken a leg or an arm, or cracked his spine, his capacity for pity and understanding would likely be severely diminished, but probably he'd still have stuck to the accident story.

I went to sleep finally, and footsteps woke me. I roused under protest, muttering, "Oh, *quit* it." I thought it was Angus just arrived from Halifax and getting himself something to eat. And then I realized what I was hearing: the pacing.

Instantly the tiredness and the irritation were gone. I shut my eyes and spoke inside my head.

Angus Mor, is that you? Are you the pacer, or is it someone else I've been tuned to all this time? Was it you that Bob Kendrum's grandfather Murray heard? Did he ever know or even suspect who it was?

Angus Mor, is that you?

Night. Moonlight. Two open graves. Hard breathing; fragments of voices, words understood and yet not understood. Two open graves. Suddenly all the moonlight concentrated in a strip of white fire; a sword unsheathed all at once—I heard the faint clashing and saw the basket hilt. There was writing on the blade. I couldn't read it, the letters seemed to writhe and shimmer and flash. Two open graves.

A sensation in my chest of an unbearably held breath bursting free in anguish, and an instant reproof as violent as a hand clamped over the mouth. The blade cold under my lips as I kissed it, and then the sword was extinguished. Sheathed? The sounds of spades, and falling earth, the hard breathing and a strangling sense of haste, dread, and agony.

It was awful. I couldn't endure it any longer and sat up, shuddering and very cold as if winter were in the room—and it *was*—and reached for my robe. The motion broke the spell. The sounds so vivid and terrible died away like sounds in a dream, but the pacing went on. Sometimes the feet hesitated, as if the walker were overtaken by his thoughts and stopped in his tracks. Then he would begin again. Huddled in my robe, my extra blanket pulled up, I lay back and shut my eyes, closed myself into the private dark with those footsteps, and waited.

Flowers. More like a picture than the real thing. A color photograph. Of course not! Was it a painting, intensely detailed? A flat disk of white flowerets; a spray of narrow pointed green leaves; scarlet berries glistening like fresh drops of blood. Along with this image came new sensations: smoky scents, small flames licking around a heap of something. Peats? The rough texture and wool scent of whatever was wrapped around me, the floor hard beneath me. Lying by a peat fire, wrapped in a plaid—I could see by the dim flickering light the dull stripes and squares of the tartan. Others sighed and spoke in their sleep. The flowers and berries were tormentingly bright in my mind. Rising up, pulling the belt tighter around my middle; the buckle was broad and heavy in my tired fingers. Tired from digging and then filling the graves.

Whose graves? But I—*he*—didn't want to think about that. *Francis.* The red-haired woman, and the taste of hatred in the mouth and the power of it crooking the fingers, flexing the thumbs for murder. Again *Francis*, and her face, and loathing. Could it be *Frances* instead? *Her* name?

No time to ponder, we were somewhere else now. The flower image persisted but was continually interrupted. It was like the interference on a shortwave radio when you're trying to follow an overseas program. It was confusing, dizzying me even while I was lying still. I *knew* I was lying still, but at the same time I was being knocked about by impressions. Stone heights arching overhead, pale light through narrow windows, massive fireplaces with cold ashes, tapestries, emptiness, desolation. The castle, I thought, and with the recognition I was wrenching at the doors and cupboards and wardrobes, and lifting the heavy lids of chests.

Someone kept shouting from a distance. I couldn't have repeated the words, but I knew the summons was for me. . . . Clothes in a chest. A tumbled mass of velvets, brocades, lace. My hands burrowed through it. A small stab in the palm of my hand, but a good pain, a victorious pain. I could have yelled aloud in triumph. A few drops of blood on my palm, like the berries—I licked them and the taste was as good as the pain. Then I was running down narrow deep stone stairs between damp walls that breathed cold, and out into a great blaze of morning.

Into the stone courtyard, the peculiar and threatening vacancy, the dark tunnel leading out. The beckoning man, who must have been calling me.

This time I made it. Or rather Angus Mor made it. Outside to the sea loch glittering under the April wind.

19
CHAPTER

I WOKE about nine-thirty the next morning, with the swallows in full swing. Bob Kendrum's rooster's challenges were borne across the valley on a cool wind that blew my curtains gently into the room. I felt rested and lively. I washed up and hurried downstairs in my robe with my notebook, to write everything down while I had my coffee.

There was already a potful keeping hot on the stove. It was explained by the presence of Angus's Jaguar in the yard. There was neither sign nor sound of Angus. While appreciating his coffee, and the bowl of fresh cherries on the table, I hoped he wouldn't come in to scatter wit and charm while I was trying to get my mind sorted out.

He didn't. By the time I'd put down everything in an impressionistic shorthand of my own which I hoped to be able to read later, I realized he was still conspicuously absent.

I went upstairs to dress. I intended to go to the farm this morning and see how Hector felt after his fall, and I was looking forward to the walk.

When I came down Robbie and the twins had just come in. Robbie said "Hi!" and tore by me on his way to clean up. I passed the bowl of cherries to the twins.

"Have some. From your uncle," I said. "How's your other uncle this morning? Hector, I mean."

"He's lame," said Calum, "but he thinks he'll live. I didn't know that ladder was so weak. It sure didn't look it."

"Uncle Angus is down there," Ross contributed. "Looks as if they're going to drink coffee and talk all morning. They get going like that once in a while. Sometimes our dad—" He stopped, and went into the pantry to dispose of his cherry pits.

Calum looked out the window. I said brilliantly, "Well, I'm off for a walk." Not to the farm, that was certain.

Robbie ran downstairs in his Sunday suit. "Okay if I go home to dinner with the guys afterward?"

"Sure."

"Well, I thought I'd ask, just in case you had a big dinner planned."

"Are you kidding? I didn't even remember it was Sunday!" I lied.

"Boy, that must have been some dance!" Ross said.

"It certainly was," I agreed. "My legs still feel it. There was a fight, too."

All three looked envious. "The Mounties come?" Calum asked.

"Nope. But somebody about seven feet tall stopped it by telling them the Mounties were on the way. He was the only man who could yell louder than they could, so he got through to them."

"Fergus Muir," said Calum with a sigh. "I wish I'd been there."

"Listen, I'm ready," Robbie said. "We going?"

"You could have dinner at our house," Ross said politely to me. "My mother and sister would like it."

"I would too, but I have to get some work done. Do you men know how many descendants Angus Mor has? And I have to list them *all*."

"We're descended through our father and mother both," Calum said.

"Hey, doesn't that make you idiots or something?" Robbie asked. This started a spate of teen-age jokes that carried them out the door. I put a handful of cherries in a plastic bag and went straight across the road into the woods. Just as I stepped inside their shadow, I heard a car coming, and waited out of sight to see if it turned into the yard. It went straight on past. Stuart was driving, his face drawn and gaunt. From this one glimpse I thought he had grown very thin just since last Tuesday in Halifax.

I put him out of my mind. I like exploring woods, and this forested hillside didn't disappoint me; I was glad I hadn't gone to the farm. I crossed a wet, ferny little room with late white and purple violets in it. In another place I found the spotted leaves of trout lilies. Bunchberry blossoms and the other tiny white flowers of home grew on dry slopes, and birds were with me all the way, either companionably like the chickadees or warning me because of their nesting sites. When I reached the top, I didn't find any ruined chapel, or a view, only more woods, violets, ferns, birds. I sat on a warm knoll long enough to eat my cherries.

"I'll be back again," I promised out loud when I left.

I worked up in my room, went downstairs at noon and fixed a light lunch which I ate on the front doorstep, walked around and picked and ate a handful of strawberries. Then, feeling smugly virtuous, I returned to work. In late afternoon I showered and put on one of my more fortunate bargains, a markdown from the Fremont Specialty Shop, where in my right mind and with my salary I do not often shop. It was a daffodil linen sundress with broad straps over the shoulders, and had its own shawl. It made me feel rich, and I thought piously that it would serve me right if Daisy Ross wore her gardening jeans this afternoon.

I did my hair up on top of my head, with becoming little tendrils escaping here and there. When I came downstairs and discovered that the Jaguar was gone, without my having even glimpsed the owner, I was unreasonably annoyed.

"So ignore me," I said aloud. "Who cares?" It was somewhat unfair of me, since I'd stayed out of sight up in my room most of the day.

Rowan was waiting for me to pick her up by the mailbox. She too was dressed up, in a silky rose-flowery print, and she carried well the soft, feminine lines. "Aunt Daisy's influence," she said. "Without even trying, she can convince me I'm dressed either like a kid or a slob. And don't *you* look elegant this afternoon!"

"Aunt Daisy's influence," I said solemnly. We giggled.

Daisy Ross's small house was on the next hill, charmingly set among maples and firs. The Jaguar was parked by hers outside the garage. "I didn't know *he* was going to be here!" Rowan said happily. I said nothing, reflecting sourly that of course Miss Ross could invite anyone she liked, but it would have been nice to be warned. Rowan, singing out, "Here we are!" led the way around the house to a deck built out on the southwestern side. Angus and Daisy arose to meet us. She looked pleased, Angus looked amused, and I wondered if he'd just been making a joke at our expense.

Don't be paranoid, Noel, I coldly advised myself. Just think of what you know about his house that he doesn't know. . . . I was glad I'd dressed up, though. These two looked so expensively casual.

Rowan kissed her aunt and uncle. Angus pulled a chair around for me beside his, and made a big to-do about being sure the sun wasn't in my eyes.

"Thanks for the coffee this morning," I said.

He lifted one hand graciously. "Any time. Now tell me something: Have you met any ghosts yet? I set out to bring you a Ouija board."

"Is that supposed to be sophisticated humor?"

"No, it's about on a level with the twins' jokes. I've been wondering ever since that night at Alec's if you and Uncle Bob had gotten together yet."

"What's this?" Daisy asked.

"Oh, Uncle Bob kept hinting about things," said Rowan, "and Aunt Christy kept shushing him."

"What things?" her aunt persisted.

"The *supernatural*," said Angus hollowly.

"Oh, those things. I'm more interested in what's new and visible."

"Jamesy's run away," said Angus. "How's that for openers?"

Rowan choked on her wine and hastily set the glass down. "When? Are you *sure*?"

"According to his father, he came home from somewhere in late afternoon, and just the younger ones were there. He picked up some stuff, told the kids he was never coming back, and took off."

"Oh, poor Jamesy!" Rowan mourned. "He was so miserable yesterday afternoon. Maybe if we hadn't been at the Bain Place, he'd have talked to them and they could have calmed him down."

"What's that all about?" her aunt asked. Rowan explained. I thought, So this brings it all together. Jamesy pushed Hector, and then ran. Scared foolish that he'd killed his uncle, or that he hadn't and Hector would talk.

The glory went out of the day. Depressed, I turned partly away from the others and gazed out at the pastoral landscape. *What is so rare as a day in June?* we had recited in school. I'd read it to my own fourth-graders less than a month ago. *Then, if ever, come perfect days.* How long before they realized that every perfect day was Disaster Day for someone?

"How's Len taking it, I wonder?" Daisy asked.

"Oh, you know Aunt Len," Rowan answered. "You'll never be able to tell if she's worried or relieved."

"Len couldn't care less," Angus said lazily. "She's got another bun in the oven."

"Oh, dear God! If ever a man's being driven crazy by his children, it's Stuart Kendrum, and yet they keep shucking them out!"

"That occurred to me too," said Angus, "but I thought I wouldn't mention it to him. He came around to the farm this morning and raised a little hell. He blames all the trouble on Hector, for having the gang at the Bain Place. He says they gave Jamesy drugs. All Hector answered was that he hoped the boy would stay away and make something of himself, that he wouldn't be the first Kendrum to leave home in a rage and then make good. He told Stuart to relax, offered him a drink, and Stuart shot out of there, burning rubber." He added somberly, "He was absolutely white. I never saw him so upset."

Rowan and I looked at each other and away. Stuart could be a very sick man, perhaps a dying man—or afraid of dying—and the others ought to know. But that would be up to Rowan, and for some reason she was fighting shy of it, maybe dreading Stuart's anger. I'd never say anything, any more than I'd mention the intact ladder. My business was the genealogy, and what the house held for me and no one else.

"What are you dreaming about, Noel?" Daisy asked me.

"Your view," I said quickly. "I always thought I had to have the ocean, but this is really something. The colors and the shapes change with every passing cloud."

"Ah, yes," she said with pleasure. "I'm never tired of it."

"Well, we can't do a thing about Jamesy and his father," said Angus, "so let's consider it a duty to enjoy ourselves as much as possible."

"Fresh drinks all around," Daisy said, rising, "and I've got some more of these tasty little doodads in the kitchen. Come on in and see the house, Noel."

The inside lived up to the promise of the outside, and I thought seriously that for a single woman a house of her own would go a long way toward satisfying the nesting instinct. It was worth thinking about from time to time, just in case. Daisy Ross seemed on perfectly good, even happy, terms with herself and her house, and that was what made it even more worth considering—just in case.

When I went out on the deck again, Angus was saying to Rowan, "I'll see what I can find out, though I don't know how in hell I can work it." He gave her shoulder a little squeeze. The way she gave me a sidewise glance from those gray eyes, I knew she'd told him about the Halifax meeting.

Daisy, coming behind me, missed this. "Angus, are you going to show up in a kilt for the Gathering?"

"Well, I've got the legs for it," he said imperturbably. Rowan winked at me, and he caught it.

"What's that for?" he demanded.

"Have you written the Impostor yet?" I asked.

"Oh, you know about him, do you?" said Daisy.

"I've given her the early family history, magic rowans, fake earls, and all. She's inclined to believe in the impostor theory, because of my noble bearing."

"But *you* wouldn't be the Earl," Rowan objected.

"Don't niggle, my child," he said severely. "What was the occasion for the leer and wink?"

Rowan smiled at him. "The fact is, when we were in Fraser's that day we agreed you'd look smashing in Highland dress. And I knew Noel would be embarrassed if I told you, so I winked at her."

"She doesn't look embarrassed," said Angus. "She's trying not to laugh. What did you really say, Noel?"

"I think you'd better let her save it for a tête-à-tête, Angus," Daisy advised. Rowan stood up.

"I have to go. But I hate to pull you away, Noel."

"No, it's time for me to go, too. It's so beautiful here, it's like the land where it's always afternoon, but I haven't seen Robbie since he left for church this morning, and he'll be looking for supper."

"You'll come back again," Daisy said. "I'll make sure of it."

She and Angus walked to the car with us and saw us out of the driveway. We intended to wait until we were decently out of sight before we burst out laughing. But as we swung onto the road we met three youngsters from the Corner trudging home from somewhere, and we gave them a ride. So we discussed neither Angus's legs nor Jamesy. I left Rowan off at her mailbox, and the kids off by the closed store, and drove home.

20
CHAPTER

ROBBIE WASN'T THERE; he'd be at the farm now, doing chores. I changed from dress into slacks, and was deciding what to assemble for sandwiches when Angus drove into the yard. He went into the ell, and I heard him moving around in there. I tried to concentrate; onions or not? Hard-boiled eggs, yes. That was easy. I put some on to boil. I was tearing off lettuce leaves in the pantry when he knocked at the kitchen door and followed the knock in.

"Hello again," I said sparklingly, not looking around.

He stood in the pantry doorway. "Now tell me about the wink."

"Aren't you getting a little paranoid about that?"

"All I want to know is what made the light of deviltry flash across that until-now quiet face of yours."

"Nothing much," I said. "I just wondered if the reason you put down the kilt-wearers is that there's something wrong with your own legs."

"My dear girl, I have macho knees and magnificent calves." We both began to laugh.

"Have a sandwich?" I asked. "It's strictly a build-your-own proposition."

"Great! I brought home some good cheese and cold cuts. You'll find them in the fridge somewhere. Got any onions?"

"Yes, if you'll slice them."

"I'm so fast they never get to me."

"Impervious to onions, possesses magnificent legs—Superman!" I started the coffee.

We had quite a collection on the table by the time we sat down to it. Robbie hadn't come in yet, and I thought he might be eating at the farm.

At first we were busy eating. When he started to build his second sandwich he said, "I told Rowan that if you'd come in and stay the night with her sometime when I'm in Halifax, we could go to dinner, a show, dancing—whatever you'd like."

It was done offhandedly, more like a courteous gesture than any personal desire of his own, and I wondered if Rowan had thought up the whole thing in the first place and he was just humoring her. "It sounds good," I said, busy with my own food, "but I have to think about Robbie. My time isn't completely free."

"Robbie could easily spend the night at the farm or over at Alec's." He got up and went to the stove for the coffee pot. Back to me he said very quickly, "But if you're not interested—"

"Oh, but I am!" I hadn't expected to say it quite like that, but now I knew I did want to go. "It's just that—"

"Just *what?*" He came back to the table. "It doesn't commit you to anything, Noel. It doesn't compromise you."

"It's not that!" I said angrily. "You make me sound like a fool!"

He grinned, and refilled my cup without asking.

"Darn it, I'd love to go!" I said. But when I said it I felt the wrench of leaving the house for a night.

"Good. It can't be till after the Gathering. But it's a firm date. You won't back off, will you?"

"I won't back off."

"There are times when you have a secretive look. It makes you a different Noel. Mysterious, baffling. What do you think of? *Whom* do you think of? Some seafaring man back home?"

"How'd you guess?"

"I've got second sight. I try to keep it unknown so nobody will think I'm a nut."

I laughed. "That's the trouble with having some special gifts. . . . But you guessed right," I lied. "Micah Jenkins, captain of the *Mollie Pitcher*. How does that grab you?"

He considered. "Sounds as if you invented him on the spur of the moment. The ship too."

"No, he exists, but if he didn't, the tourists would have invented him."

"Voltaire said something like that about God. I just threw that in to show that I'm educated. Are you getting over Micah Jenkins, or do those long looks and flights of the spirit mean you're wondering how faithful he's being while you're gone?"

"I don't wonder, I *know*. Let's say there's nothing to get over, but I'm just as happy not being in the same town with him. Happier."

"I think there *was* something to get over."

"What there was—well, I can't make it clear to you because you're not a girl."

"By George, that's a remarkably keen observation. That brain of yours is wasted here. Tell me, when did you first begin to realize that I was of the opposite sex, if you'll forgive my plain speaking?"

"Well, *actually*—that's how they always begin—it was the first time I met you. There was just something about you—that walk, that air of careless power—and the way you tried unsuccessfully to be quiet while you put the groceries away. To the trained eye all the clues were there, you see."

He threw back his head in laughter. "I have to tell you, your description fits perfectly my ex-lady."

"Is that *ex* or x as in x-rated?"

"Both. Now tell me what I can't understand because I'm not a girl."

"The trouble isn't getting over Micah. It's getting over myself for being attracted to him." It couldn't be the drinks, I hadn't had that many, and the food and strong coffee should have taken care of them anyway. "Knowing what he is, and being ashamed of myself because there was once a time when if he singled me out I was ready to cave in." I knew why I was babbling. Micah was nothing to me any more, but Angus Mor was everything, and it was very hard to sit in this house with its owner and Angus Mor's descendant, and put my mind safely on anything else.

"Go on," Angus happily encouraged me. "Did you ever cave in? I suppose it's none of my business."

"When he showed up at my door with his bedroll on his shoulder—he's very rugged and thinks mattresses are for effete snobs—"

Sandwich halfway to his mouth, Angus froze. *"Well?"*

"I did not cave in. I asked him what did he think he was doing."

"Immortal words," Angus murmured.

"And I tried to slam the door, but he almost got in. We had quite a tussle and he left, and then I thought of how long I'd waited for a personal signal from this—this—"

"Oaf?" suggested Angus. "Beast. Animal."

"No, I like animals."

"Try sex maniac. Anyway, you repented of your hasty conduct and called him back."

I shook my head. "No. And after that he never gave a sign that I was even visible except to pull the nearest girl a little closer, just to show me what I could have had."

"And you died inside, as they say. You longed for another chance."

"No," I said honestly. "But I was afraid that if he ever did come to me again, I'd kid myself into thinking he must really be in love with me—to come back, you see. And I'd give in. I know what he is, and I know what I am, so—" I shrugged.

"And what are you, Noel?" he asked very softly.

"Brave, kind, trustworthy, loyal—"

I was making fun of myself, but he said seriously, "And you expect the same of others. You're a dreamer, Noel. I hope you do find somebody like that, but it's a pretty impossible yardstick for the common man."

"What I really want," I said, "is someone tall, dark, thin, an elegant dresser with a sense of humor and a Jaguar. And oh yes, good legs for a kilt."

"Good night, Noel," said Angus. "I'll see you in the morning." We both began to laugh. He carried his dishes to the pantry.

"Don't you have to go back tonight?" I asked.

"No, I'm taking tomorrow off. I want to finish sorting some stuff down cellar, and Stuart will be over."

"He must be worried sick about Jamesy."

"Yes, and it's impossible for him to give in and just go along with the stream. Stuart lives by the Kendrum motto—'While I breathe I fight.'"

"That's a pretty good motto."

"Yes, if you've got a chance of winning. However, most of the Kendrums have never been noted for estimating their chances beforehand."

"You're one of the intelligent minority, I suppose."

"Do I sound that smug? Let's see, I said good night some time ago, didn't I?"

"Good night," I said sweetly. There was a whistling outside, and a noise at the door, and Robbie came in.

"Oh, hi, Uncle Angus."

"Good evening, kinsman," said Angus in a deep voice.

Robbie chuckled. Angus left by the door into the ell. I asked Robbie if he had eaten yet. "Sure! I had supper at the farm. But I could eat something else. What are you having?"

"Build-your-own sandwiches. Help yourself."

"Thanks, I will!" He switched on the table lamp and got happily squared away. Virginia was going to be delighted with him. I wished that she could come to Brierbank and see him being a Kendrum among Kendrums.

21
CHAPTER

THERE WAS a voyage across endless seas. Curling white crests and green water to the edge of the world. A consuming horror that wasn't fear of the sea, I knew that. Something else. Heartbreaking. . . . Child crying. The creak of timbers and masts and explosive slat of sails, the water forever knocking at our sides as we ran. . . . Small, dim, suffocating area, must be the cabin. The tartan bundle in a hammock was the center of the fear and the heartbreak. Crouching by it, looking into the pallid, sweating young face above the rough folds of the plaid, and seeing instead the new graves by moonlight. The face was Robbie's. No! *Calum, Calum,* my heart mourned.

White moonfire writhing along the blade of a sword, the unexpected chill of it under my lips. . . . The graves again. A man's face, thinned to the bone, seamed with exhaustion, the eyes gray as rain; familiar to me, familiar enough to squeeze my throat in an agony of held-back tears. A smile moved his tired mouth.

Father. Not mine. His.

Nearby the child whined, a woman whispered to it. The graves again. Another woman's face suspended in the shadows behind the swinging, smoky lantern like a devilish lantern itself; sparks in the hollows of the eyes, the hot glow on the tumbled red hair, the long mouth saying, "Your father is dead."

That tidal wave of hatred that lifted one up, bore one forward to crash upon her in a killing smother. But she had vanished and the wave withdrew, leaving only a word, a name. *Frances.* I was sure of that now.

No time for hatred, no room. Leaning over the hammock and swearing, "I will not give my brother to the sea."

The air was stifling, stinking. I—Noel—whispered, "If you could only get him out on deck."

Head turning as if he listened. The woman sang to the feverish child. "My heart's darling, my little hoodie crow, sleep," she crooned.

I was the one who listened, who turned my head, yet I was watching too. Up onto his feet, my feet, needles and pins from crouching so long. Lift off the hatch cover and meet the shock of pure cold fresh air, the blue blaze of sky, the smell of salt, the sun on the full curve of rust-brown canvas, and the strength of it on my face.

Someone had to help him move the boy. The woman, or some man from above decks? It was confused, at least for me, but then his memories wouldn't have lingered over that part. The important thing was to get the younger boy outside, pallet safely wedged, where he could at least die in the sunshine. Tuck the plaid tightly around the skinny shoulders. Its blue and green and red glowed indefatigably through the dulling grime. The small face so still, dark lashes and tumbled black hair. But breathing. . . . Lean close and say into the nearest ear, "While we breathe we fight."

I woke up as if I'd been shot out of a cannon into a net. I was out of breath, and my heart was beating so hard I could hear the throbbing like something outside my skin. My fingertips still remembered the texture of the plaid and the boniness of the boy's shoulders under it. My face and nose still remembered the cold air and warm sunlight and the briny scent that dizzied my brain with its purity.

I thought weakly, Enough of this and I'll wear away to a wisp. Sitting up in bed I oriented myself not by stars—the moonlight was too bright—but by an attempt at logic. I hadn't heard the pacing that usually went with these experiences. Perhaps it had been a dream from start to finish, based on a few known facts and the conversation over drinks, with Angus quoting the Kendrum motto. To retain precise tactile details from a dream wasn't strange to me, I'd done that all my life, and sometimes I'd remembered them a long time. Who needs movies? I joked feebly. I make my own.

Still, I'd better write it all down and stop thinking about it. I got out of bed and put on my robe. The moonlight was so bright I didn't put on a lamp. I sat down at the card table and opened my notebook to a new page, and wrote the date and the time.

The next sentence came as rather a surprise, because I hadn't planned it.

"The name of the boat was *Kirsteen.*"

I read it in bewilderment. Where had *that* come from? Had someone said it in the dream, or had I heard someone in this life say it? I was sure it wasn't in Robert Kendrum's records. Never mind. I wrote after that, in large letters, "CALUM SURVIVED."

Of course he'd survived. He'd grown up to work for the Northwest Company, like many another Scot before and after him.

I went on to write everything down, knowing there was no way of ever verifying it. I could simply be recording exceptionally vivid dreams. But if that were so, what about Bob Kendrum's stories about the fiddling and the pacer? A purist might argue that Rowan's name had put the idea of the rowan flowers and berries in my head, but nothing had suggested the other experiences.

When I'd finished I was wrung out with weariness, and fell back into bed to sleep like someone under drugs.

I didn't expect to wake up not only early but without a hangover, and full of energy besides. I had housewifely resolutions to dry-mop, plan out our dinners for a week, wash out a few things of mine, and then work on the project. I was going to keep everything else out of mind during the day and try to do the same at night. I wanted to be as sure as I could be that I wasn't manipulating my own thought processes.

I was even up before Robbie for once, but not before Angus. The coffee pot was hot, and down in the cellar someone was whistling and clinking; Angus must be already sorting over the treasures on the bench and in the old packing boxes. The bulk-head was open to the rising sun.

I mixed a double batch of bran and raisin muffins while drinking my first cup of coffee, put them in the oven, and started bacon frying. Then I went out and called down the steps, "Angus, do you want a hot breakfast with us?"

"I thought you'd never ask."

"It'll be ready in fifteen minutes."

I wondered what the ex-lady was really like. I imagined some lean, febrile, fey type with marvelous cheekbones and peculiar sex habits like the obligatory kinky heroines in most books nowadays.

He came up shortly and washed up in his own quarters before coming to the kitchen. Robbie descended from his room, surprised to see me, and pleased with both the breakfast and male company.

"We're going to start haying over at Uncle Bob's today," he told Angus importantly. "Oh, Noel, Aunt Janet says if you'd like wild strawberries the field down front should be full of them. If you don't want 'em, she does."

"You tell her I love them and I'll pick some, but she's got priority." Then I remembered. "For heaven's sake, your uncle here *owns* them."

"Never mind, everybody else can pick all they want as long as they'll supply me with strawberry shortcake, strawberries and cream, strawberry pie, strawberry jam—"

"Hey, knock it off," Robbie moaned.

A truck door slammed, and Angus jumped up and went to the back door. "Stuart, come on in and have a cup of coffee!" he called.

Stuart came in, holding his shoulders stiffly; he looked as if he hadn't slept—he was hollow around the eyes and below the cheekbones.

"We've got some warm muffins, too," I said. "How about bacon and scrambled eggs?"

He shook his head. "Coffee'll be fine, thanks."

"Sit here, Uncle Stuart," Robbie invited. "I have to go to work."

"I wasn't planning to be here so early," Stuart said, "but I was driving around and it looked as if everybody was up, so—" He let it trail off. From the way he lifted his cup with both hands, I knew he must have felt shaky. I wondered in pity if he'd been driving around all night.

"Gosh, I wish they still used horses for work," Robbie said, "even if I do get a chance to drive the tractor. Uncle Hector tells us about it. . . . Good breakfast, Noel. So long." He went out just as the twins' truck came along.

"Look," I said to the men, "I'm going upstairs and get busy. You two take your time and finish up the muffins."

I took the dry mop and left them. I spun out the upstairs chores as long as possible, but there wasn't really much to do. Housework gives me all kinds of symptoms which can be alleviated only by my leaving it off *at once*.

When I reached that point, I went to the head of the stairs and listened. The men were getting up from the table and I could tell that Angus was helpfully collecting the dishes and carrying them to the pantry. His words, spoken softly, were indistinguishable, but the tone was that of reassurance. Then Stuart said clearly, "You don't know what the boy's capable of. Len could never see it in him—that's been my cross."

"He's on his own now, Stuart. Start thinking about the other three kids, and the one coming."

Stuart groaned. They went out.

I did my small washing in the pantry sink and all the time I could hear sporadic conversation down cellar, some hammering, more clinkings and clankings, a puzzled discussion about the use

of some odd tool Angus had discovered. I took my laundry out
and hung it on the line I'd strung up from one pine to another.
Stuart left while I was doing this. I waved, but he didn't re-
spond. Angus padlocked the bulkhead, then he came to meet
me.

"Have you ever been to Peggy's Cove?"

"Only by postcard, when my friends went."

"Then let's go right now. We'll never have a better chance.
Everything's pretty quiet, but by next weekend the place will be
swarming."

I hesitated—I don't know why I can never plunge—and he
said quietly, "Please. You'll be doing me a favor."

"Stuart?"

"I couldn't get anywhere with him, and it depresses me like
hell. Of course I'm the youngest, so advice from me isn't welcome anyway, but I thought he could use a little aid and comfort." He rubbed the back of his neck hard. "Well, he's the way he
is, and I can't do a damn thing about it. He'll have to dree his
own weird."

"His *what?*"

He gave me a rueful grin. "One of the gloomy sayings passed
down from our ancestors. He'll have to endure his own fate, or
destiny, if you like that better. Are you going with me?"

"I'll have to leave something for Robbie—"

"We'll swing down to the farm and tell Aunt Janet. She'll feed
him tonight if we aren't back in time."

I packed half the contents of the refrigerator in my canvas
tote bag and he made a fresh pot of coffee and filled a thermos
bottle. We were fast, purposeful, and not talkative. Provisions
ready, we separated to change.

We met again at his car, looking—I fondly thought—like the
glamorous models in an advertisement for Jaguars. Never mind
the ex-lady, never mind his reason for asking me. (Because I just
happened to be there and he wanted company.) For a day we
were to be on stage as Beautiful People.

It wasn't a role to which I'd ever aspired, but it could be the kind of fun that's a good antidote for other problems besides unhappy brothers. I needed to keep my mind off what had happened last night. When such experiences began to dominate my waking hours, I could be in trouble. But I knew by the way I felt when Young Angus drove us out of the yard that so far I was still pretty normal.

"I was going to pick strawberries this afternoon," I told Mrs. Archie.

"They'll be there tomorrow and probably more of them."

"You'll pick too, won't you?" I asked. "And let me give you a cup of tea afterward?"

"Yes, you may, and now go along and have a fine day."

22
CHAPTER

W E HEADED toward Halifax, but turned off at Middle Sackville to go to Upper Tantallon. All my life I've started out on long drives with this happy anticipation, and I can agree with Stevenson that sometimes to travel hopefully is better than to arrive. I'd never ridden in a Jaguar before and was secretly impressed by this particular status symbol. The weather was glorious, the scenery beautiful, and we had left everybody's troubles behind us. I didn't feel obligated to make social conversation, because I was under no illusion that Angus was smitten with me. The knowledge freed me from self-consciousness. I was doing him a favor today, and he didn't know he was doing one for me.

From Upper Tantallon we drove down along the shore of St. Margaret's Bay to Peggy's Cove. Naturally it was better than any postcard, and we had it almost to ourselves. The sea was quite calm except for a deep slow swell. When we were hungry we went back to the car for the bag of supplies, and carried it out to the lighthouse.

There we went on playing our roles with a good deal of enthusiasm. I wondered once if his ex-lady or ex-ladies ever took part in such simple pleasures, and if he were just doing something that bored him but which he thought I might enjoy. I couldn't tell, and I took everything at face value. We cut off thick hunks of Mrs. Archie's bread and ate it with the cheeses and thin slices of ham and roast beef, and some southern peaches that must have cost the earth. The coffee was good. Not as poetic an item as wine would have been, but nothing could have tasted better out on that special rock by the lighthouse.

We talked about ourselves and our work, our friends, our likes and dislikes. I'd tossed my camera in on top of the lunch at the last minute, so we took pictures of each other like tourists on holiday, and got a passing birdwatcher to photograph us together. That snap was going to be a hot item to pass around when I went back to Fremont.

Leaving Peggy's Cove, we went on to Shad Bay and Terence Bay, where we talked to fishermen on the wharves and took pictures of the broad-beamed, high-bowed Nova Scotia boats painted in strong reds and greens and yellows. I felt as if I could go on being a tourist forever, if I could always have these leisurely conditions in an uncrowded June day.

Then we drove up to Halifax and crossed the Narrows to Dartmouth, and followed the road eastward to Oquiddic Harbor. Our silence seemed utterly relaxed and companionable. He pointed out things I might be interested in, and sometimes I asked a question, but otherwise we were quiet.

When we turned northwest to follow the river home to Brierbank, I roused up and grew tense for the first time since we'd left home in the morning. This was the way Angus Mor had come; this was his river. I wanted to say something, but the matter had become so personal with me that I was afraid of somehow giving myself away; as if my voice wouldn't come out right, or something.

There had probably been solid forest all along here once. Even now there were still long stretches of undeveloped, though cleared, country, so that the river was rarely hidden from us by buildings. Sometimes it flowed placidly without perceptible motion. In another place it became white water foaming noisily over a rocky bed. They'd have portaged there, I thought.

We left it to go off on a side road, not much more than a lane, and drove into the shady dooryard of a large mid-Victorian sort of house with broad porches and unexpected gables adorned with gingerbread. The yellow paint looked either freshly applied or freshly scrubbed. Vines flowered richly over the railings.

There were two cars in the driveway, one shiningly conservative, the other an old and raffish sports car. A black and gold sign over the open double doors of the carriage house read "Wm. Henderson, Antiques."

"You see, I had an errand in mind all this time," Angus said. He came around to open the door for me—this I enjoyed since it's gone out of style in most places—and we went into the carriage house. A Pickwickian Mr. Henderson was in conference about some dishes with a middle-aged couple, and a thickset bearded young man was poking around the shelves of old ship models in a corner. I went at once to a case of dolls, and Angus, whistling softly to himself, picked over some books. The couple left, with Mr. Henderson promising to let them know if he discovered a footed compote of Vaseline glass in the Mikado pattern, then he and Angus disappeared into another room. I left the dolls for a table of not-very-old, inexpensive but charming little dishes, and I found among them a china bowl and five matching sauce dishes, in a pattern of tiny pink roses. It was only ten dollars for the set, and I chose that for Mrs. Archie; then I rummaged around for something equivalent for Mrs. Bob. It turned out to be a white china cracker jar with a farmyard scene on the side, featuring bantams.

While I was lavishly throwing my money around, it occurred to me that to find something for Angus's house would be a gracious gesture. But I didn't want to get just any useless trifle, and I wouldn't have time to paw around the shop in search of the right thing, if I knew what that was and could afford it. I went to the books, wishing I'd noticed if Angus had been drawn particularly to one. I doubted it. They were an uninspiring lot, mostly novels by extremely minor nineteenth-century lady writers. Anything really good and valuable Mr. Henderson would have locked in a case, like the dolls.

The man in the corner sighed despairingly. "I don't know," he said as if to himself, "why I couldn't have found something like this in some relative's attic." He was tenderly holding a small vessel in his big hands. He gave me a look of humorous despair. "It's hell to be poor."

"You said it," I replied with feeling. "What kind of ship is that?"

"It's an exact scale model of a seventeenth-century shallop, and it was made by one Josiah Craddock, who died around 1830 of yellow fever, while he was a ship master in the West Indies trade. I've been looking for a Craddock model for years. And from the price on it, it must be solid gold under all the dirt."

"I'm sorry," I said, meaning it.

"Thank you," he said mournfully. His nose had once been broken, and with his deep tan and his beard, he could have worn a ring in his ear and with the proper costume passed for a seventeenth-century seafaring man.

"Maybe Mr. Henderson would let you buy it by installments," I suggested.

"Or I could steal it," he said, and then grinned. With obvious reluctance he set it back on the shelf, just as Angus and Mr. Henderson came back. They were each carrying a framed painting, which they set side by side on a deacon's bench and then stood off to contemplate them. So did I. They were well done, not primitives. The man was severely handsome and long-jawed above the broad cravat. The woman wore a frilled cap and a fichu. Her face was plain but she had an expression of solemn sweetness.

Angus was looking very pleased with himself. "Captain Angus and his wife, Sophie," he announced. "I got them off a very elderly relative. She wanted them to go back to the house where they belonged."

Mr. Henderson made small murmurs of approval.

"Mr. Henderson's been cleaning them and repairing the frames," Angus went on. "This must be the way they looked when they were first done." The colors were clear and fresh, the eyes bright with life.

"Are they signed?" the seafarer asked suddenly.

"Oh yes," Mr. Henderson assured him. He pointed to the righthand corner of Sophie's portrait. "You can just make it out. Samuel Coombs. His work is very much sought after these days. A pair like this could bring a phenomenal price."

"I'm not entirely unprincipled, Noel," Angus said. "I pointed out to Cousin Eugenia that she could sell these for a bundle, and she was horrified."

"Quite properly," said Mr. Henderson. "Of course if everyone felt that way, where would we antique dealers be?" He twinkled at us.

The boat lover said, "I don't have the right kind of elderly relatives. They've already sold anything that would go for a bundle, or even five dollars." He turned back sadly to the shallop. "I could make her a new suit of sails," he murmured.

"Well, Mr. Henderson," Angus said, "when are you coming to see the house? The work's done now."

"Just where is the house in relation to Brierbank Corner? I've been there to appraise some things."

Angus gave him directions. I heard him, but the words were just so much sound as I looked at the painting of Captain Angus. This was Angus Mor's son. As a baby he had been held in Angus Mor's arms. Calm, severe, yet not remote, he gazed out from the frame; if one gazed back long enough the eyes would soften among lines of weathering and humor, the long mouth would curve in a faint smile. The jaw was admirably suited for holding onto a fiddle. He must have been a merry man when he played for dancing. *I have heard you, Captain Angus.*

"What are you doing, Noel, hypnotizing yourself?" Angus asked from a long distance.

Answering him, I was like someone startled from sleep, out of bed, on my feet, and in motion before I was awake. "Trying to imagine what everything was like when that was painted."

"Anyone could write a novel just starting out from those two paintings," said the stranger.

"And I wouldn't be surprised if this girl produced it completed at breakfast some morning," said Angus. "Well, Noel, shall we get the Captain and his missus back where they belong?"

I paid for my dishes, and Mr. Henderson wrapped and boxed them as if they'd been Spode. He went to the car with us to see the paintings carefully placed in the back seat. The other man stood in the big doorway looking as if he were wondering where he could locate the devil and made a deal with him: his soul for Josiah Craddock's shallop.

Angus was as happy as I'd ever seen him. "Look, keep the paintings a secret, will you? I've got plans for the night before the Gathering. I'm going to hang the pictures side by side over the living room mantel, and we'll have the family all gather round. We'll build the first fire since that chimney was rebuilt, and drink a toast to Captain Angus." He slapped me lightly on the knee and laughed aloud. "If he's still around he'll be sorry he can't drink with us. A great man for a dram, Captain Angus."

"Why shouldn't Angus Mor be around, then?" I tried to sound frivolous. "Why not him as well as the Captain? After all, he built the original house, didn't he?"

"Somehow the old boy seems lost in the mists of antiquity. Captain Angus is almost within touch."

"What about his son, Angus J.? He should be even nearer."

"Angus J.," he said, "wouldn't have anything to do with such heathen foolishness. Parading around as a ghost! Heaven forfend, whatever that means."

"He couldn't have been too dull. After all, he played the fiddle like his father. And," I added solemnly, "he was a Kendrum."

"Aye, he was that," Angus agreed, with an accent. "And I never said he was dull. But *ghosts?* Never. He was of the earth earthy. You know, I was going to buy the Captain's fiddle from

another of Angus J.'s granddaughters, but I was afraid I might
hear it playing by itself in the middle of the night."

"I'm sure you would have heard it."

"Was there a faint emphasis on the word *you?*"

I ignored that. "As a matter of fact," I rambled on, "it should
be possible to hear the music without any real fiddle in the
house. The instrument was made of wood, wood was once alive,
so—" I shrugged. "Why not a ghostly instrument?"

"If you ever hear a phantom fiddle when I'm in the house,
wake me at once."

"I'll knock on the wall."

We smiled at each other, Angus enjoying the foolishness,
while I thought, Little you know, my boy.

"I wonder what Jamesy's doing tonight," he said suddenly.

"I can't help feeling sorry for both Jamesy and his father," I
said.

"You're very compassionate, you know that?"

I tried to be modest and felt slightly foolish. "It's pure selfishness," I said. "When I'm enjoying myself I want everyone else to
be happy so their misery won't spoil my good time."

"Then you could say all good works grow out of enlightened
selfishness. But if the thought of misery keeps you from enjoying
yourself, what does that make you in the first place?"

"Either the chicken or the egg."

"Somehow I can't see you as either," he said thoughtfully.
"Anyway, I'd like to think that Jamesy will strike out for the west
and turn up on some Kendrum doorstep in Alberta or B.C. He
wouldn't be the first in the clan to leave home because he fought
with his father." (But maybe the first to shoot at his uncle and
then push him out of a hayloft, I thought.) "And most of them
have done all right for themselves, once they were out from under Father's eyes. At least none of them ended up in jail or on the
gallows. Now let's think of something stupefyingly splendid.
Like Gilbert Kendrum at the Gathering."

"I can hardly wait to see him. Until then I'll think about Peggy's Cove at noon today. Thank you for a most beautiful day."

"Thank you for helping to make it so." He said it as if he was being courteous while thinking about something else far more absorbing than our day together, or Gilbert Kendrum peacocking in Highland dress.

23
CHAPTER

W E STOPPED at the house and he took the paintings into the ell, then we drove on down to the farm where I presented Mrs. Archie with my gift. She was so touched and so pleased that I wished it had really been Spode. They had finished supper, but she insisted on heating up the beef stew for us. We had big bowls of wild strawberries for dessert.

"I cheated," she said. "I've already been picking. But I'll be ready to pick more tomorrow."

"Good," I said. "I can hardly wait." I yawned at the end of it. "Right now I can hardly wait for bed, I think."

Robbie wanted to watch something on television so he stayed a while. Angus drove me home, we thanked each other again for the day, said good night, and separated. I heard his typewriter begin while I was still puttering around the kitchen, but when I went upstairs it became inaudible. I fell happily into bed and opened my book. It was only a few minutes before I developed a squint and a knack of reading dialogue that I seemed to be making up as I went along. I shut the book and turned out my light, and went to sleep almost at once.

There were no adventures on the way into the depths. When something disturbed me, I didn't want to wake up and I thought drunkenly that it was only Robbie coming home. I fought to hold onto my blissful stupor, but the intrusion was persistent. How many times did Robbie have to go up and down stairs, for heaven's sake? Or back and forth to the bathroom? Or up to the attic?

Attic. My brain was unfogged in an instant, and as usual I bounced up like a Jack-in-the-box to be sure I wasn't dreaming, wasn't hearing my own heartbeat.

The house was full of footsteps. I'd never heard anything like it. They went on and on, never coming to me but never going away either.

"Angus Mor," I whispered. "Is that you? Please, *please*—" I bogged down in inarticulate yearning. Why couldn't he hear me?

Something crashed against the ell side of the wall, hard enough to jar the nearby window. A smaller crash of breaking glass followed it. I sat there staring at the dim wall as if a monster were about to smash through lath and plaster into my room. I couldn't move, and this time the blood was pounding through my head hard enough, it seemed, to jar it with every heavy throb, and my heart was knocking in my chest with the same hideous energy. I was tormented by horrible ideas of demonic possession; whose footsteps had they *really* been all this time?

"Who's there?" I shouted, and without thinking I threw my book at the wall.

No demon smashed through. There was a series of smaller thumps and thuds, running footsteps, and from downstairs a distant slam. Then silence.

Sanity returned, bringing with it a freezing but very lucid fear. I went through the back door of my room into the passage, and knocked at the door into the ell. Nobody answered, and in a way the stillness was worse than the noise. I opened the door into the loft, lit by moonlight from the window in the gable.

"Angus," I called softly. Still no answer. I went timidly across the threshold. The bed was empty, the bedclothes ripped off and hurled around, one pillow on the rug beside it, another thrown across the room. A lamp had been shattered in the middle of the floor.

A light went on below and shone yellow up the stairwell. I made a wide circle around the glass and went to the head of the flight.

"Are you there, Angus?" I called.

"Yes," He sounded strange.

"Are you all right? Did you fall downstairs?"

"Come on down. . . . No, first throw me my robe. It's on a chair. Can you see?"

"There's moonlight." Trembling with reaction now, I felt as if I had ten useless fingers on each hand. The dark wool robe showed up plainly and after a clumsy grab at it I threw it down the stairs.

"Thanks." A hand took it from the landing.

"I'd better get my own robe." My teeth wanted to chatter. "Then shall I come back?"

"Yes. *No.* Meet me in the kitchen. And watch out for broken glass up there."

"Yes. The lamp."

I got my slippers on the wrong feet for starters, then couldn't figure out how I'd tangled up the sleeves of my robe with the sash. When I was assembled after a fashion, I listened at Robbie's door. I could hear his deep breathing. Downstairs Angus had turned the heat on under the teakettle and was pouring Canadian Club into a glass.

"The hot water's for you," he said. "Don't women always want a cup of tea in a crisis?"

"No," I said, turning off the burner. "Not this one. It depends on the crisis. What happened?"

"Just a nightmare," he said. "I have bad ones now and then. I should have warned you. If I scared you I'm sorry as hell." He looked into the glass. "It was a beaut." He drank the whiskey in one long swallow. "Want some of this?"

"It sure was a beaut," I said. "You threw your lamp halfway across the room, and now you're gulping whiskey like an alcoholic on the morning after."

"Maybe I was having the DT's," he said, with a little sidewise smile. But he couldn't hide the strain and the jumpiness. He'd had a severe shock. A terrible nightmare could do it, but the words *He's lying* loomed as large and black as if written in Magic Marker on the clean wall.

"You might as well tell me," I said. "I'm not going to go all nervous and hysterical. Somebody ran down the stairs, and a door slammed."

"*I* ran down the stairs."

"He wasn't barefoot. He wasn't the pacer, either." That came out without intention. I heard it with dismay and hurried on. "Or *she* wasn't barefoot. If you had a girl friend visiting, well, I guess it's none of my business, and I'll say good night."

I started to get up and he put his hand on my shoulder and pushed me back down into the chair. "What did you say? 'He wasn't the pacer, either.' What does that mean?"

"Nothing," I said, blank with innocence. "Well, a joke, maybe. Bob Kendrum was telling me his grandfather used to think he heard someone pacing."

"I've heard that," he said in exasperation. "It was the house shifting. You know an old house is full of sounds anyway, and this one has water running beneath her most of the year, from all the springs on the side of the hill back of us. Keeps her heaving and settling. But, needing excitement on the long winter nights when the nails popped out of the wall with frost, Murray Kendrum invented a ghost with boots on."

You could see him growing expansive, relieved to have a new subject to take me off the original one. I could have been tactful and gone along with him, but I said, "Who was it who ran downstairs?"

"I don't know," he said simply. He sat down opposite me at the table, his big shoulders slumped. "I didn't want to tell you this, Noel, but I guess I have to tell somebody because I can't keep it to myself. I fell asleep reading, and then I woke up with the light *out*, and someone moving around. I mumbled 'Who's there?' and the next thing was a pillow over my face and someone pressing it down with their whole weight."

"Oh, my God!" I whispered. "*Angus!*" I felt sick enough to throw up.

"He'd managed to pin one arm down, kneeling on it." He rubbed his right forearm and around his elbow. "He wasn't too heavy a bastard, and I had the strength of desperation, I suppose. So I heaved myself up a bit and him with me, enough so he was thrown forward and crashed against the wall at the head of the bed. I made a big sweep with my free arm, hoping to hell the lamp would smash and wake you and bring you running, and that would send *him* running." He was pale and sweating, his eyes had a watery glisten. "It did, and the next thing I knew the pressure was off and he was running downstairs. I wasn't as fast as I should have been, but I'd almost passed out once. I was so damn sick and dizzy when I did get up it's a wonder I didn't fall downstairs. And if that happened—" He gave me a weak grin. "I hoped that when you investigated you'd have the forethought to walk in backward with your eyes shut, to spare us both embarrassment."

"I'll keep that in mind the next time," I said, "or you could always wear your pajamas. . . . But, Angus, don't you have *any* idea who did it? Do you have any enemies in your work?"

"You mean some crazy actor who's gone bonkers because we wouldn't let him play the Prime Minister in the documentary we made about Parliament? It wouldn't be me he'd be after, love. Incidentally, the part of the Prime Minister was played by the Prime Minister. And I can't see some writer losing his marbles because we slightly edited his script for 'Vancouver, Diamond of the Dominion.'"

"And then coming here, hiding his car God knows where, walking how many miles to sneak in and suffocate you with a pillow? It does sound far-fetched, doesn't it?" I couldn't stop the occasional shudders, and I went into one of the rockers where I could curl myself up and shove my hands up my sleeves. He got up quickly.

"You need a drink as much as I do."

"No, thanks, it would make me sick. Did you lock your door after he left?"

"Yes. What about these?"

"I've never thought about locking them! Not here."

He went into the front hall and I heard the bolt shoot home, then he walked through to the back door and locked that one.

When he came back he said, vigorously, "Locking up is just a gesture now. I don't think we're surrounded. Brierbank in itself is as safe as Eden, even if Stuart does think Hector invited the serpent in when he let the Bain Place." There was more color in his face. "Maybe there was a partner waiting in a car out on the road, maybe not. But he's long gone by now. He won't be back because I've been forewarned, and I do have an automatic, by the way." He sat down at the table and leaned his elbows on it. "I'll tell you what I'm pretty sure he was after. Captain Angus and Sophie."

I said stupidly, "What?"

"The portraits! You must know there's a big business in stolen antiques. Look, Henderson told me he'd been offered twenty-five hundred dollars for the pair by someone who saw them in his workroom. He said that if I ever wanted to sell them he could get me even more."

"You don't suspect Mr. Henderson!"

"Good God, no! But he has people working for him and they have friends. Someone could have prattled on about the paintings in all innocence. What about the chap looking at the boats? He was pretty interested in the portraits and he was there when I gave Henderson directions on finding this house." He sank his head into his hands and groaned. "They always said I talked too much for my own good, and they were right. It's almost killed me."

I thought rather regretfully of the man fondling the ship model. He'd had nice eyes and a certain rough-hewn sincerity of manner. "But usually that kind of burglar isn't a killer."

"Nothing's 'usual' any more, love," he said with a pitying smile, either for me or for himself. "He couldn't find the paintings, and while he was looking, I woke up. He's like the thief who shoots the shopkeeper before he runs. I can understand thievery, though I never wanted to be a thief. But the destroyer in cold blood, whether it's of a person or an animal or a twenty-two-hundred-year-old redwood—that's the one I want to string up without a trial and leave him swinging in the wind for the ravens to feed on."

"Me too," I said fervently, "and don't anybody dare tell me that makes me just as bad."

He thrust out his hand and we shook hard on it.

"Where are the paintings?" I asked.

"They're against the wall behind my desk, and you'd never know anything was there. I'm trying to keep any of the family from seeing them. I guess my visitor thought I'd have them under the bed." He rubbed his arm again. "He had a damned hard bony knee, grinding away there."

"Have you got any liniment for it? Aspirin? A heating pad?"

"I've got everything, love; I've got my life. I'll stay awake the rest of the night rejoicing. What about you?"

"Aspirin and a book for a while." I uncurled from the rocking chair.

"Something calming, I hope? Like Jane Austen, or the Essays of Montaigne. How about Proust? I'm just showing off, of course."

"Of course. No, it'll be *The Lord of the Rings*. It never fails me."

He walked to the foot of the stairs with me, his hand lightly under my elbow. "Well, if you feel an attack of nerves coming on, knock on the wall and I'll knock back." We laughed, softly so as not to disturb Robbie, and said good night.

I took two aspirin in the bathroom, with no real hope that it would calm me down. I looked out at the pallid streamer of the dirt road passing the house, and wondered with a chill at my stomach if the man had really gone or was hiding in the barn.

Of course he's gone, you fool, I answered myself. For all he knows, Angus is waiting for him with a gun. Just the same, for the first time in my life I wished for a mild tranquilizer. Then I remembered telling Robbie about comparing myself with the

French aristocrats on the tumbrils. How would I be feeling now, I thought, if I'd discovered an actual murder in the ell instead of an attempt at one?

I went back to bed. I couldn't put my mind on my book, so I turned off the light and lay back, gazing at the luminous shapes of the windows and the far-off dream landscape rising beyond the river in the moonlight. The brook sang on through the night. I knew at last, without knowing how I knew, that the danger had been really removed. For now.

But how far had Jamesy gone? Or had he gone at all? If he had tried twice to kill his Uncle Hector, and his three cousins along with his uncle, why not Angus? Maybe he wasn't a born killer, but drugs could set the torch to his frustrations and resentment.

This time I was really cold. Emily Dickinson spoke of the narrow fellow in the grass, and zero at the bone. The snake couldn't give me that, but my own thoughts could. Jamesy Kendrum; the gray eyes, the black hair, the long jaw — all seen as in a distorting mirror.

Trying to warm myself in bed, with robe, socks, and extra blankets, I wondered until my head spun, and then I fell asleep in my cocoon.

When I woke up, feeling as if I'd had a night on the town, my first thought wasn't *Jamesy;* it was the knowledge that the pacing had wakened me before the row began next door.

24

CHAPTER

THE NEXT MORNING Angus was waiting in the kitchen for me when I came down. He was dressed for town. The metamorphosis from last night's rumpled and shaken man was more than a matter of clothes. He was hardly yesterday's good companion, either. He behaved like a man who has had too many drinks the night before and thinks he may have been indiscreet, and in the chill air of morning wants to leave no room for misunderstanding or expectation. I sipped my coffee and listened with what I hoped was an air of cold preoccupation.

"Would you please not mention to anyone what happened last night?" he asked. "It's no use making people jumpy about something that will probably never happen again."

"Like the shots," I said.

That startled him. After a moment he said, "Yes, like that. But I'm taking the paintings back to Halifax with me and locking them up in the office safe. And I'd advise you to be sure the doors are locked at night."

I must have given him an odd look, because humanity broke in and he said quickly, "Oh, look, I don't really expect it to happen again, but it's just a matter of insurance. Be ready, and that'll take care of it. Of course if you want to take my nephew and flee, I don't blame you."

"No way, chum," I said. "As Robbie would say if I merely breathed a hint."

I couldn't tell what his reaction was. "Well, I'm off. Enjoy the holiday."

"You won't be here?" I inquired politely.

"No, we'll be filming the celebration in a small town in Manitoba."

He headed toward the ell door and I said after him, "Thank you again for a nice day yesterday."

"And for a perfectly splendid midnight, eh? Thank *you!*" He laughed, and was gone. Listening to the Jaguar driving out of the yard, I knew that I could not have mentioned Jamesy to him; Jamesy was one of *theirs*. Hector must have known who pushed him, and that would have to be enough, as long as Jamesy left me and Robbie alone.

Mrs. Archie and I picked wild strawberries that afternoon. She had invited us down for strawberry shortcake that night, so I helped her hull berries while we thirstily drank tea in Angus J.'s kitchen.

For the rest of the week we had a private strawberry festival. I helped Mrs. Archie pick for her jams and shortcakes and pies, and at home Robbie and I ate berries by the quart. I'd never had so many in my life, but I could never get tired of them. They were new to Robbie but he was hooked after the first taste. Wild strawberries are one of the ephemeral beauties of life.

On Saturday Mrs. Alec drove the twins and Robbie to Halifax to spend the holiday weekend with Rowan. Hector would make do with Bob Kendrum and Mrs. Archie to help with the chores.

Dominion Day was both cool and bright, and there was a picnic at the farm. In the past there'd been much more, when communities met for games and huge picnics and fireworks. But things had gotten quieter, and the older ones regretted this; they felt the children were being cheated too. I used to feel cheated myself when my father told about the big Fourth of July celebrations when he was a boy, and he'd envied the wholehearted involvement of his father's generation.

For the meal at the farm I baked two big sheet cakes, a molasses-spice recipe known in our family as "Mamie's Delight."

The crowd gathered around long plank tables under the apple trees. There were quite a few Brierbank people there, and friends and relatives from out of town. Someone had brought out a very old lady who was to visit at the farm for a few days. She sat in an armchair with her feet on a stool, smiling the whole time.

The children took turns on the swings, and the inevitable soccer ball appeared. Everybody looked delighted with the day and the company except Stuart, who wandered gloomily around, making an effort to be responsive when somebody tried to talk to him, but not doing well at it. Mrs. Stuart was as pretty and festive as a decorated birthday cake. You'd never have guessed that there was anything wrong. I began to wonder about her intelligence.

I ate with a married Brierbank couple my age, and the wife's bachelor brother, a Navy man who was fun in a quiet, deadpan way.

While we were clearing away before the desserts came on, Mrs. Gilbert Kendrum caught me alone at the back door. I was crushing down the paper plates and napkins in the trash can to make more room.

"I haven't forgotten the conversation at Alec's that Sunday night," she said. "Have *you* seen or heard anything in the Angus J. house?"

"Should I have?"

"When someone answers like that, I'm suspicious."

We both laughed. I said, "Let's say I've had some interesting dreams, but I think they're spun out of what I've been hearing and my own imagination. That's always given me some great spectaculars in living color."

"Just the same, our great-great-uncle Murray heard things, he always swore to it. I say 'our' because Gilbert and I are cousins."

"And Murray is Bob Kendrum's grandfather. Bob told me about some of the things." I was courteously wary.

"I'd like to get someone in there, a true psychic or a genuine medium."

"Is there any such thing?" I asked.

"I believe so. There are charlatans, of course, but I know there must be really gifted people who don't talk about it. They don't sell hope and consolation, they simply accept this gift as they do the color of their eyes, for instance."

"I suppose you're right," I said, giving the paper plates another strong shove. We talked about ESP for a while.

Finally she said, "I hope you're keeping a record of those dreams. If we ever should get anything from the house, it would be interesting to compare notes."

"Oh, I'm writing them all down," I assured her giddily. "I may want to write a costume novel some day. It'll be a combination of *Macbeth, Gone with the Wind,* and *Lady Chatterly's Lover.*"

"Speaking as a librarian, I can promise you've got a sure thing there." She was so nice, and I was afraid I'd been too flippant.

"I *am* keeping a record," I said, "because they seem pretty far-out even for me."

"*Good!*" she exclaimed, softly because Hector was bearing down on us. "Hello, Hector. Are you running around the popple tree to make room for wild strawberry pie?"

"It's more of a slow crawl," said Hector. "I've already tried your cake, Noel. I don't know who Mamie was, but I know why she was delighted."

"Where was the original poplar tree?" Mrs. Gilbert asked. "Or was there ever one?"

"On the front lawn of the old house," he said. "Big feller. Noel, Captain Angus used to tell the kids to go run around the popple tree to shake down their dinner."

"I wonder how far and wide that saying has gone," Mrs. Gilbert said. "So that poplar tree still exists, doesn't it? In a manner of speaking." She nodded at me as if she'd proved a point, and walked away.

"Does she mean we've got a ghost poplar tree to add to the other spooks?" Hector grinned. "Don't tell Bob. He'll be hearing the wind rustle through the leaves. Come on over and meet Aunt Helen. She's not really an aunt, she's a second cousin to Bob, and I'll be cussed if I can figure out what that makes her to *us*, but she's always been Aunt Helen."

Aunt Helen held my hand in both of hers. The grip of those delicate old fingers was surprisingly strong. "So you are staying in my great-grandfather's house," she said.

"You're going to come and see it, aren't you?" I asked.

The Kendrum eyes sparkled with youthful determination. "I most certainly am! I spent many a summer in that house when I was a little girl." Her voice was fragile, but not her mind. "In those days the sun always shone, the lambs and the calves were always little, the strawberries never stopped growing. And the cream was so thick and *yellow*." She laughed at herself. "I was a greedy-gut. Still am."

"That's why you're so hale and hearty, Helen," Hector told her. She looked up at him in a way that brought back for an instant the merry handsome girl she must have been.

"She was my first older woman," Bob Kendrum said.

"Dear Lord, yes," she sighed. "The summer I was trying to make an impression on the new minister—he was a bachelor, poor soul—I had this little shadow. I never could catch the Reverend alone. I'd have sold that imp to the gypsies if I could have managed it. Now I'm glad I didn't, Bob. I'd have missed you all these years."

"So would Christy." They laughed together, but I hadn't been passed by for shared memories.

She said suddenly to me. "You're writing up the genealogy, they tell me." Before I could say I was simply typing it, she tightened her grip on my hand.

"My grandfather remembered his great-grandmother Jeannie taking him on her knee and telling him about a castle, and a terrible battle. She said the battle was the end of things. . . . Afterward, when he was grown, he thought it must have been Culloden, and the castle must have been Strathcoran."

The picnic was going on, dogs barking, children shouting, a

cheerful gabble of voices all around, but none of it was in my world. I sat on a bench beside Bob, and Hector squatted on his heels with his back against an apple tree. They were listening with all their attention, but the words were for *me*, as if some bond of kinship existed between the old woman and myself, but only she and I knew it.

"And they crossed the sea," she said. "There was something about an island. When they left it, the heather was in bloom." I thought Bob Kendrum moved, but I didn't look around at him.

"The voyage was so frightening she thought it went on for a year and she'd never live through it. She was little. About five, she said. A boy was very sick, but he didn't die. The boat had a woman's name. Something like *Christine*, I think."

My hand must have communicated something to hers. She spoke in an odd, bemused voice, as if she were growing sleepy. Her eyes looked it.

"When they came into harbor, she thought it was Scotland again, but they didn't stay there. She cried because she didn't want to go on another vessel. She lay down on the ground and wouldn't move. Angus Mor picked her up and carried her aboard. He was a big strong boy. Almost a man."

His name touched me like a branding iron, burning the letters into my skin. Bob Kendrum said eagerly, "Where did they go next, Helen?"

But she had dozed off, as quickly as that. Bob looked cruelly disappointed, and I felt the same way. Hector stood up and stretched. "Sounds as if they landed one place and then went on to Georgia."

"But where?" Bob demanded irritably. "I never heard all this before! Of course Jeannie was gone before *my* grandfather came along, but you'd think somebody could have set it down on paper!"

"I wonder how much more there is," I said, watching her light breathing. "But you can't force it. It has to come by itself."

"And it may never come." Bob was gloomy. "Savannah,

Georgia, wouldn't look one damn bit like Scotland, even to a five-year-old. So where did they stop first?"

"What difference does it make?" Hector said. "They could have put in anywhere—Maine, maybe, or even up here in Cape Breton—and changed to another boat to sail down the coast. The thing is, they got to Georgia, they survived and grew up, and then they came to Nova Scotia. Come on, Bob, brace up. They're bringing out the strawberry pies and Mamie's Delight." He winked at me.

Christy came over to us. "What have you men done, talked Aunt Helen to sleep?" She fussed gently with the old lady's sweater and the blanket over her knees. "Noel, your cake's a real old-fashioned treat."

"Why, thank you!" I tried to beam ingenuously. "I'm looking forward to wild strawberry pie."

I had been, but not now. I couldn't have eaten. I said I was going into the house for a drink of water, but I kept right on going around the kitchen end of the house to the far side.

I sat down on the grass in the shade and stared out across the fields, trying to steady myself. Aunt Helen's story had confirmed what I already knew, that I was getting Angus Mor's story from Angus Mor himself.

I can't express the jubilation, the sense of wonder, and the humility that I felt because I had been the one chosen to receive. I think I'd have sat there under a spell for an hour if the geese hadn't discovered me and stood staring at me through the fence and talking about me. They made me laugh, which had the effect of restoring me to my diurnal personality.

I went back to the picnic and carried on through the rest of the day without letting my consciousness drift. I was becoming very well-disciplined in that.

I didn't leave the picnic until I was sure there was nothing else I could do to help out. Aunt Helen had gone to her room for a nap, and I knew I might never get anything more from her. When I returned to the quiet house, I wrote down her story at once in the section of my notebook allotted to word-of-mouth stories. It wasn't very thick. My section was much more rich and detailed. Anyone reading all this, I thought, would be sure I was writing a novel, or should be.

If it hadn't been for my absolutely reliable checkpoints I'd have been skeptical myself. As it was, I went again through all the family notes and Robert Kendrum's papers to see if I'd missed the name of a boat. Nowhere was there a vessel called *Kirsteen*.

"Something like *Christine*," Aunt Helen had said. And I'd known it already! I hugged myself for lack of anyone else to squeeze in my joy and triumph.

The other fact, less exciting but still mystifying, was the mention of two boats. Hector could have been right, but I had heard the phrase about an island, and I wondered now if they had been carried by a small boat from Strathcoran to some off-shore island, stayed a while, and then sailed on a larger boat to America. No wonder the first stop looked like Scotland to her— it was still Scotland.

But it wasn't likely that the boy Calum would have been so sick on such a short trip. That had to be on the long voyage. Jeannie's memories were blurred around the edges, or else the confusions had come in the handing down and passing on. But I was pretty positive about the stay on an island, because the battle of Culloden had taken place in April, and the heather didn't bloom until late summer.

They wouldn't have hung around the valley all that time, expecting a raid at any moment. Besides, I remembered standing in the cold wind out on that headland. It had felt and smelled like a Maine spring. If the heather was in bloom when they finally set out for America, the departure was from somewhere else, unless this was another mix-up in Jeannie's recollections. But Bob Kendrum had spoken about the heather too, and it could well be one of those small but true facts that somehow survive from generation to generation, while larger realities disappear or at best become fragmented or obscure.

25
CHAPTER

THE BOYS CAME home from Halifax Monday afternoon. According to Robbie the celebration had been spectacular, and besides that they'd not missed a thing worth seeing in the sister cities. I received a minutely detailed description because, he told me with generous condescension, I'd seen nothing at all that mattered on my one brief day in Halifax. "I know," I agreed humbly. "I want to go again."

"You'd better. So long." He'd taken to wearing a broad-brimmed straw hat Mrs. Archie had given him, and he took it and left. It seemed to me that he'd changed and grown even in the two days he'd been gone. One wouldn't think of him now as a small boy or even a smallish one. In a couple of years he'd be dating girls who would find those black-lashed gray Kendrum eyes irresistible. Already I pitied the losers.

More important, he had begun to emerge from his own conception of himself as a fatherless child, and to see himself as a potential man among men.

Mrs. Archie was bringing Aunt Helen up that afternoon, so I went back to setting the tea tray. I had certain nervous quiverings in my stomach, not that I was blatantly hoping for any revelations but my receiving system seemed to be tuning itself up regardless, just in case. Mrs. Archie never missed a thing; I only hoped I'd be able to keep my face and hands still. Not *too* still, but just expressive enough to be natural—

"Hey, Noel, I wanted to tell you something."

I dropped the spoons, and Robbie picked them up. "Wow, you were way off."

"Way *out* is more like it. I thought you were at the farm by now, hugging Billy Boy and scratching the pigs' backs."

He grinned. "Darn it, I promised to bring them all a present from Halifax, and I forgot! Look, the twins and I have this idea. The day before the Gathering we want to start up the river by canoe from Oquiddic Harbor, and re-create the famous journey, see?"

I gave him all my attention. "Go on."

"Of course, they had a couple of canoes and a lot of dunnage, their tools and grub and so forth. We'll have just one, our bed-rolls, and enough food for overnight. We'll camp at this place the kids know, then the next day we'll arrive down here where Angus Mor stopped and said, 'This is the place.' We'll time it so we get here right in the middle of the Gathering. How's that?"

For him it was so simple and so perfect that he could no longer contain his joy. Light seemed to shoot off him in all directions as from a prism. "Only a week away," he gloated. "Gosh, if this weather only holds. Aunt Priscilla says no dice if it's stormy."

"I suppose you three would just as soon start off in thunder, lightning, or in rain, to quote the witches in *Macbeth*."

He grinned. "'When shall we three meet again?' Surprised you, didn't I? Want to hear me do 'Is this a dagger that I see before me?'"

"I would love to," I said, "but let's get back to the trip. It's the kind of thing I'd like to do myself, but forgive me if I make responsible noises. Just how safe is it?"

"You've seen the river!" he said impatiently. "It's not the Wide Missouri, or the Colorado with all that white water and deep gorges! It's right close to the road in most places, for Pete's sake. And the twins have done it already."

"Listen, I'm on your side, but you'll have to let me off the hook. Mrs. Alec approves unless the weather's rotten, right?"

"Right!" he snapped.

"Then let me check with Hector, and that'll be it. Okay?"

"Well—" he began grudgingly.

I didn't give him time to dwell on it. "What's going to happen when you arrive? Anything special?"

"Rowan's organizing that. It's supposed to come as a complete surprise to the visitors."

"You wearing kilts?" I asked mischievously.

He looked horrified. "Are you *kidding?* They probably didn't wear kilts by then, anyway. Rowan wants to fix us up with something like old-timey britches and boots, but I think the canoe trip is enough."

"Which one are you going to be?"

"Well, Ross was born first, so he's Angus Mor, and Calum and I flipped a coin for Calum the First." He was very stiff around the mouth.

"And you got it!" I cried with enough fervor to make up for my earlier reservations.

"Yep. Calum lost the toss so he's Donald Muir. I offered to swap, but he's a good guy." He left, declaiming, "'The bell invites me. Hear it not, Duncan: for it is a knell that summons thee to heaven'"—his voice dropped a sepulchral octave—"'or to hell.'"

Mrs. Archie, Aunt Helen, and Mrs. Bob spent the afternoon with me. This time there were no messages from anyone's past but Aunt Helen's own, and I was relieved not to have to be on my guard. She reminisced about the life she had known in the house; she told us in detail where certain pieces of furniture had been placed; she recollected funny or sad tales. She peopled the house for us, crowding it with life. She called oxen and horses, dogs, even cats, by name. She and Christy got going on folk medicine, starting off with a joke about nanny-plum tea for measles, and I asked if I could write down some of these facts. They were both pleased and productive. They also praised my marmalade cookies.

"You fit in so well, Noel," Mrs. Archie told me when we

cleared the table. "Nobody knew what to expect, but the minute I laid eyes on you in the dooryard that day I said to myself, 'That girl is *all right!*'"

"Thank you," I said, actually blushing. "I feel as if I should shuffle my feet and say 'O shucks.' But hasn't it been a nice afternoon?"

"Yes, and there is something else to make it a good day. Len got a card from Jamesy. He's in St. John, and looking for work. Len was so pleased. I think she really worries, but with Stuart the way he is, if she gave over to it full time that household would fall apart."

I couldn't ask without being awkward, When did she get the card? When did he get to St. John? So I said, "Poor Stuart. It must be awful to be like that."

"Well, maybe if Jamesy gets a job in St. John, Stuart'll stop fussing about him. Out of sight should be out of mind. If that sounds hard-hearted, it probably is."

"Everybody knows you've got a heart of marble," I said.

Robbie and I went to the farm after supper to watch a special on Newfoundland, and Hector assured me that the canoe trip was perfectly safe. We had cake and tea afterward, and came home amiable and sleepy. I'd read only a few pages before I was too drowsy to go on.

I was aroused by voices and in my foggy state I thought somebody had come in downstairs, though I'd been obediently locking doors. But Angus could be back, bringing someone with him. One of his ladies. My mind cleared rapidly. Maybe even the ex-lady with the air of careless power. Some nerve! Even if it's his house, I thought, it's *my* kitchen while I'm here.

"You can't do it," a woman said. With those four words and the way they were spoken, I knew at once where they came from, though I didn't know the speaker.

"Why can't I?" a man asked. "Don't you think I love her

enough? When I was a boy she was like my little sister. Now she's a woman, and I love her."

"I didn't raise her for *that*," the woman answered bleakly.

"Oh? And did you raise her to be the Widow MacDonald at twenty-three and remain so all the rest of her days?" The heat of his anger scorched me.

"She'll have plenty of chances," the woman said. "She'd have married again, and well, long before this, if it wasn't for you. God knows she adores you. She always has, and it's been a worry and a fear to me ever since she started to grow up with no eyes for another soul in the world but you."

He said harshly, "So you pushed her into young MacDonald's arms."

"He was a good boy. She'd have grown to love him in time, if he'd lived. Do you mind how she wept when he died?"

"For pity. We all felt it, remember. Give over, Annie. I'm about to claim my Jeannie."

"*No.*" Her stoniness was that of complete dedication to a cause, no matter how grim. "I pray to St. Bride to rid her heart of you, because if she doesn't it will be a hard life for Jeannie to keep another man's house, sleep in his bed, and bear his children. And she's so proud she may choose loneliness, and that will be worse. A woman may not love her husband, but if she has children from him that's better than loneliness."

"Annie my darling, you would condemn us both to loneliness for the rest of our lives. And why, woman? Tell me *why.*"

"Because when you go back, how could she take her place as your wife?" she cried passionately. "It's one thing to be a farm wife here, milking the cows, making cheese and butter, spinning the flax and the wool. As long as you're a farmer, she'd be useful to you, and give you sturdy children besides. But when you go back—oh no, Angus," she mourned, "it could break both your hearts before you're done."

"*Go back!*" he exploded. "In the name of St. Bride, go back *where?* To *what?*"

"I didn't rear you to curse like that, my boy!"

"I didn't curse." His dangerous patience reminded me of someone else. "I'm calling on your adored saint to make all things clear to me."

"It should be clear enough, even to a thick-skulled Kendrum. My daughter wasn't born to be the Countess of Strathcoran."

If he'd exploded a moment ago, his pause now was like the ear-ringing silence that follows the explosion. I lay holding to the sides of my mattress, stiff with anticipation. Finally he spoke, very gently.

"I am a farmer in Nova Scotia. The fourth Earl of Strathcoran died at Culloden, his sons died of a lung fever, and if his wife had a boy in her belly nineteen years ago, he is the fifth Earl. If it was a girl, or didn't survive, the title went to Patrick Kendrum of that Ilk, who had the good sense to sell his soul to George the Second."

"If you went back," she said stubbornly, "you have the proof to unseat him. If Strathcoran means nothing to you, why did you risk your neck searching for it when her men could have ridden in at any minute and put a sword through you on the spot? You'd have gotten us all murdered, Angus James Chisholm Kendrum." Her laughter crackled with a scornful challenge. "And you say you don't *care!* "

"I went back because it was mine, and I was a child who thought possession was important. I couldn't take his sword, but I could take that. And I believed then that some day I *would* go back, and put a dirk to that long white throat of hers."

He didn't have to say the name. I knew it already, by the hatred I could almost taste. *Frances.*

He laughed suddenly. "One day I shall sell it to build my Jeannie a finer house, or to educate our children."

She whispered, "You could not. You would not."

"Wouldn't I? It's no holy relic. I don't want what it proves. While I breathe I fight, and now I'm fighting for my Jeannie. It's not the Earl asking; it's a Canadian farmer *taking.*"

After that there was no answer, only the clock striking a half-hour downstairs, and a little breeze making a slight noise through the screens and fluttering the curtains. *Bob will be hearing the wind blowing through the leaves.*

That sentence drifted across my mind like a free-floating luminous object. I hadn't heard the rustle of long-gone poplar leaves, but I had just heard the fifth Earl of Strathcoran renounce his heritage.

I carefully loosened my grip on the sides of the mattress, took a few deep breaths, half-expecting the top of my head to come off, and sat up. My reaction was far different from anything I had felt so far. The session had been too profound to produce ordinary chills and associated dithers.

The first thing I thought of, very slowly but with great clarity, was that I must write it all down while it was fresh. The second was regret that I couldn't tell it. I believed it, but I couldn't expect anyone else to see me as anything but an addled and hysterical young female. Bob Kendrum might go along with it, but even Mrs. Gilbert from Truro, for all her interest in ESP and psychic influences, wasn't likely to fall for this romantic plot. By the time I'd written it out, I was a little doubtful myself. I told myself brutally that I might have discovered a form of self-hypnosis that could make me a fortune as a writer of Gothics.

After I'd set it all down, I couldn't relax. I kept thinking about the proof-object. I knew all about the search for it, and that he'd carried it around his neck in a deerskin bag. But the not-knowing what it was and what had become of it was tormenting me. I'd discard one fancy for another, toss the whole subject away from me in exasperation, and turn around to collide with a fresh and stunning impact against the fact that the family myth was a truth kept secret for over two hundred years.

And I couldn't tell anybody.

Food always helps. I went downstairs and made tea, and had toast with some of Mrs. Archie's new strawberry jam. Afterward I put out the light, pulled a rocker over to the front windows, and sat with my feet braced against the sill and tried to think.

I believed—no, I knew—that Angus Mor was returning over and over again and I was reading his mind. The telepathy had begun the night I was as far away from here as Sussex, and it had probably been an accident.

I was sure that he wasn't aware of me, it was as if I were a captive eavesdropper. But I was aware of him as I'd never been aware of any man in my life. I didn't care now if I couldn't tell about him.

I didn't want to tell. I wouldn't take a chance on tarnishing it by having to defend it. But he would be with me for the rest of my life.

I knew that without fever or neurotic excitement. It was an element like wind, earth, fire, and water. Coolly I reviewed the occasions when I heard him pacing. I knew now that each time I'd heard it, something violent had happened afterward, either here in fact or in his memories. So, clearly, in the case of what was going on here, he was reading someone else's mind. If I heard him pacing again, what would I do? Whom could I warn?

Again there was that prospective barrier of ridicule, alarm, or pity.

If only I could reach him so he could tell me who was in danger. Why can't I? I demanded greedily. Why can't I have the satisfaction of knowing that we have done the incredible, touched hands across two centuries?

I hugged myself in my robe, squeezed my eyes shut, and called him in my head, but I knew it was only a gesture. The time was not now. It would come as everything else had come, when it was least expected.

This knowledge was as calming as a hand stroking my head and the side of my face. Keeping my eyes shut I imagined that hand, strong, dry, and warm, stroking and soothing.

I am not asking but taking.

After a time it wasn't hard to keep my eyes shut, my lids were so heavy. I hated to leave this lovely trance to go up to bed, but I'd be cramped and cold before morning. It was all right, I knew I'd sleep now.

26
CHAPTER

I FELT VERY WEARY in the morning. Robbie had gone for a day's haying, and I got into the car and drove toward Oquiddic Harbor. I took another good look at the river whenever it was visible, which was most of the time. As Robbie said, it wasn't the Wide Missouri, or the Colorado, all white water tearing through deep gorges. In the uninhabited areas the narrow stream shimmered quietly along, and at other places there were little settlements of houses. The boys could camp just about anywhere with perfect safety, as far as I could see.

I left the highway on which Angus had driven us home from Halifax that day, and went off along a shore road until I came to a long white sand beach with seas glittering and breaking under the morning wind. I parked on worn turf beside the road and began to walk. Around the farthest point of the sand beach there began a rugged shore of all sea-polished rocks that rolled under my feet, while the sound of surf beat against my eardrums and sometimes the spray flew into my face. I met only a pair of golden retrievers and their middle-aged people, all equally amiable.

The salt wind scoured my cheeks and tore at my hair. The thought of the old house deep in the country, the warm moist heat rising from the ground, the serene river flowing among wooded or flowering banks, suffocated me. I saw myself as this haunted girl roving through the nights without sleep, and I didn't want to go back to her and her feverish schizophrenia.

From this distance I could clearly see the Other One, though she, in her night world, couldn't see me.

What was happening to me in that house? My joyous belief and commitment now appeared to me as the burgeoning symptoms of a deadly virus that lies dormant in the body for years and then suddenly reveals itself.

I was frightened and revolted, I wanted to run, but I couldn't run away from my brain. Angus Mor had changed, as quickly as this, from hero to monster; a figure of nightmare and I had created it.

Oh, the poor man! I thought. He'd be turning over in his grave if he knew what I'd made of him! I tried to joke the truth away, as if that would prove me sane beyond question. But it was gallows humor.

I had to go back finally. I was as dry as the highest-flung driftwood, freshly burned with both sun and wind, and tired from keeping my balance on steep slopes of shifting stones. I was hungry and thirsty, and that was reassuring. Surely if I were losing touch with reality I wouldn't care if I ate or drank.

At a crossroads there was a small supermarket, if that isn't a contradiction in terms, and I bought a chilled can of ginger ale and some wheat crackers. Feeling more earthy all the time, I picked out the ingredients for a spaghetti sauce and green salad.

I had my mug-up as I drove along. Going through Muir's Grant I recognized houses, bridges, even particular cows and horses, and I began gradually to shed the revulsion I'd known back on the shore. At the turn-off to Brierbank Corner I met a tractor driven by a man who'd been at the holiday picnic, and we waved. After that I reached my own road with a rather nice sense of returning home.

I decided I wasn't going mad, but that I should talk to some reliable researcher about the experiences. Yet it wouldn't be right not to tell the Kendrums first, and I didn't want to risk their reactions. I didn't want to see the change in their eyes and hear it in their voices. I wanted to remain the Noel Paige they'd liked and accepted, not the one I'd glimpsed from the distant shore.

"You don't have to make up your mind now," I said as I drove over the culvert where the brook ran. I waved to the cows. "Live one day at a time. Or rather one night at a time."

I came to the end of the pines thinking determinedly about a swim in the river and then a good lunch with a large pot of tea.

We had spaghetti that night. Robbie told me that I was a super saucemaker, and handsomely invited me to attend a soccer game in the schoolyard. I missed Rowan's company, but I sat on the doorstep with the minister and his wife, an elderly couple who were so nice I felt ashamed of not having gone to church. They were semi-retired after many years in a big city parish, and it occurred to me that Mr. Barry must surely have met some odd characters in his work, including psychics, and so he might be someone to whom I could turn.

Just the possibility of it was comforting. It made me feel as if I were in complete control of myself. Someone who was really freaking out wouldn't be thinking reasonably like this.

No. There was nothing the matter with me except cowardice; I was trying to scare myself into backing off from a superb adventure. Sitting there on the school steps, applauding the players, I made up my mind to take all I could get. If I rejected this chance, I would regret it for the rest of my life.

I went to bed that night neither expecting nor rejecting, and I went to sleep. I roused once, thinking I heard the pacing, but I wasn't sure of it. Usually I snapped awake as if someone had flipped a switch in my brain, but after the heights and the depths of the last twenty-four hours I was like someone drugged. I thought drunkenly, What happens, happens. And sank again.

The morning was dark, foggy, and cool, and I slept until almost eight. I hurried into a warm jersey and slacks, planning to build a fire. But when I went out into the hall, there was the tang of an applewood fire already in progress. From the bathroom window I saw the Jaguar in the yard. I recollected dimly the footsteps, and guessed that I must have heard Angus coming in. He wasn't in the kitchen but was whistling something brisk and jiggish in the ell. "Good morning!" I sang out cheerily. "Thanks for the fire and the coffee!"

"Enjoy, enjoy!" he called back, but he didn't come in. I made a juvenile grimace at the door, thinking, I don't want you to come in *anyway*. I toasted thick slices of bread on top of the wood stove. Angus's typewriter began, tentative at first and then gathering confidence and speed. I moved into a rocker and propped my feet on the stove hearth, and ate my breakfast. If you knew what I know, my boy, I thought smugly, you wouldn't be able to keep away from me.

But of course he would. At best he'd cock his head and listen tolerantly, while wondering how to get me out of here fast. He might be disturbed for a few minutes, or even a little regretful, but that was all. Angus hadn't fallen for me. He was charming because that was how he'd always managed people, ever since he was small, and in his line of work an effortless charm was as priceless as talent or unlimited money. He *liked* me, but then he liked almost everybody, and I was just one of the crowd. If I told him what I knew, I'd be instantly separated from the crowd — oh, I'd be a standout, all right — but for only as long as it took to ease me offstage forever.

I sighed. I didn't know why. But the sound was a lonely one in the quiet kitchen. I *was* lonely. Not for Angus, surely not for Micah, but for myself. . . . I think I might have gone on then to discover why, as inevitably as the compass needle swings north, if I'd been brave enough to follow where that trembling needle pointed. But Stuart's truck drove into the yard, and I was saved.

When the truck door slammed, the typing stopped next door, and I heard Angus go out and hail his brother. In a few minutes they came into the ell, and Angus knocked on the kitchen door.

"Any more coffee in there?"

"Yep!" I called back. "And I can make even more." I got up

and put another stick of wood in the stove, and pushed the coffee pot and the teakettle forward. The men came in. Angus's hair was rumpled as if he'd been running his hands through it, but he managed to look elegant even in jeans and a rugger shirt.

Stuart was rumpled but in a different fashion, as if he hadn't combed his hair when he got up or bothered to shave. The start of his beard and the blackness of his eyebrows emphasized his pallor. Aplastic anemia, leukemia—I wouldn't look at Angus in case he was thinking the same thing and neither of us could hide it from the other.

Stuart was bundled up too, as if it were really cold. He even had a scarf on. "Temperature changes gave me a sore throat," he said in a restrained and oddly apologetic voice. "It'll do it every time."

"Sit by the fire, Stuart," I said, "and I'll get some cups."

"Mine's on my desk." Angus went to the ell to get it, and brought back a bottle of whiskey. "How about lacing your coffee with this, Stuart?" he asked. "Warm up your bones."

Stuart waved the bottle away. He refused cream too, and took a gulp of coffee so hot that just to watch him swallow made me wince. Then he sat back, unzipped his jacket, and loosened the scarf. "Thanks," he said, looking straight ahead. "Well, I guess I'd better tell you about it."

"You don't need me," I said. I added more coffee to my cup and started for the stairs with it.

"You can stay," Stuart said surprisingly. "It's nothing personal. Not the way you think." He sounded as if his throat hurt very much, and he took another mouthful of hot coffee. I came slowly back. Angus sat at the table with his arms folded on the edge, his face serious and attentive.

"I was mugged last night," Stuart said. At our expressions he burst into harsh, painful laughter. "Progress comes to Brierbank."

"For God's sake!" Angus was on his feet. "What do you mean, *mugged?*"

"Ambushed. Bushwhacked." He drank again, and tenderly stroked his throat. "Len and the kids have gone to Kingston to visit her sister for a few days. I had supper at the Manse, and we talked over the work to be done inside the church." His voice faded to a strained whisper, he took another drink, and I refilled his cup. "I came home around ten, put the car away, and when I came out of the garage somebody jumped me from behind and jammed an arm across my windpipe."

I *had* heard the pacing, then. The warning.

Angus was staring down at his brother as if he'd never seen him before. Stuart went on. "I don't know how I got away from him, to tell you the truth. You feel so damned helpless in a grip like that. I threw myself around to beat hell, got my hand behind me reaching for anything I could grab—" His eyes shifted toward me and then back to Angus. "Kicked behind me too. Made contact, maybe with his shin or his ankle bone. Anyway, he lost his grip just in time. I was starting to black out."

"*Good Christ*," Angus whispered. I sat down unsteadily on the nearest chair and laced clammy fingers together.

"I don't know what came next. Maybe I did black out for a few minutes. A car went by, which might have scared him off. I don't know which way he ran, my ears were roaring so I swear I couldn't hear anything for ten minutes afterward. I picked myself up finally and went into the house. Got my shotgun and loaded it, and then had a good stiff drink."

"Did you call the Mounties?"

"What good would that do? He was gone. Maybe the car that went by was his chum's, coming to pick him up."

"Why you, I wonder?"

Stuart shrugged. "With them all on drugs these days, they don't have to have a reason. They could have been prowling around in the dark, half-stoned. Isn't that what they call it?" He gave Angus an ironic grin. "You're the expert."

"We won't debate that right now." Angus's tone was dry. "You think they were hanging around your place, maybe with an eye to breaking in, and then you came home, so—" He slashed a finger across his throat.

"Could be somebody Jamesy's met on his travels," Stuart said broodingly.

"Oh, come on now, Jamesy wouldn't set them on you."

"I didn't say that," he answered irritably. "But if he told them about his home town they likely saw it as a nice little plum ripe for the picking." He shrugged. "I found my billfold empty at the end of my driveway this morning."

"Nice of them to leave you that. Did you have much in it?"

"Fifty-six dollars." Stuart drank as if he were through with talking.

"It ought to be reported," Angus said.

"What could I tell? No more than I've told you."

"They might find something they could go on. They're the experts."

Stuart made a sound that could have been a snort of disgust or a cynical chuckle. I looked past the back of his head at Angus and shaped the words, *You wouldn't call them either.*

Go fly a kite, his expression said.

"Did you get any sleep last night?" he asked Stuart.

"Not till it was coming daylight."

"You should have slept late, then, not come over here."

Stuart roused up angrily. "What was I going to do with myself? There's a drawer downstairs I'm not satisfied with, and I'll tend to that, and then I'll be finished here." He got up. "Thanks for the coffee," he said in my direction, without actually looking at me.

"Oh, you're welcome. Your brother made it."

He went out by way of the ell, and Angus followed him. I heard the bulkhead doors being opened, and when I took the cups to the pantry, Angus was talking below me, his voice raised as if Stuart was across the cellar from him.

"Have you seen the cooper's adz I found in that old tea chest? It has to be Angus Mor's."

Stuart's answer was indistinct.

"Well, it's from his time," Angus defended himself. "Oh, it could be the Captain's, I suppose."

Stuart began to plane the drawer that didn't suit him, and he was only a few minutes getting it right. They came up the outside steps, and Angus watched Stuart drive out of the yard. Then he returned to the kitchen.

"Crime Wave Hits Brierbank," he said morosely. "Obscene, isn't it?"

"The crime wave could be the same man," I suggested. "The one who tried to get you. Is there any place where a man could hide? He'd be pretty safe if he only moved out after dark. Most people go to bed early around here."

"Or watch late shows on TV," he said. "Some of them are so hypnotized they wouldn't hear the church bell ringing in the end of the world. So I suppose somebody could be camping out in an empty barn."

"Like the one over on the Bain Place, where Hector fell that day. That has its own road in, and everything."

He creased his lower lip and pulled at it. "Maybe the word ought to be passed around. We don't have to scare people by telling what's actually happened, but any empty place ought to be checked out. And how to get that over without blowing it will occupy the rest of my day. In the meantime, let's you and I check out the Bain Place."

We separated to get jackets. He snapped the padlock on the bulkhead doors, and we drove out. I was glad to get away from the house, even on such an errand. I was so wrought up about the pacing I could hardly think of anything else.

"I wonder if you're psychic," Angus said suddenly.

I jumped. "*Why?*"

"Don't leap at me, dear heart. It's about this barn; what if you're right?"

"I mentioned this barn for the perfectly logical reason that it's the only empty one I know about, and Rowan and I were there a short while back."

"Don't be huffy. If you were psychic it wouldn't automatically turn you into an Untouchable. Logic, on the other hand, can be very depressing when it's used by a good-looking woman to flatten my widely romantic nature."

"Your widely romantic *Highland* nature."

"That's right. Two centuries of Canadian ancestors haven't stopped me from being a true Gael. So if you had second sight I'd consider you an honorary member of the clan."

"Thank you," I said. "For lost opportunities, and vanished hopes."

He laughed. We went through the Corner, quiet in the foggy morning, up the hill past the church and the Manse, and then turned off onto the old road. The Jaguar moved quietly and smoothly toward the clearing. Fog floated in gauze streamers through the trees, smelling of the distant sea. Birds had the place to themselves till we came, and the river was like black glass. The old boards on the barn were dark with wet.

"At the risk of looking foolish—" Angus took a small automatic from the console. "I told you I had one, remember. You stay in the car."

"I will not."

"Then keep behind me. This is the most banal dialogue. I'm feeling sillier by the second."

Feeling rather silly myself, I kept meekly behind him. We went around to the single door at the back. The silvery wet grasses looked undisturbed, but I never take anything for granted. Angus opened the door. The rusty latch crunched and grated, and the dim essence of past use came warmly out to us.

"Anybody here?" Angus called. There was the hollow silence of vacancy. We went in past the stalls. The stairs were there in the corner, as I'd imagined them.

We went all through the barn, into every odd corner, and found no trace anywhere of recent occupancy.

"Well," Angus said finally, out on the main floor, "I'll put this thing away. I'm glad nobody saw us creeping around with catlike tread."

"So you see, I'm not psychic," I said. "I'm sorry."

"The hell you are." He grinned, and patted me on the back. "But you're brave."

"Yes," I said, making a quick decision, "because I'm going to say something that you probably won't like." If I waited for a reaction to that opening statement I might not go ahead, so I didn't wait.

"Look at the ladder," I said.

He glanced at it, and back at me, mystified. "What about it?"

"Hector said a couple of rungs gave way under him."

"He must have come back and repaired it, or hired Jared to do it."

"Angus, there aren't any new rungs there! You can see for yourself. It looked just like that the day Hector fell. Right *after* he fell."

"Do you say Hector lied?"

"If he did, it was for a purpose, to protect someone. I think he was pushed off the edge of the hayloft." Instinctively we both looked up at the loft. I had all my courage now, and hurried to get everything said before I lost it. "And I think he was too shaken up by the shove and the fall and our coming upon him as we did to realize that we could see for ourselves the ladder was intact. As it happened, I was the only one who saw it, and I've never mentioned it until now."

"Why the silence, and why break it now?" Was he inimical? I wondered.

"Jamesy came through here ahead of Rowan and me that day. We were up at the farmhouse when he showed up, and when he saw us he rushed back to his bike and tore off down the track into the woods. He must have been furious—badly upset, anyway—to see us there, and he was already mad with Hector. It was the day after he rode his bike round and round in the new corn and then tried to leap the river like Evel Knievel."

"So you think he shoved Hector off the edge of the hayloft."

"I think it could have happened that way," I said quietly. "He could have roared by, parked the bike, and sneaked back. The next day, Sunday, we heard he'd left Brierbank. And now I wonder if he's back."

"And if he jumped his father last night." Angus spoke so stiffly that I thought I had offended him beyond apology. Dismay nauseated me but it was too late now. I had to go through to the end.

"And if he jumped you last week." Without thinking I gripped Angus's arm with both hands. "Angus, it's an awful thing to mention, and I know I've got no business to."

He put his free hand over mine and squeezed it. "Yes, you have a right. You're staying in my house where you could be endangered, and you saved me from being suffocated with a pillow. You also have a responsibility for young Robert. But Jamesy! Good God! Here, let's sit down."

The boys had made a bench of a thick plank laid across two nail kegs, and we sat there in the dim silence of the barn.

"If you're right," he said, "do you think Stuart knows, or guesses?" He shook his head hard as if in violent repudiation of the whole idea. "Jamesy was always a nice kid. Not a mean bone in him, I'd say. Good with animals. If you'd ever seen him beaming over a newborn foal, you'd know an entirely different Jamesy from the one you've seen."

"Look, I haven't seen him as a *killer*, for heaven's sake! But if he's happy around horses he doesn't seem to be happy anywhere else. You know as well as I do what drugs can do to somebody with a lot of grudges boiling around inside. *If* he's into drugs," I added pointedly. "If he isn't, then—" I didn't know what to say.

"I'm glad you added those two big ifs. I know anyone can love animals and hate human beings, but I'd think Jamesy's style is rampaging through a cornfield on his motorbike rather than physical assault. And supposing he does have a grudge against his father—which we all know he has, Stuart being damned hard to live with—and against Hector because he thinks Hector got Basil to fire him. What has he got against *me?*" Angus sounded bewildered. "I always liked him, and I thought he liked me."

"I don't know," I said inadequately.

"Of course if he's turned against the whole family on general principles, I'd be counted in with the rest. Maybe that's it. But whoever rammed that pillow over my face meant to kill me, and Jamesy would have to be far gone to do that." He couldn't keep still; he sprang up and began walking the barn floor. "It's one hell of a situation, Noel, if it's so, and it damn well could be."

I sat chilly and silent on the plank bench. Angus resumed his walking. "The shot fired at the pickup that day could have wiped out Hector and the three boys. Stuart was nervous, remember. He suspected Jamesy."

I hugged myself, less from cold than to stop a convulsive shudder. "Maybe I should take Robbie away," I said. "I don't know how I'll explain it to him, but—"

He stood over me and put his hands hard on my shoulders to hold me down, as if I were about to take flight. "Listen, there has to be a reasonable explanation, a way out of this nightmare. There I go using clichés again. It must be true that in an emergency nobody says anything original." He smiled, but the charm was lost on me.

"I have to take the proper steps if I know Robbie's in danger."

"You don't know that *he's* in danger. What I want is to lay my hands on Jamesy and shake a few hard facts loose. If he's really freaked out I want him in a hospital, and fast." He sat down beside me and put a companionable arm around my shoulders. I didn't object, I even began to think reasonably again, though the panic was still bobbing around in my head like a bright rubber ball in the surf.

"Hector says Mr. Hammond's nephew quit and went back to St. John. If you can find out where he lives, maybe you could find out something about Jamesy through him. Maybe he *was* here last night, but he's really gone away now."

"You are such a bright girl, Noel."

"Don't make it sound like an insult."

"Who's insulting?" He began to sing. "'Oh, Noel! Sing Noel! And merry be alway, for Noel's here and she's a dear, on this damp nasty day.' How's that?"

"The poetry part is awful."

"I admit it needs work. But can Micah Jenkins write poems? Can he sing them?"

"He doesn't have to. He needs only to stand at the wheel and *be* a poem."

"He sounds insufferable."

"Objectively speaking, he is. But I never claimed to be objective. . . . I like your melody for the 'Boat Song.' Rowan sang it for me."

"Oh, that." He showed embarrassment for the first time since I'd met him. "Look, I've come up with something. If this were a suspense novel, it would be the perfect solution."

"What?"

"Angus Mor was really the Earl's heir, and the Impostor has hired a secret agent to wipe out all the legitimate claimants."

I was happy to go along with him, keeping my secrets locked away in their special vault. "All right, who's the agent? Either he's invisible, or he's someone we know and trust. But look, wouldn't there be hundreds of claimants by now?"

"Of course not. It's the eldest son each time, and it so happens that the eldest sons have survived in a direct line from Angus Mor to Hector, who's the only bachelor in the bunch. So his brothers and their sons would follow him, I suppose, but I'm not sure of the order of succession."

"In a classic story, the killer would be the milkman or the postman, but you don't have those in Brierbank. . . . How much claim would anyone have after all these years, anyway?"

He shrugged. "I don't know. None, probably. But this is our book, so we can have it any way we want. Let's skip the details and go on to the finale. The castle of Strathcoran is blazing with a thousand candles; we've got kilts, claymores, bagpipes—"

"Secret documents!" I tossed in. "Duels on the stairs!"

"A skeleton in a chest! Dirks in the gut!"

It was fun. We threw in everything we could think of, and for me it was like calling for madder music and for stronger wine, only to be confronted by reality in the midst of it. *There fell thy shadow, Cynara; the night was thine.*

In this case it wasn't Micah Jenkins's shadow, but the conviction that I should take Robbie away. And, in opposition, the force of my rebellion against leaving Angus Mor.

27
CHAPTER

I INVITED ANGUS to lunch, but in spite of all the foolishness at the barn he was obviously a very worried man, and he didn't want to take time out to eat. He wanted to drive around to Stuart's and check up on his brother, and he wanted to talk with Basil Hammond about the nephew's whereabouts.

"I'm going to see Hector too," he told me. "If he was shoved, he knows it, and he must have some idea *who*." Abruptly he pulled me to him and kissed me on the forehead as if I were a favorite—and very young—niece.

"You're a good girl," he said, carrying the illusion further. It wasn't exactly flattering.

"I can't help feeling I'm the unwelcome catalyst," I said. That sounded mature.

He shook his head, scowling. "How? Why? No, you just happened to arrive at the point where something was about to snap. Well, I'm leaving. Cheerio." He was gone that quick, and I wondered uncharitably if he had worked up these lightning disappearances as a part of his act, but my sneer was brief and superficial. The situation was too alarming for even the briefest of snide remarks.

I made a sandwich and coffee for my lunch but I hadn't much appetite. The silence and the fog, different from that along the seacoast, began to get to me; the Corner seemed a hundred miles away, the farm equally as far. I thought, I could be murdered right now in this house and nobody would know anything about it until Robbie came home tonight.

The house felt so peculiarly empty one could hardly believe it was ever noisily full of activity; as I'd realized before, no one could be as completely *absent* as Angus Mor.

"Oh, damn and blast!" I finally shouted, and that broke the spell. I did check on all the doors, though, and then settled down to work on the project. By now Angus might have already located Jamesy, or was close on his trail, and he would be able to talk his nephew into having treatment for his drug addiction and associated problems. Everything would turn out all right, if only Angus could catch up with him before he tried something else. If he hadn't succeeded in severely damaging his uncles and his father, what about the boys, all slighter and younger than himself, and unsuspecting?

Fear for Robbie almost brought back my megrims, but I reminded myself that he was safe with Hector today, and he would be safe with me tonight if I had to sit up all night with an ax. This picture of me, glaring and embattled, struck me funny, and I laughed aloud, and after that I was all right. I didn't want to go back to Fremont yet; I didn't want to go back and look at Micah Jenkins. I loved Brierbank, the whole gentle countryside, the broad low valley running to the sea. I liked all the Kendrums. I'd even like Stuart if he'd let me.

And then there was Angus Mor.

The crew couldn't hay in the fog, so Hector had put the boys to work cleaning out an old henhouse. Robbie headed straight for the shower when he came home, then gave me a detailed description of his day. I can't say that it was the most fascinating subject in the world, but he was so proud of his developing muscles and his blisters that I would have happily listened for hours. I was saved from that because we were invited back to the farm that night to watch a special movie and have homemade ice cream.

I hated to leave, because Angus might come back with some news; and if he didn't, I wasn't crazy about returning to an empty house. Stuart hadn't said anything about losing his keys,

but what if he had, and didn't want to alarm me? I knew he had
one to the bulkhead padlock. Supposing somebody else had it
now? A mad Jamesy hiding out until after dark?

Crazily I considered loading all the downstairs furniture over
the trapdoor in the hall, but how could I explain that to Robbie?
Keeping secrets in a crisis like this one was a rather hideous part
of the crisis.

In the end I just trusted to luck. I couldn't let Robbie go
biking off alone under the circumstances; it would be all right at
sundown but not after dark, on the return. When I locked the
back door behind us Robbie laughed and said, "You scared of the
bogey man?"

"Your Uncle Angus is afraid somebody might drive off with
all his antiques."

"Around *here?*" he asked incredulously.

"Listen, Robbie, it's a big business, and the more isolated the
place the better. This place is worth a fortune because of the
family things he's collected. Even the old tools in the cellar are
worth plenty."

"No kidding," he said in mild wonder.

We had a pleasant evening with Hector and Mrs. Archie,
Bob and Christy. If Hector had anything on his mind, he didn't
show it, and I wondered if Angus had talked to him at all today. I
didn't dwell on it, and I was glad I'd come out with Robbie.
Everything began to feel more normal, and it wasn't until we
drove up the rise and around the barn that I began to be apprehensive again. The Jaguar wasn't there, and I realized how much I'd
been hoping to see it, and for a light to be shining either from the ell
or the kitchen.

My dear girl, I thought, what if it's all *Angus?* He was in
Brierbank each time something happened. He could have faked
the attack on himself and his reactions afterward. So maybe
you're better off without him in the house.

This gave me a nasty jolt in the midriff, and the cake and ice
cream threatened to rise up, but I wouldn't give in. You imbe-
cile, I told myself, use common sense.

The fog had gone away before a brisk, drying northwest wind, and the stars were bright over the wooded hill and the windbreak pines; in their light the Angus J. house faintly gleamed, stolidly foursquare to the compass, keeping its secrets to itself. The bulkhead padlock was still locked, which didn't mean someone couldn't have gone in that way and then nipped out through a house door and fastened it again. The back door was still locked, which could have been done from the inside. But once we were in and had switched on some lights, I knew instantly that no one was there.

"Boy, what a neat day," Robbie said contentedly. He went straight to bed. I took a long warm bath in the hopes of falling asleep fast and not waking until daylight. The fact that I wasn't eager for any visitation that night should prove that I wasn't bringing it all on myself, but it was no proof for anyone else. And I wasn't going to put it to the test for a good long time yet, even with that reliable hard-headed researcher. The very thought of it triggered the visceral desire to cherish, to protect, to hide a beloved illegitimate child.

Or a secret love affair that never should have happened.

After the strain of the day, and the long bath, I thought I was tired enough to sleep with no lingering in the hypnogogic twilight. . . . *And dreaming through the twilight that doth not rise nor set.* . . . Now where did *that* swim up from? Christina Rossetti. Something about remembering and forgetting. And that other line of hers that was written on my heart when I was fifteen: *Life and the world and mine own self are changed/For a dream's sake.* Then it referred to the summer boy who was like quicksilver on a tennis court, and was hardly ever seen without a covey of girls. A prototype of Micah Jenkins.

And now it meant, or should mean, nothing at all. But it stayed in my mind like the odd jingles and isolated musical phrases that won't quit. It began to take on a deep and dreadful significance, far from the blissful melancholy it once had.

"Oh *hell!*" I muttered, bouncing up in bed. "You *chump!* You down-east chowderhead! Get up and do some work!"

But I didn't want to type in the middle of the night, and my body was tired even if my mind wouldn't rest. I lay back, practiced deep breathing, and tried to remember good, safe, unsexy poems I'd had to learn by heart in the lower grades. "The Landing of the Pilgrims" did it finally; at least I remember starting out, getting stuck, rummaging around for lost phrases, and never getting to the end of it.

I was sinking into sleep when somebody spoke.

"My darling."

"Yes," I murmured.

"Heartling of my heart."

"My Angus."

It was someone else who answered, not me. I woke all the way, embarrassed, afire with the shame of my mistake, and scaldingly hurt.

"I wish I could have carried white heather," she said. "You mind the place where it grows at home?"

"Home is here, Jeannie my darling."

"Yes, with you. But I couldn't get the white heather out of my head. That I should have been carrying it to the kirk."

"How do you know about the white heather? How can you remember?"

"Calum kept it in my mind. He used to tell me stories by the hour—I *know*, Angus. I've always known. And I hope your stepmother will burn in hell forever."

"Calum always talked too much. If he was within reach now I'd take him by the neck and shake his wits loose."

"You wouldn't. He was just a little boy trying to keep things alive for himself. He couldn't talk to you, so he talked to me, and I remembered what he said. But I never told anyone, Angus. I promised."

"You must forget it. You aren't marrying Strathcoran, you are marrying a colonial farmer who just happens to bear the Kendrum name. We will not deny that, but we will never talk of our childhood even when we are alone. Your memories of being a child in the southern colonies, yes. But my childhood is as deeply buried as my father's sword."

I listened, lying as stiff and straight as a stone effigy on a tomb, aching not with physical desire but with another kind of longing which I thought would be pain forever.

"I've always loved you," she said. "From my first memory of you. You were so *tall*." Soft laughter. "Do you mind the time I wandered too far away, and the fog came in, and I thought I was lost forever? And I sat there in the bracken howling my soul away? I remembered *that* with no help from Calum! Then you came. Twelve, you were, or thirteen? I was three, about."

He was bemused. "So little, with the bright hair and the brown eyes, and the lung power bigger than you were."

"You wiped away my tears and made me blow my nose on your fine handkerchief, and you wrapped me in your plaid and carried me home."

"You cried and snuffled in my neck like a calf learning how to drink from a bucket."

"You're no poet, are you, Angus Mor?" Then she said timidly, "Angus? I can just remember the Earl. He was a bonny man. You look like him, I think. It's strange to me to be married to the Earl."

"Hush, hush, my Jeannie," he cautioned her.

"I loved you when you carried me through the surf to the boat," she said. "I loved you when you knelt all those hours by Calum; I'd watch you in the lantern light. I remember!" she said proudly. "All Calum had to tell me was about Strathcoran, and the battle of Culloden when our fathers died."

"Jeannie, Jeannie," he whispered. "Not now. It's over."

"Angus, would the sheep have eaten all the heather now? The white heather too?"

"I don't know. Maybe she never brought sheep in. There may be nothing there now but empty cottages and byres, the heather having it all."

"That would be beautiful, Angus," she said drowsily. "Do

you mind the color of the heather in bloom, and the way the castle reflected in the loch on a hot, still, summer noon? The scent and the color of the heather, and the bees in it, and the burn tumbling down to the loch, and the birds—"

It was as if he'd gently stopped her mouth. "You must forget the castle and the way the heather looks and smells in bloom, and the whaups and the curlews rising. *You must forget.* In speech, anyway."

"But never in my heart."

"No, never in the heart. It will take us back in our dreams. But home is where you and I are together."

"Yes, Angus." Meekly. Then: "So I put you in mind of a calf learning to drink from a bucket, eh?"

They were both laughing then, and it was the kind of laughter no one else should be hearing. Heat ran over me again like a flash fire, and a cold and frightening lassitude followed it. Wearily I got myself up, wrapped in my robe, fumbled my feet into slippers, and went downstairs. It was becoming light, and I was grateful for that. Outside the world lay entranced in grays, a few stars still showing. An owl flew soundlessly over the lawn and off down the field toward the cellar hole.

I heard the brook. The burn, she called the one at home, tumbling down between heathery banks to the sea loch. A waterbird down by the river. What did a whaup or a curlew sound like? Had they found any birds in their new Scotland to remind them of those in the valley of Strathcoran?

I am tired of this, I thought drearily. It has to end. I have to forget it, the way he told her to forget. But never in my heart, she had protested, and he had answered, It will take us back in our dreams.

I will dream of him, I thought. But he doesn't know that I exist.

28

<u>CHAPTER</u>

THE NEXT DAY was fine and dry, perfect haying weather, and they got it all cut. Friday morning Hector moved the cows to a pasture beyond the farmhouse, not trusting people not to show up for the Gathering with unruly children or dogs. He gave the boys the afternoon off to get ready for their camping trip.

I asked who was going to help with the chores on Saturday night and Sunday morning, and Robbie said Bob Kendrum would come over, and Angus would be back in time to assist. The thought of Angus assisting with milking and cleaning out the barn had a certain insane charm.

"Where's he gone?" I asked casually.

Robbie shrugged. "All I know is that he told Uncle Hector he'd be back." I shouldn't mind being excluded, I thought, even if I did happen to be bang in the middle of things by coming along right after Hector's fall and saving Angus from being suffocated in his bed. If he *was* being suffocated, I added unpleasantly. And how did we know he'd really gone anywhere, no matter what he'd told Hector?

The twins had lent Robbie Rowan's sleeping bag, and the three had made a list of enough provisions to last for a week. Then they narrowed the list, and went off to the store in the twins' truck. They had ponchos in case it rained, waterproof covers for everything. But the weather report was good for the weekend.

Friday night Rowan came home from her week's work in Halifax, and after supper she brought her group over to the house to show off their songs for the Gathering. The "Canadian Boat Song" raised the hair on the back of my neck, but I wouldn't allow myself to think of it in conjunction with what I'd heard in the long nights. I told myself it was the beauty of the words and the simple setting, and the young voices.

They had Rowan's guitar, a banjo, and one gangling, straw-headed boy was a good fiddler. They had worked up some other songs from their school songbook and sang those too, and then Rowan announced, "At the Gathering we're going to finish with everybody singing 'Auld Lang Syne.'"

"Why?" Ross said. "It's not New Year's Eve."

"Don't be so crass. It's a sentimental occasion."

"Too bad we can't have a flag-raising ceremony," somebody said.

"Yeah, Uncle Angus should have a flagpole." Calum said. "Well, it's too late now. But we ought to pick out a good tree up on the hill and fell it and make him a flagpole this summer."

"Hey, it can be our present to the house!" Robbie said excitedly.

"Then I'll give him the flag for it," said Rowan. "How about some more singing? I'm all warmed up."

Eventually the session turned into an impromptu dance in the kitchen, because the straw-headed boy with the fiddle was a dab hand at jigs and reels. Even Robbie was carried away enough to let Rowan take him through the Lancers. I set out a big mug-up of everything I could find, and it was all wonderful. So much fun, so much sky-high exuberance, that it was almost too much. Warning streaked like lightning through the euphoria. *If you laugh so hard you'll be crying next*, someone used to remind me when I was a kid.

And where was Angus? Where had he really gone, where had he been since yesterday's foggy noon?

"What's the matter, Noel?" Rowan asked me merrily from across the table. "Bite on a sore tooth?"

Inspired, I said, "I was just thinking Angus ought to have a rowan tree outside the door, for luck and the family connection and so forth, and I was wondering how it could be managed."

"Oh, do you know that song about the rowan tree?" she asked. "My father taught it to us." She began to sing it, and the twins joined in with her, and everyone was quiet and almost sad until the song was finished. I led the applause, anxious to break the spell of silence, and everybody followed me with boisterous relief.

When they were leaving, Rowan said mischievously, "Well, I hope the Captain and Angus J. enjoyed the concert."

"Hey, that must have been who looked in from the front hall," somebody said. "I was wondering." They went out on a tidal wave of laughter.

Robbie was yawning and grinning at the same time, limp and foolish with happiness. "Every day I think I never had so much fun in my life, and then along comes something else."

"And along comes daylight before you know it," I said.

"I suppose. 'Night, Noel. What a super day." He went yawning toward the stairs. Everybody had carried dishes into the pantry but I went in and rinsed and stacked them, and washed the silver while Robbie had the bathroom. When he had finished I went to bed. I was resigned to being wakeful after all the laughing and the music, so I got comfortable with a book. At least I wasn't committed like Robbie to getting up at daybreak and doing barn chores. Once I fell asleep I ought to get my quota, or most of it.

But I couldn't concentrate even on P. D. James, with the music still caught in my head and underneath its bright surface the apprehension running like a silent and deadly undertow. I put out the light and lay back against three pillows, looking out at the stars over the valley. The brook wasn't very loud tonight; not so much water was rushing over its rocky course these days. Does the burn still tumble down to the sea loch? I wondered. Of course. It would be fed by mountain snows.

"Noel."

I heard my name, or thought it; I couldn't be sure until it came again. "Noel." Quiet. I sat up in bed gazing at the wall to the ell. Angus on the other side?

"What is it?" I asked in a low voice, mindful of Robbie across the hall beyond two closed doors.

"Noel."

"Yes, yes, I hear you."

"Noel."

It was like hearing voices on the CB radio calling out, when you answer but they don't hear you. And it wasn't Angus, not this Angus. I hauled up my knees and locked my arms around them till my shoulders hurt. This time I answered inside my head.

"Yes, I hear you. I hear you. Please, Angus Mor," I begged on the edge of weeping, "give me a sign that you hear *me*."

"Listen, listen. Noel. Danger. Great need. Danger."

I kept thinking I must keep my head clear, I must not panic. *Deep. Cold. Steps down. Brick and stone.* This was more a series of impressions than actual words.

"In the castle?" I asked. "A dungeon?"

"*No, no!*"

The vehement refusal was like a physical impact. We were communicating! I wondered if it was possible for a heart to stop with joy.

"A cellar, then?"

The agreement was as strong as the earlier rejection.

"Where? This cellar?"

"*Yes!*"

"What about it? What should I do?" Don't let me fail him, I was praying inarticulately at the same time.

"Behind the gooseneck and the hands."

I despaired. It was degenerating into nonsense.

"In the cellar?" I repeated. "*Here?*"

"Yes, yes, *yes!*" His urgency beat around me like roaring surf. I could only go down there and hope he'd show me where the gooseneck and the hands were. *Hands.* I saw severed hands, wearing gloves for some weird reason. Large white cotton gloves. And a long neck saved from a long-ago Christmas goose. That was bad enough, but the image of the hands might have given me doubts about my own sanity, had it not been that I was too excited, too desperately anxious to do what he wanted me to do.

"Stay with me, Angus Mor," I pleaded. "Don't desert me now." I pulled on my slippers and robe. But as I went into the hall with my flashlight I saw the line of light under Robbie's door.

I sagged against the wall, staring bleakly at that thin orange stripe. Then I went across the hall and asked softly, "Are you all right, Robbie?"

"Yeah, but the music got me all hyped up. And I've been worrying about the weather tomorrow too."

"It's going to be fine all weekend."

"Is that a promise?" He chuckled drowsily.

"Yes, it is."

"All right. I'm sleepy now anyway." The light went out. But Angus Mor had gone, and I knew it. Angus Mor's absence was always as positive as his presence.

The knowledge of desertion was stunning; my head rang with emptiness. I went back and fell limply on my bed and lay there waiting, but I knew it was no good. If he'd been there still, I would have gone on down to the cellar even in the middle of the night. But now I was chilled and shaky at the very prospect, as if I'd just wakened to find I'd walked in my sleep to the edge of a cliff.

And *had* I just wakened? Had I dreamed it all? I was back to the crazy girl again. But I am not crazy, I told myself with icy finality. Angus Mor had reached me and I had reached him.

I never heard Robbie getting himself up at five. It was well after seven when I tottered into the bathroom and tried to revive myself by splashing cool water on my face; I didn't have the nerve to take a cold shower. I felt weak and trembly, as if I'd been sick or were about to be.

Oh, fine! I thought miserably. I'm all ready for the Gathering tomorrow. I could see myself lying shut up in my room, feverish, nauseated and maybe worse, while the descendants visited the shrine. I wanted to cry with self-pity, but my coffee tasted wonderful, always a positive sign, and within a few minutes I began to feel much healthier, excited all over again, and anxious to search the cellar before anyone could interrupt me. The "gooseneck" bothered me. Chicken and turkey necks, I knew from experience, dried up into a handful of little bones. Maybe this one had been preserved in some way. Salted, tanned? It sounded as ridiculous as the "hands," but I was hopeful just the same.

I went into the hall and pushed away the rug, lifted the trapdoor, and laid it back. There was no need to switch on lights, the morning came in at the narrow windows. Since the last time I'd been down here, the place had been swept, the workbench cleared, pegboard installed, and tools hung on it. I opened and shut the deep drawers below the bench. They moved like silk, both the old ones and the new. Somebody in the past had been an artist, and so was Stuart, to build drawers like that. Some of the drawers were still empty; one held the smallish odds and ends that are found in any cellar anywhere; another had the jumble of old tools and parts that had been lying on the bench when I was here before. Angus would probably sort them and fit things together when he had time, and then figure out how best to display them like the big implements in the barn.

I looked into the still-vacant cold closet, and inspected the shelves of old iron pots and kettles, tinware, and stoneware jugs. I didn't see a preserved gooseneck anywhere and, naturally, no unattached hands in white gloves.

It was a lovely cellar as cellars go. The first three Anguses— "Or should I say Angii?" I wondered aloud—would have been very impressed. But it was going to tell me nothing, I knew without even trying for a message.

I went upstairs and fixed a decent breakfast. After that I

threw all the small rugs out onto the front lawn to shake later, and dry-mopped the floors. When I dusted the mantel in the long living room, I remembered suddenly, but as from a very long time ago, the day we'd brought home the paintings. Wasn't it tonight Angus had planned to hang them and have the family in for a showing and a toast?

Had he even thought of it since? They might be still in Halifax where he'd taken them for safety. Maybe after the attack that night he hadn't wanted to think of it.

If there had really been an attack. . . . With manic energy I cleaned Robbie's room and mine. Downstairs I washed up last night's and the morning's dishes, and was so reckless I had to take time out to quiet down before I broke half the willow ware.

29

CHAPTER

A T NOON we all set forth for Oquiddic Harbor. Hector's pickup carried the canoe, the dunnage, and the boys, and Bob Kendrum rode in front with him. I drove my station wagon, with Rowan, Mrs. Archie, Mrs. Alec, and Mrs. Bob all going for the ride. The women were all delighted with the weather for the Gathering. The boys and Rowan were high, and Bob Kendrum was almost as carried away. Hector's more moderate good humor was so unclouded, as far as I could see, that I began wondering again if the missing Angus had told him anything at all about what was going on.

But if he didn't know anything else, he knew he'd been shoved out of the hayloft that day. So he was putting on a good performance for the sake of the others. That must be it, I assured myself. Personally I wanted to be enjoying myself without qualification, so I kept thinking, At least you made contact with Angus Mor. You really did.

And then that horrifying urgency would sweep around me again like a killing sea. *Danger. Great need. Danger.*

The women were talking, but their voices were nothing compared to that one. My hands were wet gripping the steering wheel. I would go to Mr. Barry, the minister, as soon as I got back to Brierbank and lay out the whole story.

After that I was able to concentrate better on the immediate time and place. We left the boys at a quiet spot beside the road just a little way from the salt water. They wanted to pack the canoe and launch it without an audience, since the first voyagers hadn't been seen off by a bevy of relations, so we dropped them and drove back to Brierbank.

On the way Hector, driving ahead, signaled us with a waving arm as we were passing a big, solitary, white farmhouse with handsome shade trees out front and a fine set of outbuildings behind.

"Something special about that place?" I asked.

"No, he means for us to stop around the next bend," said Mrs. Archie.

We found the pickup parked off the road and we parked behind it, and we all walked into the woods a little way to the place where the boys were going to camp out. The story was that Angus, Calum, and Donald Muir had started late in the day from Oquiddic Harbor, so they had to sleep out one night on the way rather than make the trip in one day's paddling. They had built their fire against a certain huge boulder which Bob and Rowan, at least, now viewed with respect.

Mrs. Archie had asked us all to the farm for lunch. I couldn't see a way of escaping that without being conspicuous, but I would leave as soon as I could after the meal, and I'd have to do a little lying in case Rowan wanted to come back to the house with me.

But with one of these instantaneous shifts of mood I was having these days, I lost my apprehension of the unknown menace while we were having lunch, and felt so sleepy I was sure I'd have no trouble taking a nap. I offered to help with the dishes, but was refused—my sleepiness had become very obvious. Mrs. Archie was coming up later on to get the wild strawberries before the many feet at the Gathering could destroy them, and I was going to help her.

Rowan was yawning too; she said the excitement of the music last night had made her wakeful. So she wouldn't suggest coming to the house, I was pretty sure.

On the way out to the car I stopped to speak to Hector and

Bob, who were leaning on a fence rail smoking their pipes and contemplating the livestock.

"What's a gooseneck?" I asked.

"The neck of a goose," said Hector. Bob grinned.

"Oh, come on," I said. Is there anything else that's called a gooseneck, something that has no connection with a bird?"

"It's a kind of chisel with a bend in it," Bob said at once. "Old-timey kind."

Hector took his pipe out of his mouth. "Shaped roughly like this," he said. He dropped down easily onto his heels and drew an outline in the dirt. "A barn mortise router, all iron. Bog iron. They had them in the early days. There's one back at the house." He nodded his dark head in the general direction of the Angus J. house. "Might even have come from Georgia with Angus Mor."

I was sure they could see the heartbeat lifting my blouse, or a pulse in my neck; I wished Bob Kendrum's eyes weren't so intensely keen. I made myself lean back nonchalantly on the fence rail. "All right, now tell me what are 'hands'? And don't say it's what's on the ends of my arms."

Hector laughed. "If you're still thinking of tools, they're wooden handles made for tools."

"More old-timey talk," said Bob. "'Hands.' I remember my grandfather calling them that."

"That must be what all those odds and ends of wooden shapes are I've seen in the cellar," I said, still nonchalant. "You can see they're well-worn and polished with use. I'll have to look at them with more respect. Well, thanks, both of you. I came across those words in my reading last night, and I was curious."

I tried to leave without haste. I have a hard time being deceptive; I always think I'm giving myself away. My forehead was wet by the time I'd gotten the station wagon backed out on the road and headed for home.

I certainly wasn't going to take a nap now; I'd never been so wide-awake in my life. But I wouldn't take a chance on going down cellar until Rowan and her mother drove past. Rowan might still think of some reason to stop in. I had the back windows open so I'd hear the car going by without having to stand watch. Sure enough, they went along about a half hour later.

Now the hot sunny silence of a perfect July afternoon settled down on the Angus J. house and the roses, the motionless pines standing in pools of hot shade, the flowering field slanting down to the sky-colored silk ribbon of river glimpsed through the poplar leaves that always trembled in a breeze that only they could feel.

Now.

I went down through the trapdoor, and was crossing the floor toward the bench and the drawers where I'd seen the "hands," when somebody drove into the yard.

"Oh, damn, damn, *damn!*" I whispered. I darted back to stand against the wall beside the bulkhead steps, in case anyone knelt down to look in the cellar windows. They were open and screened, and I could hear perfectly the footsteps on the walk.

"Anybody home?" It was Stuart's voice, stronger than it had been a couple of days ago. He knocked at the back door, and then opened it. Silence. He was beholding the opening in the floor.

Why hadn't I locked the door behind me when I came in? But he had a key to the bulkhead anyway.

"Hello!" I called heartily. "Be right up!" I grabbed one of the tall stoneware jugs off its shelf and set it on the wide stairs. "Wait a minute, Stuart, don't go away." I went back and got another one, then brought them both up with me, giving him what I hoped was an artless, excited, girlish smile. He stood looking at me with his hands on his hips, as if my frivolity were beneath contempt when life was so grim.

"I wanted to make some field flower arrangements for tomorrow," I explained, "and I remembered seeing those jugs when Angus showed me the cellar. I didn't think he'd mind. Do you? They'll be perfect, don't you think?"

He made an ambiguous sound. "I guess I'll have to wash them," I said, looking fastidiously at my hands. He replaced the trapdoor and I pulled the rug across with my foot, then carried the jugs into the pantry, made a big thing about washing my hands, and returned to the kitchen.

"Well, how are you?" I asked. "Your voice sounds a lot better."

"It's all right now. I was looking for Angus. He came over to the house that day, and I haven't seen him since."

"Neither have I," I said. "He must be out of town."

"Then you don't know where?"

"Haven't the foggiest."

He seemed dispirited. "I thought you might know. You two seem pretty friendly."

"If having a meal together now and then, and going on a picnic to Peggy's Cove, is friendly, then we're friendly. But otherwise your brother's very private. Why don't you leave a note for him in on his desk?"

"It's nothing that can't wait." He turned to go, his face so dark and rigid that I couldn't help a gesture. He looked lonely, and I knew the family were still away.

"Stuart, would you like a cup of tea or coffee? Have you had any lunch today? I'll fix you something."

"No, thanks." He was halfway out the door. "But I appreciate it," he said awkwardly. He walked out to the truck. Bemused, I watched him turn in the yard and go out the way he'd come.

I didn't get a chance to lift the trapdoor again before Mrs. Archie came in. Well, if the gooseneck is there it's not going anywhere, I consoled myself, and nothing terrible is going to happen this afternoon.

Mrs. Archie had a wide-brimmed hat to protect her fair, freckling complexion, and I put on shorts and a sleeveless blouse. We picked for several hours, sometimes close, sometimes separated. There was a peaceful somnolence about the afternoon. I found some beautiful berries among the ferns that grew thickly around the cellar hole, and I wondered how long it had taken for meadows to replace the original forest, if Annie and Jeannie had

ever been able to pick field strawberries on this slope, or if the
fruit had come much later.

I kept out a quart of strawberries for myself and Robbie, and
gave Mrs. Archie the rest. Over tea I offered to come down that
night and help hull them.

"Thank you, dear," she said, "but I won't be able to do anything with them tomorrow so I'll put them away tonight, hulls
and all. They'll ripen a bit more in the cellar and we'll have saved
them from the feet of the mob. Maybe Monday when the
Gathering's over we should have one more giant strawberry
shortcake."

"Speaking for the boys and myself—wow!"

We laughed. "I wonder where they are by now," I said. She
named several locations where they could be, we talked about
how perfect the weather was for them, and then she got up to go.

I had walked to her car with her when Angus drove into the
yard. He got out of the Jaguar and stood looking oddly at us; he
had a curious resemblance, in expression, to Stuart.

"What's the matter, love?" his aunt asked him.

"I've got one hell of a headache," he said.

"For goodness' sake, take something for it and go to bed," she
ordered. "You want to be fit tomorrow."

"Oh God, the Gathering," he groaned. "Don't anyone offer
me two cents, or I'll hire radio and TV time to call it off."

"Do you feel that bad?" she asked worriedly. "Should you see
a doctor?" She went up close to him, as if to feel his forehead,
and he laughed and put his hands on her shoulders and gave her a
little shake. "I'm fine. An hour out here and I'll be a new man."

"Not too new, I hope. We love the old one."

We watched her out of the yard; she waved as she went by
the barn and out of sight. I had a peculiar feeling of alienation
from him; a new self-consciousness made me unwilling to look
directly at him. I did finally, and to my relief he wasn't watching
me and guessing at my erratic suspicions. He was staring at nothing that I could see.

"Want something to eat?" I said brightly.

"No, thanks. But I want to talk. Come on in."

"There's still plenty of tea," I babbled. He held the screen door open for me and I was so nervous I stubbed my toe on the threshold. He caught me by the elbow, and I laughed foolishly.

"That means either I'm getting some money, or I won't get married this year."

He didn't answer. Behind me on the way to the kitchen he was an immense and threatening Presence. "Hey, I just thought," I said. "Isn't this the night you're going to hang up the Captain and his missus?"

"They're still in Halifax. Will you shut up and sit down?" he said with tired patience. "What ails you? You're like a three-legged cat with fleas."

"That's the most glamorous thing that's been said to me this year." I dropped gracelessly into the nearest chair. "You didn't find Jamesy," I said. "Or you did, and it's all bad."

"No, but I found out where he's been. I went to St. John, and he did arrive there with Basil Hammond's nephew, who isn't a bad kid, by the way, but no earthly good around horses." He smiled, very faintly. "He's working in a garage now, which is where he should be. All he thinks about is fast cars and racing. This place was Devil's Island to him. He told me it was Stuart who kept talking drugs to Basil. He heard it himself when he wasn't supposed to be around. Of course Basil was bound to give some consideration to a father's words about his son."

He sat down on the edge of the table and looked at the floor, as if it was an effort to talk or as if what he was really thinking was taking up most of his attention. "So what about Jamesy?" I urged. "Did this kid tell Jamesy, finally?"

"Yes. After Jamesy wrecked the cornfield. Then they took off. He didn't know anything about the barn bit."

He kept on staring at the floor; he might have been reading his words there, and with difficulty. "Basil's sister is a nice woman. She said Jamesy was polite around the house, picked up after himself, and apparently went out looking for work. But she felt he was disturbed about something. Anxious, brooding, she described it. Anyway, he got up early one morning, thanked her, said he'd got it all together now and was leaving. Off he went on his bike and that's it."

He lifted his head and said, "You look as if somebody punched you in the stomach."

"I feel that way. Was that before his father was attacked?"

He nodded slowly, studying the floor again.

"Then he could have been the one, and you know it. Getting even with his father for making him lose his job. Oh, Angus, I don't *want* to think it, but if he's been home three days and nobody's seen him, it's giving me gooseflesh." I rubbed my prickly arms. "He could be hiding out in those woods across the road. He could even have stood outside here last night while the kids were singing and playing, and hating us all." Angus lifted his head and his gray eyes watched me as if he were taking notes while he waited to see what I did next. I felt like hitting him. "And why didn't you get word to me somehow, if you've known it for all this time? Why couldn't you warn me? What have you been doing?" I heard myself going shrill. It was inexcusable, but so had been his silence. He still said nothing, just kept on watching me.

"In the first place," he said finally, "he didn't say he was coming home. He could have been heading for the States, or out west. In the second place, I called Hector when I got back to Halifax last night."

"But it was none of *my* business, I suppose."

"We didn't think you were in any danger. Neither of us thinks Jamesy's a menace except to himself. Hector doesn't know who shoved him out of the hayloft. I don't know who put a pillow over my face. Stuart doesn't know who mugged him. It's too damned easy to say Jamesy's acting strange, so Jamesy has to be the one."

Because you could be the one? I thought, feeling sick to my

stomach. Is that why you won't see Jamesy as a threat? I said, "Those three boys are going to be camping by the river tonight, and everybody knows where their special spot is."

"What makes you think they aren't safe from him, if he's the one? It seems to me it's his father and his uncles he's after."

"He must resent them like hell, Angus! For one thing—even if this sounds heartless—they've got .no fathers jamming down on them, and their mothers know they exist, they're concerned about their boys. Oh, probably Len is too, but she's got younger ones, and a new one coming, and she always seems to sail along like this placid duck."

Angus's mouth twitched but his eyes didn't change. In some circumstances gray can be a very cold color for eyes. He looked ten years older than he had looked a week ago. All at once I couldn't think of anything else to say. I jumped up and went to the pantry, saying, "I'll have a drink, I guess. That's an awfully good well."

"It's a never-failing spring. Angus Mor located it with his witch-hazel divining rod, did I ever tell you that?"

"No." I drank slowly, tasting the water as if it were wine. I'd been taking it for granted all this time. I wanted to be alone to think about his first finding the water and then tasting it like this when it had settled. But there was something weird about the silence between Angus and me; for me, at least, it pulsed with all that I wanted to say and couldn't. For him—well, I had the feeling that he was absent again, except in body.

"Did anyone inherit the talent for dowsing?" I asked, returning with my glass in my hand.

"Oh, I guess a few Kendrums can find water. Some other people in the town too. It's not uncommon."

"Do you know if Angus Mor was second-sighted?"

"I never heard." He gazed absently out at the fields in the coppery sunlight of late afternoon.

"Mrs. Gilbert Kendrum has a theory that it's a genetic trait and if there were enough cross-marriages a few people could be born with very highly developed ESP. She feels cheated because she's not one of them."

Angus murmured, "Mmm," and kept on looking out the window. At least it was a change from his reading his lines off the floor.

"I suppose if you had it you wouldn't admit it," I said. "It wouldn't be *macho*."

He burst out laughing at that, and stood up. "Well, I've got things to do. Look, I'll drive down the river road tonight and check on the boys if it'll make you feel any better. After milking."

"He could come after you left them, in the middle of the night."

"I'll take a bedroll and sleep with them, for God's sake!" he said irritably, and strode into his own quarters. While I was washing up the teacups, he drove out again in the direction of the farm.

Such is the power of a rigorous training in good manners that I felt guilty of a crime against his hospitality for having evil thoughts about him, no matter how fleeting. But I couldn't get away from those cold, blank, gray eyes. It had been as if someone else, or some *thing*, had moved into the shell of his body. Supposing he was one of those born with the highly developed gift, and had already heard what I'd heard in the house?

He was the only one who'd visited the valley and castle of Strathcoran, had seen the stones and the family portraits. If by inheritance he was psychic, he would have been bombarded by impressions with enough force to shake his senses loose, and then, after that, if he'd heard some of the conversations *I'd* heard in this house—"Oh, dear God!" I said aloud, and I didn't know if I was praying for him, or for myself for being so far gone in fantasy.

I had only his word for the attack on himself. I was thankful I'd never given in to the impulse to tell him what I was experiencing in his house; I might be dead by now. I thought of inviting myself to go with him to check on the boys. Still, nothing was going to happen to them in broad daylight, and the evenings were long and light just now. Toward dusk I would drive down there myself, park off the road somewhere, and keep watch if I had to huddle all night behind the famous boulder and be eaten alive by mosquitoes. I knew I would remember the place by that splendid farm.

In the meantime I was going down cellar again to find the gooseneck and the "hands," but I would wait until he had gone, ostensibly to see the boys. I had this chilly, sickening sensation of loss because I didn't want it to be true about Angus, and if it was, I was afraid. There'd been something about the way he watched me, as if he knew all the time what I was trying to mask by my inane chatter.

It was so crazy it was almost funny in a horrible way. All I could hope was that he wasn't receiving any vibrations from me now. Maybe the business of getting seventy-eight cows ready for milking and then milked, even by machine, was sufficiently absorbing to jam the communication waves.

Still, I wouldn't take any chances on going down cellar yet.

30
CHAPTER

I DIDN'T WANT any supper but I didn't want to appear edgy in case anyone came in. For "anyone," read *Angus*. So I made a cup of soup and got a book, and sat at the kitchen table. The shades were drawn against the westering sun, and the room was filled with a pleasant pale amber light and the early-evening conversation of birds coming through the open windows. These were oddly tranquilizing and I found I was even understanding what I read. The book was one I'd brought home from the farm, a good novel by a Canadian writer, set in Montreal. It reminded me that life existed outside the small special world in which I was now an uneasy guest.

I was getting pretty good at controlling my mind, I thought once, and too complacently, because a moment later Angus put his head in from the ell, and I jumped so that the book flew out of my hands.

His smile was sardonic, if it could be called a smile. Rather more like a grimace. "I'm on my way to see the kids."

"Any news of Jamesy?"

"He could be anywhere. We're still looking." Who was *we*? "I still don't think the boys are in any danger, but I'm driving down there anyway. I may suggest they sleep somewhere else. Maybe the owners of the farm would let them sleep near the house. The kids will object, of course." Again that odd expression. "I'll see how it feels to me when I get there."

He withdrew without inviting me to go, and I was glad of

that, as I wouldn't have any normal reason to refuse him. He might not even be going to where the boys were; not until later. But I would be there by then, and between now and dark I ought to think of something I could use for a weapon, if only no more than the tall aerosol can of insect killer I'd seen in the cellar. A blast of that in the face should immobilize anyone.

No matter where he'd gone now, he wouldn't be back right away. I went into the ell and locked his outside door, returned to the hall and made sure both my front and back doors were locked, and then kicked aside the rug.

In the cellar the light fell through the narrow windows: colorless on the north side, in theatrical shafts of gold from the west. The birdsong went on. I remember particularly the whitethroat sparrow, who here was supposed to say "I love Canada, Canada, Canada" instead of "Sow wheat, Peabody, Peabody, Peabody."

Still with bolts and doors on my mind, I went to the inside door at the foot of the bulkhead steps, but that was the one thing Stuart hadn't completed. It still lacked its hardware, except for the hinges. It would have an inside bolt eventually, but for now it couldn't be locked. But I would have time to get up from the cellar between the arrival of Angus's car and his getting his door unlocked.

No matter. He wouldn't be back for a while yet. I went to the workbench, pulled out the drawer that had the "hands" in it, all the old tools, hatchet, ax, and hammer heads, chisel blades, gouges, and so forth. Cautiously I poked around in them; the old bog iron was still bright and sharp in many of them. I found the gooseneck chisel, just as Hector had drawn it for me in the dirt. I held it and shut my eyes, wishing childishly for Angus Mor to say, "That's mine. I brought it from Georgia with me."

Naturally nothing happened. But I laid the oddly crooked chisel to one side, and then I pulled out the drawer all the way and set it on the bench. I knelt, and put my arms in the long gap, reaching as far as I could. My hands touched cold smooth metal. Groping with both hands, I was able to grasp the box and bring it out. Already I'd seen it as a strongbox and I was right. It was new, and enameled dark green. I set it on the bench.

"This is it," I muttered. "But it's locked and what the hell do I do *now?* Have I got to tell somebody the whole crazy mess?" But maybe they'd listen to anything now, out of desperation after the attacks. Hector, anyway. I conjured up a somewhat comforting vision of his usual calm, benevolent expression.

Someone was unlocking the padlock on the outside of the bulkhead door, and I hadn't heard an engine. Instantly I went to pieces. I tried to put the strongbox back in and jammed it at an angle. Sweating, I wrenched it out and put it on the floor under the bench, kicked it into the shadows—I hoped—and seized the heavy drawer and tried to wrestle that into place.

Someone came down the stone steps. I glanced over my shoulder, hoping I didn't look blind with panic, and saw that it was Stuart.

"Oh, *boy!*" I let out a long, hard, gusty breath. "I was just trying to get this drawer back in. Hector was telling me about some old tools Angus Mor brought from Georgia and I was looking at them, and pulled the drawer out too far." I even laughed. "Almost dropped it on my feet and broke my toes."

Stuart's face was absolutely still. He took the drawer from me.

"Gooseneck chisel," I said. "See there? Fascinating. Hand-hammered out of bog iron. Angus should really clean these things up and mount them."

"Oh, he will," he said sarcastically. "They're holy relics to him."

As he leaned over to replace the drawer, he suddenly stopped moving, and with a chill at my stomach as if I'd somehow swallowed ice cubes I realized he was looking under the bench.

Then motion began again. He drove the drawer into place, dropped to his heels, and pulled out the strongbox.

"Where did this come from?" he asked.

"I don't know," I lied. "It's a strongbox, isn't it? Angus must

keep things in it. Insurance policies for the house, stuff like that."
I heard my voice, fast and fluttery. "It would be safe down here
in case of fire, wouldn't it?"

Stuart stood up and faced me, holding the strongbox. His
face was still quiet, with the immobility of rock. "It's mine,"
he said.

I was more incredulous than shocked. "Why don't you keep it
at home?" I asked, still trying for the light and innocent touch.

"Home?" he asked contemptuously. "With a batch of kids
who are into every corner, every crack in the woodwork? No,
this is mine alone, it's nobody else's business."

"No," I said. "It's not really yours alone, and you know it,
don't you? It's got something to do with all these things that have
been happening."

Color shot across his face like flame and the way it quickly
receded was sickening, as if suddenly he were bleeding to death.
"I don't know how you did it," he said tonelessly. "You never
heard those things you wrote. The dead don't pace the floor in
leather boots and they don't talk either. He's only a handful of
bones and dust." The blood was beginning to rise again, giving
him a darkly congested look. "But you guessed *something*, and
damn you for an interfering bitch!"

My own face burned. He'd been reading my notebooks when
I was out of the house. Thank God I hadn't written down the
love scene! Outrage took me beyond fear, but I didn't scream at
him the way I wanted to. I was still in control. "If you've been
getting in and going through my things like a sneak thief, why
couldn't you have taken your precious box away any one of those
times?"

"I told you, damn you!" His voice rose. "Because there was
no private place for it! This was *my* place till my fool of a brother
let *you* into it."

Angus, come back, I gibbered in the back of my mind. I
never meant to accuse you. Don't stay all night with the boys,
please. . . . Keep talking, Noel. Talk your stupid head off.

Stuart was watching me. Cold blank gray eyes as Angus's had been, but now I knew which were the dangerous ones. I had to keep going. Control was leaving as a giddy, senseless exhilaration took over; I was going to *find out*. I guess one never really believes in one's own doom until it has one by the throat.

"If you don't believe I heard all that," I said, "how do you think I knew enough to look behind the drawer with the gooseneck in it? I never heard of a gooseneck chisel in my life! And I didn't know what 'hands' were. But I knew the danger was behind them!"

His grayish mouth was moving but I didn't hear anything. I wondered recklessly just how mad he was; if he thought he was speaking aloud and could only hear his words inside his head. My legs were weak; very carefully, keeping my eyes on his as if trying to control a wild animal, I backed up till I could lean against the bench.

"Just where does Jamesy come into this?" I asked.

The words broke free at last past pale lips. "He was too smart for his breeches. He knew I was getting ready for something. To run away with another woman, maybe. Thought I had her in Halifax." Mirthless show of teeth. "Christ, if he'd ever found out the truth, he could have killed me after I'd done all the work, and put in the claim himself."

"What claim?"

"Never you mind, my dear." It was a ghastly parody of Bob Kendrum's courtliness. "You won't be around to see what happens. But it's going to be worth a hell of a lot of money to *someone* for me not to upset their applecart. I'll be a rich man, and to hell with this town and everybody in it. I'll never come back!"

"The Earl of Strathcoran is really an impostor, isn't he, Stuart?" I asked sociably. "That's what you found out. There was something hidden where you were tearing out partitions, and now you've got the proof in the box. So you're trying to get rid of everybody in the way. Do you want the castle, the valley, the whole works, if any court recognizes your claim?"

That *if* was a mistake. The changes in his face were becoming dreadfully familiar to me, and my reflexes were well conditioned to them. "But of course they *will*," I hurried fervently on.

"I don't want any of that rubbish," he said with disdain. "I wouldn't live in that country. The best thing Angus Mor ever did was to run away from it. But the Earl's a rich man. He'll gladly make a settlement to hush it all up. I haven't come this far to be stopped," he warned me, smiling now. "You and Alec's girl spoiled my first chance at Hector. I was waiting to come back and get him while he was out of wind. And you had to mess up the business with Angus. You can see why I hate you, can't you?" He sounded almost agreeable. "Now, Alec was easy."

"How did you do that?" I asked, sounding eager. "I thought it was a heart attack in the woods."

"It happened here. Brought on by a pillow over his face, and then I drove him out to the woodlot and dropped him. Him with his damfool ideas of a Gathering, and filling the kids' heads with sentimental trash."

"And being next in line to Hector," I said knowledgeably. He nodded.

"But why Angus? He's the youngest. Once you get rid of Hector and Alec—"

"And their boys," he reminded me. "That's tonight."

I just managed not to break into a paroxysm of shivering. "Why Angus?" I persisted.

"Because a boy out of his head with drugs makes no distinctions. He'd kill anyone for money. Look what he did to me!"

"That was a masterful job of faking you did on that," I said admiringly. Angus *must* be staying with the boys; or else time had gone all out of whack for me, and he hadn't been gone long enough even to get to the camping site. Angus Mor was very absent, after he'd gotten me into this, no doubt with the best intentions. But how could he save me anyway?

Stuart was smiling faintly but with gratification at his own cleverness, and I felt a mad lust to puncture that.

"It was a mistake to miss on Hector and Angus, " I told him.

"They're getting suspicious about those shots and being half-suffocated and shoved out of haymows—you must have done a lot of sneaking on foot through the woods, huh? Anyway, Jamesy's on his way home from St. John, if he hasn't got here already, and he told someone that he had it all together now. Angus is with the boys, and Hector's waiting to see what Jamesy's got all together."

He kept on smiling. "Hector died this afternoon," he said.

I almost collapsed then. "You lie." I wanted to shout it, but I hadn't the wind to shout. My throat felt half paralyzed, as if I couldn't even swallow.

"He drowned in the river below the cornfield, and they know it. *Angus* knows it." He was enjoying my reactions.

Angus's bleak stare. . . . What it had meant, what he must have been going through and couldn't tell me. And what I'd suspected of *him*. "How could he drown in the river?" I demanded.

His smile broadened. "Jamesy jumped him from behind, pushed him in, and held his head under water. They know it wasn't an accident, the marks would be on him. Nobody's been able to locate me to tell me, but when they do I'll have to help look for Jamesy, of course. He's rotting his brain with drugs, the way I've been warning everybody, and now he's on a murder spree. His uncle—you—"

"Oh, *no*," I said firmly. "Somebody will come."

"No. At the farm they're thinking only about the funeral."

Mrs. Archie had gone home to that, and Angus had let her go home to it unwarned. But maybe he hadn't been able to make himself talk about it, and had gone right back there after talking with me.

"You're still lying," I said. "There's been nobody by here, police or ambulance."

"They came in from the Inverness road, my girl."

"Angus will be home any minute now."

"Oh, no," he assured me. "If he's not looking for Jamesy to take him to the Mounties, he's with the boys, as you seem to think. Jamesy's too sly for them all. He'll kill Angus and the boys as they sleep and then he'll disappear. They'll never find him. And when I get over feeling sad about the way my eldest son turned out, I'll visit the so-called Earl of Strathcoran. And when I'm a rich man I'll be gone with the wind!" He laughed. It was an incongruously youthful sound, from him.

"You've got it all planned out, haven't you?" I tried for amazement and awe, and did quite well. "What a strategy! What *will* happen to Jamesy? Shall you kill him too?"

"I already have," he said casually. "I only have to get him away from where he is, and bury him where nobody'll ever look." He came toward me and I tensed for flight, but he set the strongbox on the bench. "Now," he said, still leisurely, "I'll take care of you, and then I'll burn your foolish notes, and put this back where it's safe, and everything will be fine again. Perfect, in fact." He smiled at me and flexed his hands, and placed his fingertips together in a meticulous and macabre gesture.

I lunged past him across the cellar toward the stone steps and above them the open bulkhead. He pivoted and caught me by right arm and swung me around with a force that sent excruciating pain through my shoulder, but I kept on fighting him, throwing myself about in tremendous lurches, trying to kick, anything to keep him from getting a good grip on me with both hands. I had to reach those stone steps and the sight of sky, and the merest chance of help coming along. I was slammed into the pressure tank and bounced off it into his arms; he had me then, held too tightly for me to bring up my knee or get a hand into his face, and then, panting and laughing at the same time, he threw me against the casing of the inside door.

I was exhausted, aching, my shoulder and arm felt broken, and now I knew what death was. I recognized it coming at me in those strong, long, gifted Kendrum hands. I gathered up all the breath I had left and shouted, "Angus Mor, help me!"

It was a crazy thing, but it stopped Stuart for just a second. Astonishment and uncertainty rippled like waves of light across his face. After all, how *had* I found out about the strongbox?

Then he came on again and took me by the throat. Just before his thumbs went in, his face hideously close to mine, I shouted again, "Angus Mor!" And I meant it. My anguished eyes moved upward and to the left, to the merest glimpse of the open bulkhead possible to me. Stuart couldn't help it, he had to turn his head and look too. From where he stood he could see the whole opening.

I heard the whistling gasp in his throat, I saw his face turn tallowy and felt his hands drop off. I threw my weight against his chest and he went backward like a felled tree, and I looked up and saw the figure at the head of the stone steps. A blurred silhouette against the sky: hands on hips, feet braced apart. Only two things were clear, the tartan hose and the colors in the kilt.

"Come down!" I cried. "He's trying to—" But there was no one there, no one with me, only Stuart lying on his back across the threshold. Blood was running onto the cement floor from the back of his head. His mouth was open, his eyes wide and staring as if they still were seeing whatever had forced that whistling gasp through his throat and turned him dirty white.

I couldn't tell if he was breathing, and I didn't want to touch him. Sobbing frantically, I scrambled up the steps into the sweet air of freedom.

31

CHAPTER

I WAS SITTING on the back doorstep when Angus drove into the yard. I don't know how I appeared to him but he got out of the car fast, leaving the door open, and took me in his arms. I cried out with the pain of my shoulder and he kept saying, "What *is* it? Noel, talk to me!"

"Stuart was going to kill me," I said. "Nobody'll believe me, but I swear he was going to kill me. But somebody came, somebody early for the Gathering, and all dressed up—and scared Stuart—But now he's gone, whoever he was. He *must* have seen!"

I looked around wildly. "Hush, hush," Angus said, smoothing my hair and holding my head against his chest. We went to the bulkhead with his arm around me, and then he left me to go down and kneel beside his brother. I stood where the stranger had stood, and watched.

Angus felt for a pulse, laid his head close to Stuart's chest. Then he looked up at me and said, "He's dead."

"I pushed to get away from him and he went over. Did I kill him? But he looked strange before he fell."

"It could have been the way he hit his head, or it could have been a heart attack," he said. "You're safe, and that's what matters." He spoke in very measured tones, as if he had to find each word before he could use it. He shut the bulkhead doors and fastened the padlock. Stuart had left the key in it, attached to his key ring, and Angus put that in his pocket. "I'll have to call the Mounties again. Come on, we'll go to the farm."

"They did come, then.He told me,but I couldn't believe it at first about Hector. Oh, Angus, Mrs. Archie had to go home to *that*. I can't believe Hector's dead. I won't believe it!"

"Hector's fine," he said wearily. "He's been staying out of sight so Stuart would think he'd drowned him. Hector had the sense not to struggle, but he might have lost out if something hadn't stopped Stuart." He put me into the car, and went around to get in on his side.

"What?"

"Jamesy, the way we read it. We're pretty sure he was shadowing his father today, all the way through the woods from the Corner. His footsteps are in the cornfield, dug deep, as if he charged down the whole length of it after he saw Hector disappear into the alders where he knew his father already was. When he said in St. John that he'd got it all together, he must have decided his father was losing his mind, and he came home to try to do something about it." He folded his arms on the wheel and put his head down on them. "Poor little bastard," he said, harshly, as if otherwise he'd weep. "His father's been out to get him from the first, with all this talk of drugs. Trying to drive him away. God, Stuart was always at odds with the world—resentful, acting cheated when there was no need of it—but this is insanity!"

"He told me he killed Jamesy," I said. Incredible that Stuart lay dead and staring beneath the padlocked doors.

"Yes." He kept his head down on his folded arms. "Bob and Christy had gone home, and Aunt Janet left to go berrying. Hector went out to take a look at the cornfield and he thought he heard a dog whimpering in the alders. He went down there to see, and the sound lured him all the way to the riverbank, and he got one glimpse of Stuart from the corner of his eye before he jumped him. There's a deep hole above where Jamesy rode his bike in that day, and that's where Stuart thought he could do it. . . . It looks as if Jamesy came in after them. His clothes were still wet when we found him." There was a catch in his breathing but he went on. "Hector didn't know what got him free, but he let himself float toward the home bridge, and the minute he was out of sight he scrambled up and back to the house pretty well winded with the whole thing—it's a wonder *he* didn't have a heart attack then and there."

"Is he all right now?"

"Yes, the police doctor checked him over when he came to look at Jamesy."

"What about Jamesy?" I had to keep on asking even though I didn't want to hear anything more.

"Hector called the Mounties as soon as he got his breath—no false sentiment about his brother, not with everything that's been going on—and when they took a walk down into the alders to see what they could see they found Jamesy." He had to stop for a moment before he could go on. The whitethroat sparrow kept singing, "I love Canada, Canada, Canada." The sun was down and the Angus J. house stood against a dull bronze sky, not keeping all its secrets now.

"Strangled," Angus said suddenly. "He was smaller than his father, you know. And apparently Stuart knocked him out first. . . . I came along from Halifax just after they found him. You and Aunt Janet were down in the field berrying, and I didn't stop here, I had this feeling I should go right to the farm. I arrived in time to help Hector take the news about Jamesy."

"When you came back here you knew that," I accused him.

"Yes, but while we were looking for Stuart we didn't want the truth to get out about Hector's being alive and Jamesy's being found dead."

"Stuart didn't count on anyone going down there and finding Jamesy. He was going to take him away tonight and bury him. Before or after he killed the boys, and you too if you were with them."

"But why?" Angus lifted a drained and anguished face. "Did he say *why?* It's all so insane, but did he give you any reason whatever?"

I almost told him then. Probably the lethargy that was taking me over kept me from it. "There's a strongbox down there that's his. It was hidden behind the drawer of old tools."

He gave me a wild look. "I don't want to go back in there."

"Well, I don't suppose anybody will steal it now," I said. "Let's go to the farm. My shoulder's killing—I mean *hurting* me."

He was at once concerned about me, and I was glad to have diverted his mind from the cellar for a little while.

The effects of an experience like mine are very interesting, to objectively understate the case. Having gone to the extremes of terror, the whole body fighting it with every reflex and the wild pumping of a heart that seems ready to burst, the mind plunging dementedly through chaos—when it is suddenly ended, one can hardly believe it at first.

Sitting in the car with Angus, hearing what horrors had gone on while his aunt and I picked strawberries in a summery landscape, I was oddly calmed and settled in myself, and a profound grief for the Kendrums came in like a silent flood tide on a windless night.

We drove to the farm, Angus with an arm tightly around me as much for his own comfort as for mine, I thought. This was another thing which helped me, while I huddled inside that close embrace as if I never wanted to leave it. I hadn't yet mentioned Alec, and right then I didn't know if I could, any more than they could take any more. What good would it do them to be told that Stuart had murdered Alec? If they guessed, so be it, but let me not be the storm crow that carried the news.

It was quite a night. The boys were blissfully out of it, camping just where they were supposed to be, drowsily watching their fire in the twilight before turning in. They accepted the visit from a police car as a simple formality; a check of their identities and a warning to drown their fire later.

When the Mounties and the ambulance came this time, it was by the road I knew. Angus and Hector drove up to meet them at the Angus J. house. Mrs. Archie, even more businesslike than usual, had given me a couple of aspirin and ordered me to take a long hot bath for all my sore places. She made telephone calls while I soaked. Bob and Christy were already there, and Mrs. Archie called Mrs. Alec to tell her that she and Rowan had better come to the farm. Mrs. Stuart had already been called in Kingston about Jamesy's death; now her sister there was asked to tell her about Stuart's. She had hardly seemed to react, the sister said.

Protecting the unborn again, because she could no longer protect the first-born? I wondered to myself, while everyone agreed it was a blessing for Len that she was the way she was. They were all relieved that she wouldn't be brought home until tomorrow. That some version of death had visited the farm was now known through the countryside, because two ambulance trips and an assortment of police vehicles all in one afternoon couldn't be ignored. Mrs. Archie dealt quickly with the telephone calls, by assuring everybody that Hector was all right and they'd know the rest later.

After a long time Angus and Hector drove back, and the police car behind them. The family and I sat around the dining room table drinking strong tea and answering the official questions. They already had the story of the afternoon. Now it was mostly for me to talk. I listened incredulously to my own voice, quiet, uninflected, saying that Stuart had found me in the cellar and flown at me in a rage, and told me he'd killed both Hector and Jamesy that afternoon.

The police kept asking me about the man at the head of the stairs. I had seen only the sturdy legs in tartan hose and part of the kilt, I insisted. Telling it, I remembered, as I would forever, Stuart's wheeze of terror and the way his face went dead and witless before my eyes. I trembled, and Angus moved his chair closer to mine and put his arm around me. I steadied my voice.

"All I could think was that it was someone in town for the Gathering, and wearing his outfit. Maybe he'd come over to see Angus."

Angus shook his head. "I can't think who."

"What about Wee MacGregor, whatever his name is?" I asked Rowan.

"I don't know why he'd be coming to see Angus, he doesn't even know him. He'd go to the Tolmies to show off, more likely. Unless he was coming to see *you!*" She brightened pathetically. She'd been sitting there in a stunned silence, after first murmuring, "Jamesy . . . poor Jamesy." That was what seemed to hit her the hardest of all.

The police got Wee MacGregor's real name from her, and called his home. He was in the States, expected home late tonight. No chance of his being in Brierbank. Then they called Gilbert Kendrum, and found him at home in Truro. The only thing left to do was to ask questions around the village about some visitor who had inadvertently walked into a murder scene and left again, either without knowing what was going on, or because he didn't want to be involved. That's always incredible to me, but I guess some people are like that.

The Mounties left finally, and we were all about to sag, when Angus went out to his car and brought in the strongbox. "Don't ask me how I spirited it out without their seeing it," he said. "I just felt we should all see it first, whatever is in it, before it goes to them."

"Maybe they won't have to see it," Bob said hopefully.

"Unless it gives them the clear-cut motive they're looking for," said Angus. Hector, smoking his pipe, had nothing to say. Like all of them, he looked years older. They were grieving angrily and helplessly for the boy, and they had lost Stuart twice, you might say.

Angus took Stuart's key ring from his pocket and began looking for the strongbox key. I took a quick glance around at all the Kendrum and Kendrum-related faces, and felt myself an alien from somewhere out beyond Saturn. I got ready to leave the room; *escape* was a better word. Angus found the key and unlocked the box and tipped back the lid. Whatever the contents were, they were wrapped in tartan. I saw the glow of old, soft colors under the light, but I didn't wait for anything else.

"This is a family matter," I mumbled and got up and went out.

"Noel!" Rowan called after me, and I thought Angus turned as if to follow, but I hardly saw or heard. I was half-blind with tears. *Reaction*, I thought grimly. I went out into the summer dusk to the swings and sat on one of them. The dogs went with me, sniffing companionably around. The night was scented with roses and the growing fields, and fireflies signaled against the dark. I was afraid to give way to what I felt for fear I wouldn't be able to stop, and there was no place to go to be decently alone with it. I couldn't run back to the house, though the police had finished with it; I couldn't make myself step alone over the threshold. I would be more alone there than I'd ever been in my life, because Angus Mor wasn't going to come back. There'd be no need now.

While I tried to keep my eyes squeezed shut to hold the tears in, my throat ached and not from where Stuart's bruises were. There was still something else that wouldn't leave me alone. It refused to be ignored.

In that ragged piece of tartan unfolding under the light, the colors brewed from plants and lichens were still defiantly alive after all the years, and I'd seen that tartan before. In the very old pattern book we'd examined in the shop at Halifax, yes, but much later than that. Tonight, in fact, at the head of the bulk-head steps. It was the sett called Kendrum Ancient.

Angus Mor had shown himself to Stuart tonight, and no matter what the medical examiner would say, Stuart had *known*, and had died of terror.

He'd come, he had saved me, he had gone, and I had never seen his face. He would not come back. *And I had never seen his face.* I knew then what was meant by a broken heart because mine was broken then. I couldn't even cry about it. It was too much. To be bereft of a lover you have never embraced is the worst widowhood of all.

32

CHAPTER

ANGUS AND ROWAN came out and found me in the swing. They stood close to me in the soft dark.

"You have to come in and see it, Noel," Rowan said.

"Yes, come on, Noel." Angus put his arms around me and lifted me out of the swing. "You've been in this almost from the first."

I went in with them, dry-eyed now, and blinking against the light; the others weren't surprised that I looked dazed. Mrs. Alec had been crying but was now calm. Sorrow showed in all the eyes, in different ways, except that Bob Kendrum's blue eyes were greedily alight. "By God," he kept saying softly, "now we're going to *know*."

He looked secretively at me and I glanced away.

The tartan bundle was open on the table. There was a modern notebook. And there was, I saw without any surprise, a rotting deerskin pouch, and lying on top of it, gleaming bright and beautiful, incongruously untouched by the years, a brooch of gold and enamel, such as a Highland gentleman might wear on his plaid at the shoulder.

Rowan flowers and berries. This was what he had carried around his neck and against his skin; this, I knew at once, was what he went back to search for in the castle, through all the chests and armoires, and it had given itself away to him by jabbing his palm. I felt the sudden pain now, and the taste of the drops of blood.

"Now, Noel," Angus said softly, "look at *this*." He opened the notebook. On each page another one had been carefully mounted, an old, fragile, brown-edged leaf crowded with writing in faded inks. Transparent tape protected the edges from crumbling more. In this, as in everything, Stuart had been a perfectionist. He had failed only in some of his murders.

Angus read out the first page to us. "'I, Angus James Chisholm Kendrum, born May 20 in the Year of our Lord 1730, commence this narrative on my fiftieth birthday in the Year of our Lord 1780. Not for my children or for their children; but that in the years to come the valor of my father and his comrades will be known again. And that someone will know the truth about *me*, that I must keep hidden now because it could harm my sons and their sons. But a hundred years or more from now my descendants should be safe from the contamination of a bloody striving after false glories.'"

How wrong you were, Angus Mor, I thought.

"And he lived out his life pretending to be illiterate," Mrs. Alec said in wonder.

"He says," Angus went on, "'For most of my life I have practised in secret the hand I learned at school in France so that I would not lose it. When I have written this, I will never need to write again. I shall go to my grave an unlearned, unlettered farmer of Brierbank.' And he wrote a good hand too," Angus said softly. "Strong, self-assured. The strength of it comes across the centuries."

"Quick, read how he signs it," said Bob Kendrum eagerly. I still wouldn't meet his eyes.

"No, no, don't!" Rowan objected. "Read it all first, Angus."

"We're all worn out," Christy sighed. "We've had enough trouble today for a lifetime. That poor little Jamesy." Her eyes filled. "And I keep thinking of Len."

"Christy, m'dear, you go in the other room and lie on the couch," said her husband. "I'll take you in and cover you up myself. But with what this family's gone through this year, beginning with what happened in the spring and what's befallen us tonight—if there's any answer to it in that old writing there, we deserve to know what it is."

"All right," she said meekly, and went with him.

Angus Mor's Narrative

On the sixteenth day of April in the Year of our Lord 1746 my father Angus James Stuart Archibald Kendrum died on Culloden field. Our kinsman, Ronald Kendrum, escaped, God knows how, for he was no coward, and found his way home through the mountains like a fox, bringing us the news and my father's sword.

I would that he had been the one to tell us, but it was in the night that he came, and my brother and I were sleeping. Our stepmother Frances came to wake us and tell us, and I could have strangled her with her own hair because I knew who would now come brazenly to her bed, where he had already been privily.

Enough Kendrum men had died at Culloden to turn Strathcoran into a vale of mourning and she hated the misery of it. She had always hated it there, even in the best of summer, when the heather was in bloom. She considered us all savages. And now with the prayers and the weeping and the lament of the pipes rising like smoke from the peat fires, she rode to Inverness to await her lying-in. Her lover sent troopers to escort her. He could be with her there. He didn't dare come to Kendrum country, the bloody traitor that he was. And perhaps she saw that in my eyes which helped hurry her away.

So I was the fifth Earl at fifteen. My brother Calum was ten. We would rather still have been simply our father's children than Strathcoran and Lord Kendrum. I comforted Calum as best I could, but there was no one to comfort me. I was so big, they considered me almost a man, and there was too much sorrow and fear all around us. Annie Munro, who had raised us, did what she could, but her heart was broken for the loss of Fergus. Her Jeannie was too little to understand all the wretchedness, but she was always asking for her father.

There were mostly women left, small children, and old men. The cousin who had brought us the news and the sword lay dying of a lung fever. A man rode up from Inverness, at great risk; a kinsman of my mother, a Chisholm. Through a servant girl he had heard that we boys were to be secretly done away with, so that Frances's son would inherit. She had been informed it *would* be a son. She was always a superstitious bitch, but not enough so that she expected God to strike her dead for conceiving a bastard and naming him Kendrum.

Annie's uncle, Ruari the fisherman, and I dug two graves by night in a far corner of the burial ground, and in one we buried my father's sword, and in the other his bonnet with the eagle's feathers. Over them we set up slates for stones, with Calum's name on one and mine on the other. Frances would be told that we had died of the lung fever; not strange, it was all around us.

Then Ruari was to take us to Lewis in his boat. The night before we went, when we slept in Annie's cottage, I kept remembering the Cellini brooch that must always be in the possession of the true Earl, and as soon as it was day I went up to the castle and I found it. Frances's loyal people had gone with her, hoping to save their own necks, and no one else would have stopped me had they seen me. But Ruari came after me in a fury lest the traitor troops should ride into the valley at any moment.

When we went to Lewis, to Ruari's wife's cousin Tormod MacLeod, we were named Jamie and Fergus Munro, Annie's sons. When the long warm days came we sailed for America in *Kirsteen*, named for Tormod's wife. He and his sons often went to fish on the Banks off Newfoundland. Our Chisholm kinsman had given us what money he had with him, and we took a sack of oatmeal to live on. The heather was in bloom when we sailed, and I took some with us, but it died on the way.

The passage was not dangerous, but bad enough. Little Jeannie was sick, and Calum nearly died, with something else besides seasickness, I knew. I can never forget the nightmares he had, believing he was buried in one of the graves we had left behind for Frances to find. He was haunted by the memory of the stone with his name on it, and he used to cry, Father, Father! Come and save me! Dig me out of the ground!

Annie had to tend Jeannie. I did all I could for Calum. I prayed, not knowing to what, because if there was a God, why were we here in a waste of seas instead of home with our father? Why was Annie a widow, and the valley full of weeping?

When I tired of praying I cursed, and I talked into Calum's ear so he could never lose me and go on alone wherever he was heading. One day I knew I had to get him out on deck so he would know there was still a sun. Tormod's brother helped me. We kept putting water between his lips, and brose thinned into a gruel. I never left him day or night, and he lived.

When we reached Nova Scotia, it was like Scotland again. I had never seen or smelled anything so sweet, unless it would have been the return to the sea loch at Strathcoran.

And we had just walked ashore, the land surging under our feet because we'd been so long on the sea, when I saw that arrogant oaf, that brother to Frances, Lord Darach. I'd forgotten he'd been made a baronet of Nova Scotia and took it seriously, going there to live when he ran out of credit and reputation and any pretense of honor at home.

My father had no use for him, and Frances had pretended the same. But I had no doubt that some day he'd be walking through Strathcoran like the laird himself. Neither had I any doubt—boy that I was—that *I* would return and drive out all this filth. Unless, I thought hopefully, the Red Indians killed him first; but he was too cowardly to take chances.

Hatred was like bile in my throat. And terror too, that he should get an eye on us and recognize us past the shaggy hair and the dirt. A vessel had just come in from England and he had ridden to the harbor to get his mail. I hurried Calum back aboard *Kirsteen* and below decks until someone told us Darach had ridden away again. Annie had already recognized him, but he wouldn't know her.

We spent the night in a hut at the shore, walking around

after dark to enjoy the feel and the scents of the land. Our Lewismen talked with other seamen; this vessel just in from England would be going down the coast in another day, after taking on stores and water. I gave Annie what money I had to buy our passage away from Nova Scotia.

We sailed on an early morning tide. Jeannie had already made a friend, and I had to carry her on board, kicking and screaming.

We were out of danger now and sailing down a fair foreign coast. We went ashore to walk around wherever the vessel lay over, to strengthen our legs. It was like a dream to be actually *in* the Colonies of which we'd heard all our lives. The very people looked different, and we saw men in leather clothing, and Red Indians.

We ran into no foul weather on that trip south. Calum was stronger every day. He entertained Jeannie with long stories. Annie cut our hair and tried to make us look more presentable, and scolded us into remembering our manners and a seemly way of eating. Cutting across blue seas into the warmth of the south, I dreamed of how quickly I would return to Strathcoran as a man and drive the aliens out. I grieved because I hadn't been able to bring my father's sword with me, but Annie Munro's son would not possess such a magnificent weapon.

If my father could not be buried in his own valley, at least his sword was there, even though it lay under my name.

Boy that I was, I dreamed of arriving in secrecy at the sea loch below the castle, of rallying my followers; I would be like Prince Charles Edward arriving from France, though without a bloody failure at the end. Anything is possible in the brave, innocent heart of a fifteen-year-old boy.

My followers would be few, because God alone knew how many Kendrum men would be left by the time the Royalist troops had gone through, and then Frances's people would drive out what was left. Perhaps we would all gather in America and go back together.

On that night of arrival I would dig up my father's sword,

and clean and burnish it. We'd wrapped it in a plaid to protect it as much as possible. I knew by heart the words on the blade.

"The man who feels no delight in a gallant steed, a bright sword, and a fair lady, has not in his breast the heart of a soldier."

In the night we would take the castle. I'd be merciful to the boy who'd succeeded me, but there should be no doubt in his mind about me when he saw the Cellini brooch, worked by the great artist for my ancestor Allan Kendrum when they were friends in France and Italy, and forever afterward the private possession of the Earl of Strathcoran.

Frances would not laugh again. I had no plans to execute her for what she had planned to do to my brother and me, but she should know what terror meant when I arose from the dead to confront her.

I kept all this to myself. For Annie I was becoming a serious man, ready to face and conquer an uncertain future. For Calum I was the protective older brother, and the same for Jeannie.

At Savannah the heat of the Georgia autumn nearly felled us. We were taken in by other Highlanders who had arrived long before us, and there were more coming every day. At first we could only sweat, and pant, and drink, drink, drink. As the cool weather approached we felt better, and then we had a chance to go with a widowed man, to take up his new grant far inland. Annie became his housekeeper, and I worked with Roderick Muir in the fields, Donald Muir his young nephew, and two blacks. He was a good man, and when we had been two years with him I deemed it safe to tell him our real names but not our parentage. When I came of age, Mr. Muir spoke up for me and I received my own grant of land, adjoining his. But I had never forgotten how Nova Scotia had looked to us, had felt under our feet, after the long days aboard *Kirsteen*, and if I could not go back to Scotland yet, at least I could go there. I was not afraid of Lord Darach now, supposing he was not yet dead of Indians or his own dissipations.

Mr. Muir had the proper letters written for me, the grant was made by a Crown graciously willing to forget its own disgraceful past, and in my thirtieth year I deeded my Georgia land to Mr. Muir and his second wife, and took passage for the Strait of Canso. Calum was twenty-five then, Jeannie twenty. Donald Muir went with us.

The war with France was going on, but our ship hugged the coast and we outran serious danger off the coast of Maine. We left the women with good people at Canso, and sailed along the coast to the mouth of the Oquiddic. Here we traded for canoes and went up the river. A narrow, harmless river as rivers go, in places hardly wider than the burn that falls brown and foaming into the valley at home, but we found its kindliness a blessing, and there was in the cool bright air the very perfume of freedom.

Donald's heart was given over to Muir's Grant before it ever was called that, but he labored with Calum and me to get our cabin up so we could send for the women. I found water for us on the brow of the hill above the river. Then Calum and I helped Donald to build his cabin.

With every Nova Scotian sunrise or sunset that autumn, with our first winter there, hard as it was, and then the first spring, beginning slowly as it does in the Highlands, I was becoming more wedded to this land. When, the next year, we raised the first big barn to replace the smaller shelters, it was a turning point and I could smile with sad affection on the fifteen-year-old boy who lay on the deck gliding toward Georgia and schemed his revenge. I knew I would never go back now, even if I could raise a regiment of men.

Oh, we dreamed, Calum and I. Nightmares came sometimes, but they grew scarce. The sweet dreams of home were the worst. But they too came less often. Calum went west and joined the Northwest Company. Jeannie married young Kenneth MacDonald, and by twenty-four she was a widow, her husband and baby taken off by an outbreak of smallpox. She was courted both for herself and for her farm. She sold the farm finally, and returned home to her mother and me.

We married when I was thirty-nine and she was twenty-nine, and our first son was born in the Year of our Lord 1770. He is now ten, a handsome boy who puts me much in mind of my father, but he has his mother's happy Munro temperament. Fergus was a sterling, steady man. I have two more sons in whom I delight, and a baby daughter. The boys do not know, and I choose for them to never know, who and what their grandfather Kendrum was. Their world is here, not back there in a valley corrupted with infamy and hopelessly stained by the blood of lost causes.

I believed for a long time that Jeannie didn't know. She was hardly more than an infant when we left Lewis. But Calum, that incorrigible storyteller, had given her all his own memories to keep; perhaps for the same reason I am writing this testament. On our wedding night I swore her to secrecy, and so far she has kept her vow for the sake of our sons' souls.

Once I told Annie I would sell the Cellini brooch, but I never have. I leave it with this testament in the walls of the new part I am building onto this house, in a wooden chest of my own making, wrapped in a piece cut from the plaid in which we shrouded my father's sword. I leave the finding of it in the hands of God. If He so wills it, one day my descendants, Nova Scotians and North Americans, may know what sort of men they sprang from.

Finished on the 26th day of May. Thanks be to God who giveth us the victory.

Angus Mor

The name was written large and bold and clear with a long sweeping line beneath it like the slash of a dirk.

We sat there in silence as the book was reverently moved around the table so that everyone could read the signature. How I was able to sit still and look at it, I don't know. My mouth was so dry I had a hard time swallowing, but nobody expected me to say anything anyway. When the noise broke out, my voice wouldn't be missed. Mrs. Alec was quietly weeping. Hector and Angus still looked stunned.

"The stories are *true!*" Rowan cried incredulously.

"By God, they are." Bob Kendrum was laughing like a boy; to look at him you'd think murder and sudden death had completely gone out of his mind, or had never even occurred.

"I wonder what happened to the chest he made," Hector said.

"I was going to surprise you with my surprise," Angus said in a bemused voice, "but it appears we have something to surprise the surprise with."

"You're not making sense, my boy," Mrs. Archie said sharply.

"I might as well tell you," he said. "I'd invited the Earl of Strathcoran. The genuine Impostor." He gave us a tired grin. "He's over here for some sort of industrial exhibition in Ontario."

"And is he coming?" Rowan asked.

"He'd accepted, but now—" He pushed back his chair. "I'll see if I can reach him in Halifax. I haven't the faintest idea where he's staying."

"How are we going to call it off?" Mrs. Alec asked suddenly. "There's no way we can reach all the motels and campers, and if there's a concentrated campaign by radio to notify them, heaven knows what else will be converging on us down here." She spoke with a despairing anger. "I wish there were just some way we could get it over with, once and for all!"

"Shall we have it then?" Mrs. Archie asked, shyly for her. "Some of these people have come from a long way. If they could just see the cabin site and the house, have their lunch and go away . . . and don't forget, the boys will be coming up the river in all innocence."

It was decided then to have it. If the news of the two deaths should get into the Sunday papers, so be it. The family would take turns—and this included me—acting as hosts, so that no one needed to be constantly in the public eye. The Gilbert Kendrums could help out, and Daisy Ross was another one.

It was nearly midnight now, and Mrs. Archie and Mrs. Alec went to the kitchen to make some sandwiches for us to have before we broke up. I was to stay at the farm, Angus was returning to the Angus J. house; he said that if he didn't go back now, he would never want to.

Hector and Bob were reading parts of the narrative again, and Rowan pulled the strongbox over to her and lifted out what looked to be old newspaper clippings. They contained pictures and articles about the Scottish Kendrums, and the present Earl in particular. Beneath them there was an envelope in stiff yellow paper.

"I don't suppose I should open this," Rowan said, and handed it to Hector. "After all," she said with a brave attempt at humor, "you're The Kendrum. You're the head of the family. So you open it."

He just lifted one eyebrow at her, but Bob slapped his leg and said boisterously, "By God, you are! The—how many earls would it be?"

"Calm down, Uncle," Hector said. He pulled out a color photograph. It was Stuart and yet not Stuart. Handsome, arrogant, with a high head, an aggressive chin jutting out over the lace jabot and the silver-buttoned black-velvet doublet. The full glory of the modern Kendrum tartan, reds, blues, greens, and yellows, was set off by a silver-mounted sporran, and the plaid fastened at the shoulder with a handsome brooch.

"Oh, my God," Angus said.

"*Noel!*" Rowan whispered. "He'd been in the tartan shop that day. He was having this all made for him!"

"He looks magnificent," said Mrs. Alec, sounding dazed. "I'd never believe it was Stuart. He laughed at everybody else, he made fun of Alec, he called us all fools—but look at him! All the time he wanted this—this glory."

Angus said to me, "Did he tell you what was in the strongbox? When he said he'd killed Hector and Jamesy, didn't he give you any reason at all?"

If I looked straight at him, I would be able perhaps to think clearly and tell what they wanted to know, without letting them discover what had sent me to the cellar in the first place.

"He said it was his," I began, cautiously. "The strongbox, I mean. And whatever was in it, if Jamesy found out the truth, Jamesy could have killed *him*, after he'd done all the work, and put in the claim himself." I could hear Stuart's voice as I spoke, tight, jerky, exhilarated. The experience was hideous. "I asked what claim and he said never mind, but somebody would pay a lot of money for him not to upset their applecart, and he'd be a rich man and he'd go away and never come back."

I was ashamed to be talking about him at all to his people, but they listened attentively, as if I could help them solve the enigma that was Stuart.

"He was the one who attacked you," I told Angus. "You weren't between him and his claim, but that was for misdirection, I guess." Then I almost stopped breathing, waiting for someone to mention Alec. It seemed as if I could hear his name in the room, vibrating all around me. But no one spoke it. Perhaps they were afraid to.

"So he was going to be rich, and cock a snoot at us all," Bob said. "Well, that boy was always an odd stick, no doubt of it."

Angus picked up the photograph. "Look at him! He's feeling like the reincarnation of some far-back ancestor who killed everybody between him and the title, and finally got it. I suppose this was to be produced at the moment of truth, and, as you say, Pris, he wanted the glory too. Can't you see the pure triumph in him?"

"All I can see," said Hector with a sudden lacerating brutality, "is the devil in tartan."

33
CHAPTER

ALL AT ONCE, when I saw Angus getting ready to leave, and saw the anxious affection and concern they were all showing for one another, I wanted to go back too, not for Angus's reason but for my own. I wanted to be free to move about if I couldn't sleep. My shoulder had quieted down but not my brain, and I could see myself trying to lie quietly out of the way in a strange room in a house where a family was grieving. They shouldn't have to consider me, nor I them, when you came right down to it. Not after what I'd been through.

Angus seemed pleased that I decided to leave with him. "We'll knock signals on the wall at each other," he joked feebly, and then we couldn't think of anything else to say. When we left the car in the yard we walked by the bulkhead without looking at it. He unlocked my back door and we went into the hall. Too late I remembered the open trapdoor, and shied like a spooked horse, but the door had been closed and the rug replaced.

"I did that," he said. "After the police left." We went into the kitchen, and before he put on the light there he said, "You're sure you'll be all right?"

"Yes. What about you?"

"I'll yell good night at you through the wall, and you yell back." We both tried to laugh, and then he made a heavy despairing sound like a groan and reached for me in the dark. We clung together without speaking, his face in my hair, my cheek against his shoulder. I wanted to say that I was sorry, but that was too vapid a word for such enormities, so I just held fast with all my might, feeling the hard beating of his heart, or mine. My shoulder hurt, but I wouldn't have made a sound even if I'd been in agony.

"I loved Stuart once," he said finally, his voice muffled by my hair and vibrating strangely through my head. "Maybe I'll love him again, in time. But he tried to kill you, he tried to kill Hector and me, and he murdered his own son. Right now *love* doesn't enter into it."

"If you could only see it as a terrible sickness," I murmured against his shoulder. "You kept saying earlier that he was mad."

"Maybe we should face facts," he said wearily. "What is the matter with calling it plain old-fashioned evil? Maybe Hector was right about the devil in tartan." He tightened his embrace. "Thanks for being here tonight, Noel."

Then we separated without saying anything else until later, when he knocked on the wall and called good night, and I answered back, adding, "Whoever's up first makes the coffee."

I took more aspirin and surprised myself by going to sleep. There comes a time when you have to give out.

I wakened in a cool dawn, with a mist over the river that would burn away later under a hot blue sky. I was calm, and resigned to there being nothing more in the house for me alone. There was no need. I had done what had to be done.

There wasn't any sound from Angus's side and I hoped he was sleeping deeply. I took my notebook downstairs and burned it in the kitchen stove as a final gesture. Only Stuart had known about it, and it must have touched him with cold grue like a feather of ice trailed along the unsuspecting spine. He must have seen me as a sort of witch, to be executed for that as well as for what I'd found out.

Already my heartbreak was less, though I could still remember and still be shaken by last night's anguish. Probably it would never go away completely.

But Angus Mor had been Jeannie's man, after all, and he had lived out his years with doubtless many moments of pride and satisfaction.

I'll always love you, Angus Mor, I promised him. And I thank you for appearing to me as you did.

Then I added wood to the flames so I could boil water for the coffee.

The eleventh Earl and sixth Impostor was a chubby, beaming, unpretentious man wearing shorts and a Madras shirt. He was a great help at the Gathering, just by being there. Even the diehards liked him; not knowing, of course, that they'd been right all the time. Angus Mor's narrative was not to be made public for a while yet.

The boys' landing was greeted by an applauding crowd and the piper played "The March of the Kendrum Men" as they came ashore. Rowan's singers were superb. For those who didn't yet know what had happened, the day was superb in every particular. For those of us who did know—well, I think we were all glad to have our turns onstage. For some of the family it was a period of catharsis, and the secret password was, *Do it well for Alec's sake.*

Of course the sound of the pipes turned me into a tearful jelly for Alec whom I hadn't known, for poor young Jamesy whom I'd known a little, and for Angus Mor whom I'd known best of all. I wasn't the only one affected; either you love the pipes or you hate them, and if you love them it's a violence in your blood you might never have known was there until the first skirling note roused it to a passion of rage or grief or delight.

When the Gathering was over, the Earl had a quiet meeting with Hector and the manuscript in the farmhouse living room, over the bottle of whiskey he'd brought from his own distillery. Later they walked around the farm and leaned on fences and contemplated cattle.

We all gathered together for a late supper. Worn out, and with the autopsy reports, the funerals, and the publicity to come, at least we'd accomplished the Gathering. Len's relatives were still holding onto her in Kingston, and that was covertly agreed to be a good thing.

Strathcoran was such a cozy, rumpled little man it was easy to forget that he lived in a castle and had an impressive background as an industrialist.

"Well, I've agreed not to unseat him," Hector announced dryly at the table, "and I've returned the Cellini brooch and made an honest man of him."

The Earl laughed. "But the Seat of the Kendrums in Nova Scotia deserves something from the old homestead, and as soon as I get back there I'll think what it is. This man is too modest to make any suggestions, so I'm open to ideas." He nodded encouragingly all around the table.

"Now I have to tell you something serious," he said. "I don't know how far your tragic brother would have gotten in court with his claims, even if he'd been able to clear the decks, so to speak. I'm not sure, but I assume the two boys Angus and Calum were legally dead after a certain period of time."

He paused, and it was so quiet we could hear the geese gabbling outside the kitchen windows. I could swear no one even breathed as we waited. He said somberly, "But there's no reason to doubt Angus's story. You see, we have family legends too, but nobody wanted to inquire too closely into them. Then about five years ago my son and I had the graves opened. We discovered no bones, *but*"—he stopped again, holding us in thrall by his fine sense of the dramatic—"we found the fourth Earl's famous sword in one, wrapped in the rotting remains of a plaid, and in the other what was left of a chief's bonnet, with the plant badge and three eagle's feathers."

He finished his wine and Hector leaned over and poured more in his glass.

"What it proved to us," Strathcoran went on, "was that the boys had escaped. But where or how, who could tell? They could have been drowned off the mouth of the sea loch, or lost in the mountains. Or they could have survived. But again—where or how?" He shrugged. "The discovery here moves me much more than I'm able to show. And I'm surrounded by Kendrum men who look far more like some of the portraits at home than I do. By the way, the stepmother's baby was a legitimate Kendrum. In his portraits he resembles very much his father, the fourth Earl. . . . Odd how some genetic traits survive." He waved a hand at Angus and Hector and the clustered boys. "You'd look perfectly at home in the castle at Strathcoran. Now me—" He grinned and ran his hand over his thinning hair. "I'm a sort of sport, a throwback to some short fat sandy folk on my mother's side."

"What happened to the valley, sir?" Robbie asked. "Did the troops come in and burn it?"

"No, the stepmother's lover was useful there, and she was sensible enough of her child's welfare to want to preserve all she could for him, once she'd gotten rid of the true heir. She died when he was two years old, and he had a respectable rearing by his guardian Patrick Kendrum of that Ilk, and founded a long line of quite estimable men. They never threw the crofters out to bring sheep in, for one thing. . . . And they've been good soldiers and public-spirited citizens. Even me, though there was a serious doubt for a time if I'd make it."

"You kids all look long and hard at this man," Hector commanded. "You'll never get a better chance to be close to a real honest-to-God earl."

Strathcoran laughed. "They've been looking at one right along, haven't they?"

EPILOGUE

"Good grief," Robbie said all at once one day. "I've not only got you for a sister, but I'll have you for an aunt too!"

"Are you as horrified as you sound?" I asked him.

"Gosh, I'm not horrified!" he protested. "But I was just thinking—hey, it's really *weird*, isn't it?"

"It certainly is," I agreed. "And you don't know the half of it."